THE SHELF LIFE OF HAPPINESS

THE SHELF LIFE OF HAPPINESS

DAVID MACHADO

TRANSLATED BY HILLARY LOCKE

amazon crossing

This is a work of fiction. Names, characters, organizations, places, events, and incidents are either products of the author's imagination or are used fictitiously.

Previously published as *Índice médio de felicidade* by Publicações Dom Quixote in 2013. Translated from Portuguese by Hillary Locke. First published in English by AmazonCrossing in 2016.

Published by AmazonCrossing, Seattle

www.apub.com

ISBN-13: 9781503938052
ISBN-10: 1503938050

Cover design by David Drummond

Printed in the United States of America

To Maria and Martim, the future

SWITZERLAND: 8.0

Look, Almodôvar. First of all, you weren't here.

Things got very hard, very fast. Or maybe they had always been hard; maybe the world had always been a complicated place. I don't think it all started when you were arrested, though it somehow still seems that it did. And your absence made everything worse; your decision to refuse visitors had its consequences. That is to say, we weren't prepared for you to be gone. The void you left behind was too big, and none of us knew how to live in the vast space of your desertion. But you weren't here, so we had no choice but to try. I still can't say if we managed. I just know this: you won't be the one to judge our failures. At some point, the coherence of your silence became another one of our conditions.

I imagine you there, on the inside. A place not your own, where your body had to learn to fit into small spaces, where you had to follow the laws written in the eyes of the men around you. Was it difficult? Did you ache inside those strong walls? Did you go cold with terror when you met the hardened gaze of the other prisoners? Here on the outside, everyone thinks so. Your first week there, Clara called me every night, crying, gasping, nearly suffocating. "Poor thing," she'd say, as if you were some innocent child, as if she were your young widow. "My poor love," she'd sigh. "What if they hurt him?" Your son, little Vasco—who's grown to be taller than me now—would come home from school, shut himself in his room and play violin, sheet music strewn all over the floor, the sharp vibrations from the strings humming through the walls. And Xavier. He spent every spare minute online, poring over the criminal codes in search of any loophole that might set you free. He kept saying, "That man's not going to last, Daniel. Almodôvar isn't cut out for life behind bars." Your friends would gather around tables in cafés, restaurants, and kitchens, proposing enthusiastic toasts in your honor to distract themselves from their fear that something terrible was about to happen to you. No one could make any sense of it. How could this be? You were a good man, you had an honest smile, and you always said the right thing. You were a husband. A father. A friend. Any possible explanation seemed like a fantasy. And I spent my life apologizing for you. "He had his reasons," I'd say. "We know the real Almodôvar. He's not a different person now just because he's in prison." Back then I wasn't mad at you yet.

But now I imagine you there, on the inside. I imagine your face, your gestures. The thoughts that fill your hours. And I don't think you're scared. I don't think you're in danger. I think you're doing just fine. You've found a hiding place to wait out this dark time in our lives, this long winter. You're hibernating—that's what you're doing. Your heart rate has slowed, you eat your three meals a day, and you're enjoying the comfort of the walls around you, your practically nullified existence. We might be freezing out here, but in there you stay nice and warm. You're a chickenshit little coward, Almodôvar. Just when did your world become so much more complicated than ours that you thought you had the right to do this to us? There were so many people counting on you, who depended on you. In a way, you were responsible for them. Did it all weigh too heavily on your heart?

* * *

I would have understood. If you had agreed to see me when I visited you, if you had answered my calls, if we had been able to speak, you'd have explained everything and I would have understood, Almodôvar. And I would have spared you the reality out here: your son, your wife Clara, Xavier, me, the troubles of the people you care about, this country crumbling to the ground, the whole world collapsing. I wouldn't have said a thing until you were prepared to hear it, to know it, to feel all of it. I would have waited to tell you that three months after you were arrested I lost my job, and that not long after that, Marta, who had been unemployed for nearly six months, took off with the kids to Viana do Castelo to work at her father's café while I stayed behind because I still believed in our life in Lisbon. And even though things got very hard, very fast, I kept believing. Talking with you would have been good for me, it might have helped, and I was willing to wait as long as it took.

You're a chickenshit little coward, Almodôvar.

Now I have no other way to communicate with you. And only when I find it convenient, you'll have the right to reply as you can in these circumstances; maybe we can have some sort of conversation, and it will be (almost) like old times. So here goes.

The morning Xavier left home. Let's start there. That morning was important. The month before, I had found work selling vacuum cleaners. It was all a scam, and I knew it from the start, but I had run out of options. In six months I had filled out twenty-six job applications, with no luck. My unemployment benefits were scheduled to drop off into an abyss in a few months. I was only thirty-seven, but it seemed as if my life was already over. I was scared—of course I was scared. Then I went online and found an ad for sales reps, filled out an application, and the next day I got an e-mail saying that I had been selected. Just like that: no interview, no tests. At the orientation session, they told us we'd be selling vacuum cleaners. I almost laughed out loud. Almodôvar, I would have sold real estate on Mars if it had come to that.

Xavier left home?

No, Almodôvar. It's not your turn to speak yet. I'll be the one to decide how this story goes.

The vacuum cleaner scheme went like this: the company that sold them (it was called WRU, though I never found out what that stood for) rented equipment by the week to its employees—me and everyone else who had been selected—so we could do demos. We were expected to arrange these demos ourselves, and though the company said it would offer logistical support if we needed it, I never found out what that meant either. They didn't give me a desk, just the address of a warehouse where I'd go pick up the vacuum cleaners. Everything else was done over the phone. I didn't have a contract, which allowed me to keep collecting unemployment, and I earned a commission for each vacuum cleaner I sold, between 7 and 11 percent, minus rental fees. In other words, I had to pay to work. I accepted the job immediately.

I ran all around town doing demos. I had rehearsed exactly what to say, I knew all the models in the catalogue, and I'd always have two or three of them in the back of my car. But it wasn't easy getting people to let me into their homes, and days would pass when nothing would happen, as if the world were slowly coming to a halt. Occasionally, someone would open their door, let me vacuum their entire house—their walls, carpets, curtains, and sofas—only to tell me they weren't interested. (Things had gotten bad for everyone, not just you and me.) I exhausted all my contacts: my mother's friends, everyone at my old job, girlfriends from high school I hadn't seen in over a decade, my male friends too. Marta helped. She was gone, but she still made calls, asked friends to have me over.

* * *

One day Clara called. She had heard I needed help selling vacuum cleaners, and she offered to organize a demo at your place in exchange for a 10 percent cut of my commissions. I accepted. It was a good day: I sold two. When we were done, Clara talked about you for a while, about your absence. She was worried about Vasco: he wasn't reacting, as if he hadn't noticed you were gone. She asked me to go talk to him. I did, mostly as a way of thanking her. Vasco was in his room, scribbling in the margins of some sheet music—something about a dead dog. We talked for ten minutes, his voice so much like yours when you were fifteen, the same long pauses between sentences. We mostly spoke about music; he likes '70s rock, the Who, Led Zeppelin, the Rolling Stones. He smiled two or three times; he looked good, at peace. And I didn't want to ruin it, so I didn't ask about his life, school, girlfriends, or friends—nor did I mention you.

But here's what matters: I believed in the possibility of starting over, seizing the loose reins of my life, pulling them tight. And I wasn't angry; I wasn't angry back then. I thought all I had to do was pay attention to the important things, tend to them, look ahead, calculate every step. I was convinced that if I did everything right, life wouldn't get in my way.

But then that bastard Xavier—who had shut himself in his apartment with his computer for twelve years to ponder the misery of life—decided to leave the house the very same day I had planned to do a demo at a hotel in Cascais. Here's the thing: I could sell ten or fifteen vacuums in one shot, make some money, change everything.

Xavier left his house?

The first person to spot him was Tuga, just after six in the morning, close to the shopping center; Tuga's message said he couldn't be sure, because it was very unlikely, but he thought he had seen Xavier in a dark-blue tracksuit, his cracked heels protruding over his slides, his white hair. After that, another five people claimed to have seen him. They all messaged me as if I were Xavier's father, or as if I were you.

There was also a call from Xavier from 5:42 that morning, which I had missed because I put my phone on "Silent" at night.

I called Xavier. I let it ring for a long time. He didn't answer. So I threw the merchandise in the car—six boxes of new models, vacuum cleaners that could suck out your thoughts if you wanted them to, expensive, as if they had been designed by NASA—I threw it all in the car and went looking for him. I had to be at the hotel at nine, and even so, I drove around the neighborhood looking for him, up and down all the streets where I thought he might be, stopping at all the places where he used to go before he turned into a miserable hermit; I made some calls, asked if . . . Wait, that's not true. That's not what happened. I'm saying all this as if I didn't want to disappoint you, as if your opinion still mattered. I got in the car, that part is true. But I didn't go looking for him. As I left Lisbon in the direction of Cascais, I remember thinking: If he was going to kill himself, he'd already had all the time in the world to do the deed.

Listen, Almodôvar. I don't have to defend myself. I'm not swearing an oath. I'll just say this: that morning, when I received the news that Xavier had left his apartment, my only thought was that I had to sell those damned vacuum cleaners. Even knowing that he'd probably thrown himself off a bridge. Even knowing that, in some way, you were counting on me to look after him. But I'm not like you—we've known that for a long time. And I'm not his friend like you are. Well, to tell you the truth, I don't know if I'm his friend or not. At some point, a long time ago, we were friends. Then he got all wrapped up in his black shadow, and all his words took on a supernatural anguish. And I remember looking at him, a sixteen- or seventeen-year-old kid among other angry sixteen- or seventeen-year-old kids, thinking that it made no sense, that the laws of life as we know them did not justify the existence of a person that sad. Xavier's depression came out of nowhere. As if he had invented it. I never told you this, but I'm convinced he invented his persona—that sad wisp of a guy with graying hair, empty eyes, and a cigarette burning between his fingers, drawing sad drawings in his notebooks, an eternal despair in everything around him, an air of impending suicide. I don't think he was ever sure of his identity, so he adopted his dark persona and then liked it, or got used to it, or got lost in it. It doesn't matter. That's just how he ended up, Almodôvar. Days in bed staring up at the emptiness between himself and the ceiling. Thin as if he were on a hunger strike. The tattooed numbers on the arms, back, chest—some he designed himself. His pills. His obsession with statistics. The mathematical equations on his bedroom walls. The customers he would let in at any time of day or night to give them spider tattoos—I never understood why only spiders—in exchange for a pittance that barely sustained him. And the absence of any consideration for the future.

It was this lack of future that scared me most. How can someone not think about the future? Thoughts of tomorrow, or next month, or the next ten years—how do they not weigh on someone? How can a person wake up every morning and not feel any hopes or fears about what might happen? I didn't know how to relate to someone like that. And looking back, I realized something: you were always immune to Xavier's sadness. Your ability to put up with his cynicism and the absolute indifference in his silences was almost alarming. And you never dropped him as a friend; I kept hanging around both of you only because I wasn't willing to give up on what we had once been. Besides, getting new friends was out of the question—I'm just not that kind of person.

And you wanted to save him. You'd say, "Xavier is an artist, and artists have to grapple with death and suffering." We talked so much about Xavier's inevitable suicide that at some point I started to think of it as already having happened years ago, not as something that was still to come. And yet you insisted on saving him. No one could be sad in front of him, and we couldn't leave him alone; you wanted to be there to stop the inevitable, as if he no longer was capable of making a decision about his own life.

But all that has changed now; you can't save anyone where you are.

True. But you can.

You're wrong. I didn't stay here so I could take your place. And unlike you, I never felt responsible for Xavier's life.

So what happens if he blows his brains out?

Almodôvar, the right question is: So what happens *when* he blows his brains out?

So what happens when he blows his brains out?

Xavier is an important part of us. When he blows his brains out, it will open a void we'll never know how to fill. Believe me, death does that to the living. On the other hand, we'll feel an immense relief, almost peace. But that's not even the point. The point is this: the day he decides to blow his brains out, none of us will be there to stop him.

He left home for the first time in twelve years, and you went off to sell vacuum cleaners in Cascais. You're a selfish prick, Daniel.

Hold on. You're the selfish one here, motherfucker.

Xavier's depression always makes you uncomfortable—that's why you let him skulk off to some dark corner to end it. So you can finally have your rest, your relief, your almost peace. Go fuck yourself. If everyone thought like you, this planet would be empty.

Like anyone else, Xavier needs us to respect his wishes.

He needs us to respect his life. And that requires an effort you don't want to make.

Look, motherfucker. Don't talk about effort when you're the one who refused to see us for almost two years. And I made an effort. I didn't go sell vacuum cleaners.

You didn't?

No, I didn't. I got on the highway. I drove five miles. Then I made a U-turn back to Lisbon.

Why?

About two months earlier, I had been at Xavier's house. He had asked me to come over. Our conversation didn't go well.

He was lying in bed with his laptop on his belly, his fingers poised over the keyboard. It was around four in the afternoon, but his room was like a cave, the windows shuttered, a lit lamp on the floor covered with a sweater, the walls blending into the darkness, and a dense cloud of smoke hovering near the ceiling. And despite the heat, half of his body was under a quilt. There was soft music playing, strange music, like whales crying—his usual shit. He sensed me come in but didn't move or look up to greet me. I said hello. He didn't respond, just lifted a hand, a lit cigarette dangling between his fingers. I sat on the edge of the bed and waited. I don't know if you ever noticed this: in Xavier's room, time slows down, things take longer to happen, as if our bodies become denser there, as if nothing—no gesture, no sentence, no silence—could ever really end. After about three minutes, he spoke.

"We messed up," he said.

"What do you mean, 'we messed up'?"

"The site," he said. "The site isn't working."

Can you believe it? The dude was still working on the site. You hadn't been around for over six months and Xavier had kept working on that shitty site. Because you put the idea into his head. You went on about that site for months: how it was a surefire idea, how we'd sell the business a year later with 10,000 percent profit, how we'd pay our bank loans, our children's educations, how we'd be living large. You fed him the whole movie. And we'd be doing a good thing, you said; we'd be helping people. You made it sound so good I even started to believe you. It seemed like a great idea. To be honest, it still seems like a great idea. But the truth is that you and I put in a bunch of money, money that I need now, money that might have prevented you from doing what you did, and we never saw that money again. And Xavier was supposed to program the site. He spent weeks without sleeping, and when it was finally ready, nothing happened; months passed and still nothing happened. He was right: the site wasn't working. But I had forgotten about it a long time before. Meanwhile, a year later, Xavier was still messing around with it.

I didn't want to have that pointless conversation, so I tried to be patient.

"What do you want to do about it?" I asked him. "We can't put in more money."

He closed his laptop, and his face went dark.

"There are people using the site," he said. "The problem is that none of them need any help."

In short, the problem was this: we created a social network where people who needed help could meet others who were willing to give it; for the first eleven months the site was online, twenty-two people signed up—fourteen of them never posted; four posted regularly, asking for someone to give them a hand job, or wipe their ass, or cut their toenails; three used the site to stay in touch among themselves without ever requesting any help; and one would post occasionally to offer help for anything at any time, stating that he had a nine-seater van to get the job done.

But here was my biggest concern: Who were these people?

Xavier got out of bed, his tall and skinny body seeming to waver, as if a wind were blowing in his room. He lit another cigarette and gestured toward the closed window.

"Are people still the same out there?" he asked.

"People are still people, yes," I answered.

"Don't people still need help?"

"Everyone needs help."

"So why won't they ask for it?"

"I don't know. Maybe they don't know about the site."

He took two short strides and sat next to me on the bed. I could just see his profile in the diaphanous lamplight, his eyes clouded by tears on the brink of falling. But when he spoke, his voice was steady, as if he were harboring the storm inside himself.

"I'm scared of what might happen if someone asks for help," he said.

But he didn't seem scared.

"At least we'll always have a nine-seater van." I smiled.

His cigarette trembled between his fingers, tendrils of smoke stirring in the darkness. He didn't laugh.

"We need to write in and ask for help," he said.

At this point I just wanted to get out of there, Almodôvar. But instead I heard him out, because that's what you would have done.

He wanted to create an account with a fake username and use it to write in for help. Something simple—sealing a window, taking the dog to the vet—just to be sure someone would answer.

"What happens if someone offers?" I asked.

"You'll respond and accept."

"Me?"

"Isn't there anything you need help with?"

"Not really."

"You just said everyone needs help."

"No one is going to believe that I really need help."

"If you tell the truth, why not?"

"Why can't you ask for help?"

"I can't leave the house."

"Ask for help here at home. Say you can't go out, and you need someone to go buy your groceries."

"My mom brings me my groceries."

"Then ask for something else. A roast chicken. The newspaper. A haircut."

He was quiet for a long time, moving his lips as if he were solving a complicated equation in his head. Then he said, "If someone came to help me, could you be here too?"

"Fuck off, Xavier. That's completely ridiculous."

"It is not."

"Forget the site."

"Okay, I'll forget it. Let's do this one thing, just to see if anyone answers, and then I'll forget it."

I considered it for a few seconds. It was a stupid idea, and I didn't want to have anything to do with it. You and I had already spent two-thirds of our lives trying to satisfy that bastard's every whim, just because we were afraid of what might happen if we refused. But the truth is that Xavier was old enough to hear a no from time to time.

"Fine," I said. "I'll be here when they come help you."

I forced myself to remember that moment, the significance of that promise.

Xavier let out a loud sigh, as if I had just saved his life.

I got up, feeling heavy in the head. That happens whenever I visit Xavier: I walk in, riding light on some naive wind, thinking it will be good to see him, that we'll talk for hours like we did when we were kids, but then within minutes I begin to feel the sadness in the air mingling with the smoke and the shadows, and all I can think about is leaving as soon as possible. Xavier learned to sense my feelings, as if being a shut-in gave him the power to see beyond what he took in through his eyes.

"You can turn on the light," he said.

I didn't answer. I walked over to his desk. His papers were organized into five or six piles: handwritten equations, graphs, random numbers, the usual. One sheet had a table that took up the whole page. That wasn't unusual—even the walls were plastered with tables. But its name caught my eye: "The Happiness Index."

"What's this?" I asked.

"Statistics."

I picked up the sheet and turned it over. The table continued onto the other side. It was a list of 149 countries in order of their average happiness index. The first on the list was Costa Rica; the last was Togo. Lines 127, 128, 129, and 130—Bulgaria, Burkina Faso, Congo, and the Ivory Coast, respectively—had been highlighted in green.

"What's the happiness index?" I asked.

Xavier flopped back on the bed and lay back on the comforter, his hand that held the cigarette hanging off the side. He closed his eyes.

"It's not very interesting as a stat; it lacks objectivity," he said. "But it's the best we have. It's based on a survey with just one question: On a scale of 0 to 10, how satisfied are you with life on the whole?"

He took a puff on his cigarette. Smoke slipped slowly from his nose.

Then he added, "I suspect most people who respond don't take the survey seriously, because most people don't know shit about happiness."

Can you believe it, Almodôvar? Xavier, the most miserable bastard in this entire city, the darkest soul I've ever met in my life, had decided to play the happiness guru. I could have devastated the guy in a matter of sentences, you know. Instead I just said, "So what's happening in Bulgaria, Burkina Faso, Congo, and the Ivory Coast?"

"That's where the average happiness index is 4.4, the same as mine."

"You answered the survey?"

"Of course."

He was lying motionless on the bed, his cigarette pressed between his lips, vertical. He opened his eyes and closed them again.

I asked the only question I could summon: "Why?"

"Because I like to quantify things in life, in the world. You know how I am."

"You're not scared of what it might mean?"

"I'm more scared of not knowing."

"So?"

"So what?"

"So your happiness index is 4.4 out of 10. What does that mean?"

"My score was 4.43672, to be precise. And, among other things, it means that I should move to Bulgaria or Burkina Faso or the Congo or the Ivory Coast."

"Why?"

Xavier rolled over and stubbed out his cigarette in a saucer on his bedside table that was already overflowing with butts.

"I have a theory," he said.

"What's that?"

For the first time in recent memory, I was genuinely interested in something Xavier had to say.

"A man moves to a country where the average happiness index is the same as his," he began. "Once he's surrounded by people whose index matches his, he feels more at home in his new community, more accomplished than he is. In other words, he's happier. His happiness increases to match the level of another country farther up the table. Then the man in question moves on to the new country, if only because he no longer feels at home where he is. In this next country, the man again feels completely comfortable, which again increases his happiness index, forcing him to move on to a country farther up the table. And so on. Finally, the man in question will end up living in the country at the top of the table and will be as happy as it's possible to be on this planet."

There was a long silence.

"Do you really believe that?" I finally asked.

"It's a theory. Even I know it's not that simple."

"So you're not moving to Burkina Faso?"

"Probably not," he replied.

"You don't want to move up the table?"

"Of course I do. Don't we all? But I'd have to leave this room first. And that would provoke an immediate decline in my happiness index."

He paused and looked at me. "A 4.4 is already low," he added. "Anything lower could be dangerous."

His tone was sarcastic, but it still sounded like a mathematical truth.

"I want to take the survey."

"Good luck," said Xavier, lighting another cigarette.

"How did the question go?"

"On a scale of 0 to 10, how satisfied are you with your life on the whole?" Then he added, "Don't be too quick to respond, Daniel."

I tried to think of everything: Marta and the kids, my unemployment, the money I didn't have, my Plan, my reflection in the mirror that morning.

"**8.0**," I finally said.

Xavier looked at me, surprised.

"What?"

"That's my answer: 8.0."

"I told you not to rush."

"I didn't."

"You don't speak for a minute, and then you rattle off a number that supposedly represents your degree of satisfaction with life?"

"That's my number."

"So in three minutes you reviewed your entire existence. You took everything into account, pondered all the variables?"

"Yeah, I think so. How long did it take you?"

"Shit, Daniel. I've been thinking about it for two weeks, and I still feel like I'm missing something."

"Two weeks, Xavier? This isn't a math problem."

"But it is. More importantly, it's your life. You can't solve it in three minutes. I'm telling you, most people don't know shit about happiness."

"Your number was 4.4, and I'm the one who doesn't know shit about happiness?"

"It's not that you don't feel happiness. You just don't understand it."

"And you do?"

"I understand my happiness," he said. "It's an equation, just like everything else, with variables and constants and weights that I have to string together with the appropriate operations."

"Variables? What variables?"

"Friends. Love. Time. Dreams. Thirst. Stomachaches. Hope. Jealousy. The joy of eating. That kind of shit."

"You can't quantify that," I said, and laughed.

"If you can quantify happiness, you can certainly quantify the feeling of wanting to be eight years old again, or your fear of kissing someone. Of course some variables can only be found by solving other equations first. It's a system, really. It's complicated. But life is complicated, Daniel."

Seriously, Almodôvar. Fuck that motherfucker.

"Is this what you do when you're holed up in here all day? Sit in the dark and assign values to things in life?"

He didn't answer. He just stared at me for a while, looking surprised. "You're angry. Why are you angry?"

I didn't know what to say. I looked down at the sheet of paper in my hand and scanned the list. Then I found what I was looking for: Switzerland, the fourth country in the table. The average happiness index in Switzerland was 8—the same as mine. I don't want to live in Switzerland, I thought. I looked back up at Xavier.

"You've been a recluse for twelve years—what's left to account for?"

As I spoke, I realized how mistaken I was. He had so much to account for.

Xavier sat back down on the bed, his feet dangling off the side, and searched for the right words to justify his existence.

"I know," he finally said. "It's not much. But even so, it's a life. As long as my heart is beating, it's a life. My life. And it's important for me to know exactly how much it's worth. At least I'm not fooling myself."

"Are you saying I'm fooling myself?"

Xavier's lip quivered slightly.

"Yes."

"Fuck you, motherfucker. I'm not Almodôvar. I don't have to put up with your shit."

"I'll help you solve your equation if you want."

"What equation, Xavier? There's no formula for happiness."

He nodded and fell into an agitated, indescribable silence.

"I have to go," I said.

And I left.

I didn't go back. We were used to handling him like glass, speaking to him as if sharp words could shatter him somehow. I imagined him undone on the bed. I imagined his mother finding him in shards on the bed, trying to glue the pieces of her son back together, trying to remake her child, knowing it was only a matter of time before he burst open again. But I didn't go back. I didn't call. He stopped texting me. Then, nearly a month later, he sent me an e-mail with an update on the site. He had created a user account under a fake name and requested help changing a fuse. No one answered. The weeks passed. There wasn't a peep from the other members. The guy with the nine-seater van gave no signs of life. Maybe he didn't want to help, or maybe he didn't know how to change a fuse. At the end of the e-mail, Xavier wrote: *I give up.* I assumed he was talking about the site, but the truth is he could have been talking about anything. Still, I didn't go back to see him.

It's true, I was tired of Xavier's shit, but that's not why I didn't go back. Here's the thing: I was busy trying to rebuild my own life. It was still crumbling down around me. The money I made selling vacuum cleaners didn't come close to covering my expenses, even after I cut down on smoking and canceled my cable, my phone service, my health insurance. Even after I stopped eating out, buying clothes, going to the movies, going out for the occasional beer. Even after I reduced my grocery list to the most basic items. I tried to renegotiate my mortgage with the bank, but that was useless. Rich and poor, everyone had the same problems.

But it wasn't just an issue of money. I missed Marta, her weight on the mattress at night, how she'd look at me after we put the kids down to sleep, her assured way of speaking. When we talked on the phone, when we saw each other, I'd force myself to act as if everything were fine, as if the distance didn't affect us, as if our money problems and my situation were temporary, a kind of vacation. She did the same. And during those early months, everything seemed fine. But it wasn't. And my kids. Their pain became a block of ice in my chest, making it suddenly impossible to breathe.

Each month I'd drive to Viana to see them. My in-laws own two little apartments in the same building in the city center; they lived on the ground floor, while Marta and the kids lived above them. We'd stroll along the beach, braving the wind, then stop for lunch in restaurants with a view of the sea. At night, the kids would come lie on the bed between Marta and me, and we'd morph into a four-headed creature under the duvet. When I was back in Lisbon, we'd talk online every day, sometimes on video-chat, so it was almost as if we were together. But it wasn't enough—nothing could replace touching them, smelling them. A terrifyingly obvious crevasse began to open between us. They said nothing; they understood the situation, and I never sensed that they blamed me for the separation. But the truth is that something had changed. Especially with Flor: she didn't look at the camera when we talked, and she'd write to me with those detached abbreviations like "kk" instead of "okay." She'd use English words but also emoticons interspersed throughout sentences that I didn't understand at all. I tried to remember being thirteen. Had I been like her? I don't know. My memories are too conflicting to trust. With Mateus it was easier: we hardly spoke, but we'd play games online, exchange videos we found. It was a form of communication, at least. And, though brief, our conversations possessed a frankness that seemed nearly impossible in our situation; the words of my nine-year-old son were so real and full of meaning, too truthful at times.

One day I interrupted a game I was playing online with Mateus (we were throwing darts at Madonna's face) and typed: *On a scale of 1 to 10, how satisfied are you with your life on the whole?* He took so long to respond I thought he was writing a longer answer. He finally said, *It's hard to say. Let me get back to you tomorrow.* Then, four days later, I got this: *6.8* ☺. Which meant that I—unemployed, separated from my family, with one friend in prison and another on the brink of suicide—was happier than my own son. Still, he was happy with his number—Mateus wasn't as generous with his smiley faces as his sister. The thought of it made me reconsider my 8.0. I realized I hadn't taken into account my own children's happiness when I had calculated my number. I stopped and tried to think of anything else I might have left out of the equation, as Xavier called it. There were my bouts of insomnia. If I included those, my number would go down at least two or three decimal points. Then I tried to find something that would make my happiness index go back up. My cardiovascular health: at my last visit, the doctor had said I had the heart of a man six years younger. That was good enough for me.

Anyway, all this to say that the morning Xavier left home, I was afraid our last conversation had provoked him. Almodôvar, if Xavier wants to kill himself, I won't stand in his way, but I don't want to be the one who pushes him over the edge either. So I went looking for him.

Daniel, let me take back what I said. You're not a selfish prick. You're an egocentric bastard.

Back to the morning Xavier left home. I pulled into the neighborhood just after 9:30. I parked the car. I tried to call him. His mother answered his phone. She was at his place; someone had told her that her son had gone out, and she had run straight there. There was still no sign of him. No one knew where he was; he had left his phone at home. His mother was crying. I didn't ask why.

"Try to calm down," I told her. "I'll find him."

I imagined what it might be like to be Xavier, dragging around all his thoughts, feeling his heart race at the slightest disturbance around him. I imagined living locked up in a room for twelve years out of fear, disgust, or plain lack of interest—we can never know for sure, right? I imagined going out on the street after all those years as a recluse, the shock of it, the force of the world invading my eyes, my chest.

If I were Xavier, where would I go?

I realized that that was the wrong question. The real question was: Where would I go if I wanted to kill myself?

I didn't have to think about it for long. The answer came as quickly as the question: the train tracks.

Remember, Almodôvar? Remember all those suicides that happened when we were kids? I do. They don't keep me up at night, but I remember them. Xavier must have remembered them too.

I started the car and sped off.

How had we never thought of it before? The train tracks. The lesson was stored somewhere in our subconscious. Case studies. The whole strategy published in the newspapers. We knew the most surefire spots, the most effective ones. Don't you remember? Keeping track of them had been a game, a kind of hobby for us. We were young, and those people seemed so far away from us, like in a movie. Don't you think Xavier might have fantasized about doing it himself? He must have, once his spirit unraveled; back then he was still happy.

I set off for the station. Most people were staring hard at their own feet, as if they feared the ground would drop out from under them. I walked toward the tracks and peered through the fence. No sign of a body. Then I realized that if someone had thrown themselves in the path of an oncoming train, there would have been panic. Someone would have called an ambulance.

I got back in the car and drove along the line, prepared to spot an ambulance, a gathering of people. I scanned the tracks. Maybe no one had seen anything. Maybe the engineer felt nothing more than a slight tremor when the train struck Xavier's body.

I tried to calculate how much Xavier's happiness index might have fallen after our conversation. Two-tenths of a decimal point? One-half? A whole point? Maybe I wasn't that important. Maybe it had nothing to do with me. Maybe the day had simply come for him to leave home and throw himself onto the train tracks. It pained me to think that could be the case. In spite of everything, I still wanted to be important to Xavier.

You are . . .

I know. I'm a selfish piece of shit. Fuck off, Almodôvar.

I drove along seven miles of track. Nothing. I stopped the car again and scrolled through all my messages about Xavier. Tuga, Cabral, and Rose had all seen him near the shopping center, so I turned back.

At that hour of the morning the streets around the shopping center were quiet. If Xavier passed, it would be easy to spot him. I drove in circles along the same streets, first in one direction, then the other. At one point, a group of nine or ten kids—most of them around fifteen—broke into a run as if someone were chasing them. I stopped the car and got out. I tried to see what was happening. Nothing. Everything else was still; it looked like a movie set. The kids disappeared down a ramp leading into the shopping center's parking garage. I got back in the car, drove another hundred yards, and parked.

I called Xavier's house again. His mother answered. She had stopped crying, but Xavier still hadn't appeared. I hung up and went into the shopping center. I roamed the halls. I rode the escalators. I peered through shop windows. The world seemed so normal there, everything in its place, so well proportioned, diligent people at work behind the counters, an absence of shadows. Maybe Xavier had left home looking for precisely that. Maybe there was no reason to be concerned.

I studied a map of the shopping center to find my bearings. I had searched everywhere besides the restrooms. See, Almodôvar? I didn't just leave. I traipsed back through the hallways and searched the men's and women's rooms, stall by stall, floor by floor. No Xavier.

By the time I left the shopping center, it was pouring rain. The wind was blowing in no particular direction, swirling drops in the air without bringing them to rest on the ground. I sprinted to the car. I started the engine, but didn't drive. I sat and thought about all the places Xavier could have gone after spending twelve years locked inside. Every last place in the world seemed possible. I considered those four countries: Burkina Faso, Bulgaria, the Ivory Coast, Congo. Maybe that was the answer. Maybe we'd never see him again. We could sleep knowing he was living among people who were as satisfied with life as he was. We'd just have to find a way to be happy for him.

I looked at my watch: 12:08 p.m., six hours since he had disappeared. Enough time to have killed himself in twenty different ways. Enough time for anything. We would have known by then if something had happened. Bad news travels fast; people can't rest until they've blabbed about a tragedy. But I couldn't be sure. Days can pass, even weeks, before someone notices a cadaver in some random place. I thought: If he throws himself into the river, he'll be swept up in the currents, poured into the Atlantic. He'll take a few laps around the planet and slip from ocean to ocean before his body is washed up on a beach somewhere, already so decomposed that no one would guess that a man could have existed within it.

Then the passenger door opened. Xavier got in. He acted so calm, so natural, as if we had agreed to meet at that very place and time. He was soaked and ran his hands over his face and hair. Then he finally looked at me with profound relief. It was clear that the past few hours had been hard for him. He said nothing, just looked out the window, his lips pressed tight, his eyes darting around, as if he couldn't believe the real world around him.

"Where were you, Xavier?" I asked.

He didn't respond.

"Xavier."

He looked at me, smiled, and began to cry.

"What are you doing here?" he asked.

"I was worried about you. Everyone is. You disappeared."

"Yeah."

He was about to say more, but didn't. He looked down at his hands resting in his lap, his fingers struggling to remain interlaced.

"Were you about to make a big mistake, Xavier?"

He looked at me and grimaced.

"What?"

"Were you thinking of making a big mistake?"

"What kind of mistake, Daniel?"

It was a conversation I didn't want to have. Instead, I pounded the wheel and shouted, "I've been looking for you for hours. I've been everywhere. Fuck you, Xavier."

He stayed silent for a moment, his chest rising and falling. Then, in a very quiet voice, he said, "It's hard enough to be in this car with all that rain outside. The yelling doesn't help."

That's right, the bastard was playing the victim. Then I suddenly thought about the vacuum cleaners in the back of my car. I could drop the guy off at his place and drive to Cascais. Make up some excuse for missing my morning appointment. The world was still turning, and every minute that passed was a minute lost.

"What did you come here to do, Xavier?"

"You thought I was going to kill myself."

My heart skipped a beat.

"Don't talk nonsense, Xavier."

"You thought jumping off a bridge was my only reason for leaving home," Xavier said, through a half smile.

Look, Almodôvar. I wasn't angry. On the contrary.

Xavier righted his lips again and went on.

"Don't worry. I would have thought the same. Look at me. The fact that I'm still breathing goes against all the odds. I could have won the lottery, but I'm alive instead."

I laughed.

He didn't. He just let his head fall back against the headrest and closed his eyes.

I looked straight ahead. The rain was still falling, but the street had disappeared behind the misted glass.

We stayed like that for a long time. Then he turned and looked into the back.

"What's in the boxes?"

"Vacuum cleaners. I have to sell them."

He nodded.

"Do you want to know why I left home?" he asked.

"Why?"

"I was looking for Ávila."

"Who is Ávila?"

"Fernando Ávila."

"Our seventh grade math teacher?"

"Yeah."

"What happened to him?"

"He called me last night around five in the morning. He said some kids were following him. They wanted to jump him."

"And he called you?"

"Yeah, we're friends."

"You are?"

"He visits me sometimes. We talk math, he lends me physics books, that kind of shit."

"For how long?"

"I'm not sure. They told him I didn't leave my house, and he showed up to ask if I needed anything. It was during my third or fourth year at home."

Did you know about this, Almodôvar? Did you know Ávila visited Xavier? And it was important to him, so important that Xavier left the house for him. How did I not know this? Are there more people visiting him we don't know about?

"Does he still teach?" I asked.

Xavier shook his head.

"He was fired about five years back. One of the parents accused him of touching a kid, though the kid never actually came forward with any details. Other parents joined the protest, some teachers too. It turned into a witch-hunt. The school never gave him a chance, just asked him to leave. No one would hire him after that; the rumors had jumped the school walls. He started drinking. Or maybe he was drinking before that, but afterward he lost all moderation. He spent his days just hanging around. He'd stop in a bar, drink anything they put in front of him, then move on to the next one. Every so often he'd wake up underneath a park bench or at the feet of some statue. When the money ran out, he started begging. I helped him a few times. Last year he started giving blow jobs here in the shopping center bathrooms for ten or twenty euros a pop."

"Shit, I didn't know Ávila was gay."

"Does it bother you?"

"No, of course not. But he visited you?"

"Fuck off, Daniel."

"I'm just asking."

Xavier urgently clutched at the door handle, as if he was about to open it. But then he froze, suspended in his unfinished gesture. He didn't dare leave the car.

"You left home after twelve years just to look for Ávila?"

"They wanted to beat him up. The dude had no one else."

"You could have called me," I said.

"I did call. You didn't answer."

"I turn off my ringer at night. It wasn't personal . . ."

He didn't respond.

"And now?" I asked.

"And now what?"

"And now where's Ávila?"

"I don't know. I looked everywhere." He sighed.

"Who wanted to jump him?"

"Kids. Fucking homophobes who were never even his students. They whisper about him in school hallways like he's the bogeyman. Kids chase him down the street screaming *faggot*; they tell him to take it in the ass, spit on him. He's usually too drunk to turn around."

"Kids?"

"Kids."

Then I remembered, Almodôvar.

"I know where he is," I said.

Xavier took his hand from the door handle.

"You do?"

I started the car. The windshield wipers took up their dance. I made a U-turn. Xavier said nothing, trying to follow what I was doing. When he saw that we were entering the parking garage under the shopping center, he said, "I checked this place when it was still dark out. Ávila wasn't here."

"I . . . think he is," I stammered.

I drove through the poorly lit passages of the parking garage, past rows of parked cars interspersed with empty spaces, the air filled with silence and the occasional snort of an engine. From time to time, someone would cross in front of us and disappear into a car. I drove slowly so we could peer into the spaces between the cars. I imagined Mr. Ávila's legs sticking out from under a van. We stopped for a moment in front of the elevators going up to the shops. When a man got out, Xavier squeezed my arm tightly. We watched him closely as he paid at the machine and, with heavy bags in one hand, looked around for his car. Somehow, Xavier wanted to believe that our solution lay with that man, that he would solve everything and get us out of there fast. Except I had seen those kids. We kept going.

I drove down another level, where there were only a few parked cars. The cement absorbed the white fluorescent lights. There was no sign of motion, only a few places where the kids could hide. I advanced along the pathways, disregarding the arrows painted on the ground. I made a slow figure eight, which brought us back to face the ramp up to the level we had just left.

"What's that?" asked Xavier.

I followed the direction of his gaze. There were two vans parked against the back wall. Everything seemed still. I looked harder, but the vans appeared to be empty. And then I saw it: on top of one van there were two people lying belly-down, side by side, heads toward the wall; from our angle, we couldn't see their heads, just their restless legs.

I put the car in first gear and drove around a column in the direction of the vans.

"Turn off your lights," said Xavier.

I turned off the headlights and drove as slowly as I could without stalling.

"Are those the kids?" asked Xavier.

"I think so."

Look, Almodôvar. I had no clue about anything. I was acting on instinct, my muscles operating on some kind of mechanical impulse. And I was trying not to think. If I had been thinking, I would have gotten the hell out of there. I had too many of my own problems to play the hero for my seventh grade math teacher.

"What are they doing?" asked Xavier.

I didn't answer. I steered to the left. More of the bodies on the van came into view.

"What are they holding?" asked Xavier.

He was right: they were leaning over the edge of the van's roof and holding something in their hands—something with a light.

"Phones," I said.

"Look at those guys," Xavier whispered.

Crammed into the few meters between the truck and the wall were other people, five or six, maybe more, all staring at the wall as if it were a TV. They were just kids, no older than fifteen, sixteen, wearing baseball caps, puffy jackets, sneakers, skinny jeans, backpacks—the whole uniform. Were we ever like that? I don't remember. Their faces were half-covered, bandannas over their noses and mouths.

My foot delivered a steady, gentle pressure to the accelerator; the car maintained its speed, the engine noise reduced to a faint purr. The kids didn't seem to notice us. They were distracted by something else.

"No sign of Ávila," sighed Xavier.

As I recall, that was the last thing he said. After that, he shut down. By that I mean he just sat there, taking it in, his lips pressed together in a hard line, reactionless. He shouldn't have been there. Imagine, Almodôvar. You leave your house one day after twelve years and one of the first things you see is a bunch of hoodlums in an underground parking garage doing terrible things. We were close to them—maybe fifteen yards away, maybe even closer—when one of the kids on the van saw us and alerted the others. They all turned and looked, their movements synchronized, like in a play. A space opened up between two of the kids who were standing, and we could just make out what was behind them: Ávila was lying on the floor, huddled against the wall. His hair was matted and moist, his shirt was filthy, and he was naked from the waist down. A kid with his back to us was making a game out of spraying our mathematics professor's body with piss, while the others stared down at my car as if it were a bull.

The seconds ticked by. I turned to Xavier. He was staring back at the kids, but he didn't seem scared. He had an incredible calm about him, as if he had long since been preparing for that very moment. My hands were on the wheel, my right foot on the accelerator, my whole body tensed, and yet I couldn't decide what to do next. Then one of the kids took a step forward. He had a soda can in his hand. He took a sip under his bandanna and then tossed the can at us languidly, like a girl. The can traced a short arc and bounced off the hood of the car, making a racket that echoed off the cement.

The kids laughed.

Keeping the clutch to the floor, I pressed the accelerator. The engine roared. I thought: How is this happening? I just wanted to make sure Xavier wasn't lying on the train tracks somewhere and then go sell vacuum cleaners in Cascais.

"Get lost!" yelled one of the kids.

I released the clutch and the car shot out in their direction. They hesitated, believing for one long second that nothing could happen to them. Then they suddenly scattered. Only then did I hit the brakes. The car didn't stop right away; the tires skidded on the cement.

One of the kids fell across the hood and then sank to the ground next to Xavier's window. We only came to a full stop as we bumped into the rear of the van.

I looked around. The kid who had been pissing on Ávila was standing in front of the car, staring at us. Ávila was still huddled against the wall, not moving, as if he were waiting for us all to leave so he could get some sleep. I looked into the rearview mirror; the kids were starting to pick themselves up. I kicked the car into reverse and sped backward, aiming for them as they ran. Then I drove back toward the van.

"Xavier!" I shouted. "Xavier!"

He didn't move.

I opened the door and got out. The kid next to Ávila backed up a few steps but didn't run. He was short, no older than twelve or thirteen. His face was masked by a Portuguese flag bandanna, his head was shaved, and he had a thick gold hoop in one ear like a pirate. He buttoned up his fly, all the while staring at me. He didn't move when I approached Ávila; he just lit a cigarette and stood there watching me. I grabbed Ávila under his armpits. His clothes were soaked; there was blood on his forehead. The smell of piss stung my nose before it reached my stomach. When I hoisted him up, he let out a groan and turned his head in my direction, though I'm not sure if he actually saw me. I dragged him to the car.

"Want some help?" the kid asked.

I looked at him; his shoulders were trembling with laughter. I let go of Ávila with one hand to open the door to the backseat, and he collapsed to his knees. Then I saw the three vacuum cleaners. Xavier was just sitting there looking at me, waiting for me to figure it out.

Clearly, Almodôvar, there wasn't enough room in the back for all the vacuum cleaners and Ávila. Something had to go. And I'm sure that from the comfort of your cell, the decision seems simple. Only, it wasn't. I'm not ashamed that I had to think about it. Leaving behind one of those vacuum cleaners meant paying for it in full. It would be a lot of money, money I didn't have. But the kid was still standing there behind us, silently smoking his cigarette, waiting. Leaving Ávila and going for help would have been a death sentence for him. I could have called the police, but the other kids were starting to regroup, and we wouldn't have been able to hold them off for very long. I called out for help half a dozen times, loudly, my voice vibrating in the tight space between the floor and the ceiling. Then I pulled at the edge of one of the boxes and let it tumble out of the car. I wedged Ávila into the empty space as spasms of pain hindered his every movement.

I was running back to the driver's side when I realized there was someone near the ceiling. A kid on top of the van was holding the phone, pointing it at me: he had been filming everything. The others seemed to have disappeared. I got in the car, put it in reverse, and then turned the wheel until we were facing the exit. That's when I saw the second kid, who was also still on the van, lying facedown, his chin against the metal roof. Just as I noticed him, he peeked up at us. His face wasn't covered, and the flash of his image was enough for me to recognize who it was. My first thought was, What is he doing here?

Almodôvar, it's all your fault. You were gone. People needed you, and you had to go rob a gas station as if the rules of life didn't apply to you. Otherwise, tell me why your son Vasco was lying on top of that van filming a gang of hoodlums pissing on an old drunk. You abandoned your son. It's possible that nothing would have happened, but it did.

It was a matter of seconds. I didn't stop the car. I didn't get out to speak to him. I left him behind with the vacuum cleaner. I won't ask for your forgiveness. As I sped out of the garage, the kids bombarded us with their backpacks. Xavier's window shattered, as if by magic, the glass transformed into hail that spilled into his lap. He screamed, threw up his hands, and brought an arm across his face, his skin and clothing glistening with broken glass. Then we drove up the ramp toward the exit.

"Are you hurt?" I asked.

He just sat there, his hands on the dash. There wasn't any blood. He only spoke when we approached the exit.

"We have to pay for the parking," he said, his tone strangely relaxed.

Almodôvar, we wanted to get out of there fast, but we had a red-and-white card to validate before we could get through the gate. And I thought: Just go, ram through that shit and no one will ever catch us. But no one acts on those impulses in real life, so we turned back to look for a pay station. I had a feeling that our carelessness would cost us a lot, that the little bastards were already organized, hidden among the cars, waiting for us to pass—that we would never leave that place.

We found a machine next to the elevators, and Xavier, his hands still on the dash, whispered, "I don't have any change."

"Seriously, Xavier?"

He gave me a bewildered look. Then he shifted his gaze an inch to the backseat and whispered, "We have to get him to the hospital."

"Fuck off, Xavier. Stop talking."

I got out to pay. I could have called security, asked for help, filed a report. But we just wanted to get out of there.

By the time I got back in the car, the stench of piss had become unbearable. Thirty seconds later, we were on the street. The rain had stopped and the world had just become more complicated.

At the hospital, we filled out all the paperwork, made statements to the police, gave them our information, and promised to cooperate. I didn't report your son; I didn't even tell them there had been two little bastards filming it all. Xavier was anxious: he shook the glass out of his hair and coat, and a rain of little diamonds bounced off the sidewalk in front of the hospital entrance; he smoked a whole pack of cigarettes in just over an hour; around three in the afternoon, he locked himself in the bathroom and stayed there until we left. I called the hotel in Cascais and explained the situation. The woman I spoke to understood. We talked for a few minutes, and in the end she said that she'd get in touch to plan a new demo, but that she didn't have any spots left for that week. I did the math: the rental fee for the five vacuum cleaners, plus the one I had left at the parking garage, plus the broken car window. The damage was over nine hundred euros. I didn't have nine hundred euros.

Ávila was hospitalized with a head injury. By the time we left, he had come to. He heard us talking, gave us a weak wave, and made some noises we couldn't interpret. I had the feeling he didn't know who we were. They had cleaned him up; he looked like our math teacher from twenty-five years before—he didn't even look that much older. Xavier asked him what had happened, but he just blinked.

When we left the hospital, Xavier said, "I want to go home."

He was like a child.

"Fuck you, Xavier," I said. "We're going back to the garage. I want to see if the vacuum cleaner is still there."

"I'd prefer it if you dropped me off at home first."

"And I'd prefer it if you're weren't such a cowardly little shit."

He looked at me with a trace of indignation. I knew I was being unfair, given that he had left home on his own to go look for Ávila—but I didn't say so.

I drove back to the shopping center with Xavier riding in the back, far from the broken window, in case it started raining again. We entered the parking garage and explained what had happened to the first guard we saw, asking him to follow us down to the lower levels. The guard got into the car. At that hour, both levels were full. It didn't even look like the same place, and it was hard for us to find the spot where it had happened. Then Xavier suddenly pointed.

"It was there," he said.

The vans were gone.

So was the vacuum cleaner.

All that remained was a puddle of piss near the wall.

CYPRUS, GERMANY, MALTA, NICARAGUA, THE UNITED KINGDOM: 7.1

Almodôvar, you don't know this, but I had a Plan. I had it written down, step by step, on 126 pages of a black notebook, a sort of daily planner for the distant future. Every now and then I'd reread it to refresh my memory. From time to time, I'd add a point, or alter a point, or tear out an entire page. The Plan was not definitive; I've never been so naive. For example, on page 12, where it said *Never weigh more than 172 lbs.*, I had crossed out the *172* and written *180*. On page 37, under the heading *When I get married*, there was a long paragraph that I had redacted with a black marker, and I had written *Rethink*. Page 61 is the continuation of a point on child-rearing that I'd written on page 6, added nine years later. Pages 23 and 24 were torn out.

The original version of the Plan was based on good sense. I hadn't written anything outlandish; I'd never suggested anything that was beyond my powers. I remember writing it out and thinking: All of this is possible, if you do everything right, if you stay focused on each step, it will all happen. So I fought every day for nearly a decade to make sure that those words would come true. I believed in work, in what I could accomplish through sheer physical and mental strength. I made changes to what I'd written because I had changed, my ideas and ambitions had changed, or at least adapted to changes in the world. But not a single line of my Plan mentions vacuum cleaners, monthly trips to see my kids, or days with so many unfilled hours. My question is this: When had the world changed so much that I had lost my ability to adapt, and the Plan stopped making sense?

I thought about it a lot. My only conclusion was this: I never could have predicted this situation. I never could have imagined that I'd lose my job with the agency. I had started young, at nineteen, and I learned quickly: all the logistics of a trip, the geography of every country, the bureaucracy of each destination. I was able to create a fourteen-night itinerary for anyone, anywhere on the planet, after talking to them for ten minutes. Five years later, they had moved me from one of their agency branches to their main offices. I started to manage projects. I had an office of my own overlooking the avenue, an annual budget of almost a million euros to manage. The director trusted me—the new kid, adept at all the new technology—to compete with the growing demand for online travel bookings. Not even at its most optimistic did my Plan take into account such success. And I gave it my all. I had keys to the office; every day I was the first to arrive and the last to leave, my dedication absolute.

But we never had a chance. The Internet is a tsunami; you can't fight it. All we could do was jump on the wave and ride it, hoping to reach land before we went under. It happened so fast. The first round of firing was in May of 2010. Three months later, they closed their branch in Porto. My budget was suspended indefinitely, all pending projects on hold until further notice. More people were fired. At the end of the year, we received an e-mail from the director announcing a wage reduction across the board. He asked everyone to make a special effort at such a critical time; he repeated *We are a team* three times in ten lines. The next month, no one was paid. In March, they shuttered the Lisbon offices.

I was lucky. They kept me on until the end; I witnessed it all. During the last month, there were three of us working in a space where fourteen people had been. One afternoon, the director appeared and bluntly announced that there was no more work, the company had filed for bankruptcy. He didn't apologize and seemed to be just as shocked as the rest of us, his hands trembling, his eyes staring into space. We hurriedly packed up our things in boxes. The building would be vacated the next day so they could rent it as soon as possible. They promised us a severance that they never paid. The case is still pending in court.

I wasn't afraid, I remember that much. See, I had the future written in a notebook that I had read dozens of times, studied, and pondered, and the words lent me strength, became instinct, my certainty about the future unwavering. The agency's closure was nothing more than a setback—and my Plan had room for setbacks. I believed I'd find comparable work at another agency within a month. I thought: This might be a good thing. I was thirty-seven years old, and there was such a thing as staying in the same job for too long. A change would be good for my career; I'd have new projects, new colleagues, new perspectives. So I got organized, updated my CV, sent it out to dozens of agencies—and not just in Lisbon, but in Porto, Algarve, Madrid, Seville, and Brussels. My days were as full as they had been when I was working: I sent e-mails, made phone calls, browsed job sites, filled out applications, met with recruiters, went on interviews, shook hands, smiled, looked serious at all the right times, spoke with confidence. It was as if looking for a job were a job in itself.

Except there were no jobs, Almodôvar. That year, I spoke with my old boss on the phone a few times. He'd call me for no real reason, just to chat, tell me about the trips he and his wife were taking, trips they had postponed for a lifetime because of work—even though his work had been traveling. He guffawed as he told me he didn't miss our old office, which was still for rent, he said, abandoned. He was fifty-three years old and claimed that forced retirement was the best thing that had ever happened to him. He'd always end the call by asking me if I had found a job, and before hanging up, he'd make it a point to say: "If you hear of anything for me, let me know."

Almodôvar, despite all his enthusiasm, my former boss didn't want to be unemployed. And he was counting on me to find him a job.

What I'm trying to say is that the world had stopped. I wasn't even forty, and my life had stopped moving forward. And my Plan didn't say a thing about that. I couldn't have planned for my world to stop, just as I couldn't have planned for Marta to move away with the kids. Even so, I wasn't afraid. I spent a few nights poring over that notebook. What had failed? Where were the loose ends? I couldn't find any flaws. It was a good plan. A just plan. It had all been viable. Even so, I tried to rewrite everything, adapt my idea of the future to the new limits of reality. I pondered the alternatives:

Delete a marriage.

Delete a child.

An apartment with two bedrooms instead of three.

An apartment an hour from work instead of thirty minutes.

Any job instead of the right job.

Any life instead of the right life.

No version seemed better than the first. Any compromise seemed wrong. I didn't know how to live in this new version of the future. My life was already made, and there was no going back. All I could do was fight.

For half a year I continued to wake up early. I would sit at the computer and look for jobs—any jobs. When I found work selling vacuum cleaners, I tried my best. It seemed like a way out, an opportunity. Then Xavier left his apartment, and I lost that vacuum; I suddenly owed a lot of money, and WRU suspended my contract until I paid them in full. I couldn't afford to pay them in full. I was jobless again—though it's naive to think that selling vacuum cleaners had ever been a real job.

That was in November. I started to look for work again, but there was nothing. I did the math: the money I had left in the bank against my house and monthly expenses. If nothing happened by February, I'd miss my mortgage payment. I thought about selling the house, which was too big for one person, and buying a smaller one. But that would mean letting go of the hope that our situation was only temporary, the hope that Marta and the kids might come back home to Lisbon.

On the other hand, time stretched out before me, and I didn't have enough gestures or thoughts to fill it, to stop myself from getting washed away in surges of boredom. Night and day became one—I had no reason to distinguish them—and my insomnia no longer bothered me, so I began to sleep for two or three hours at a time, regardless of whether it was light or dark out. Maybe I was keeping the same slow time that exists in prison. I imagine you've grown used to it by now. Only I didn't want to do that, do you understand? I didn't want to slow down.

And then there was your son.

After that day in the parking garage I couldn't stop thinking about him. It didn't seem possible that he had been there. When had he become that kind of person? When had he ceased to be the kid I watched grow up, the one who rode bikes with us on Sunday mornings, the one who used to ride on my back to soccer practice? What had happened to him, inside of him, that had led to that moment? What hadn't happened? Then I thought: Maybe it doesn't matter; kids do stupid things every day, test the limits. We made our mistakes. Remember that night at Sesimbra Beach when we broke into an ice cream kiosk at 2:00 a.m.? We stole five or six huge cartons, filled our three freezers, gorged ourselves on ice cream for weeks.

But that's not the same, is it, Almodôvar? So he didn't piss on Ávila like all his friends did, but maybe he just didn't have to go. Or maybe he was waiting his turn and would have done it if Xavier and I hadn't shown up. But whatever the case, he was there with the group, he did nothing to prevent what happened, and he watched it all with a phone in hand, filming the whole scene. Shit, it wasn't good. It wasn't the kind of behavior you'd expect from a human being.

One night, during a quick nap, I dreamt that you and I were in your cell, sitting on the floor, our knees drawn up to our chins. Time was passing quickly, months, maybe years, and we just talked: women, soccer, Xavier, memories. Dumb shit. It was a good dream, all those years condensed into less than ten minutes. When I woke up, I thought: I want to talk to Vasco. And then I decided I wouldn't.

You could have called Clara.

Almodôvar, I did call Clara. Because, ultimately, Vasco is her son. He's yours too, but you're the bastard who removed yourself from all of this.

Clara asked me to come meet her at the clinic. We talked in the cafeteria next to the waiting rooms. And despite the uniform, despite the name tag, Clara didn't look like a nurse. Sitting there near all those patients writhing in pain, she seemed more like them. She squeezed her eyes shut, as if the effort to keep her body upright were growing unbearably painful.

When I asked if she felt okay, she said, "I'm just tired."

Almodôvar, the thing is, when you were arrested, your in-laws had to start helping Clara with money. Your mother-in-law sent money for three or four months but stopped when her own rent went up. Clara got by like this for almost a year. It was hard, but it was doable. Then her mother fell in the shower and broke her leg in three places. She went four months without walking. She recovered partially through physical therapy, but never completely. Clara's father did his best to help his wife with the cooking, the constant churn of laundry, the grocery shopping. But it soon became clear that he needed help too, so they hired a maid. It was no extravagance: his old age demanded it. Between the cost of physical therapy, the medicine, and the maid, they couldn't keep sending money to Clara. So in the end, she had no choice but to pull double shifts at the clinic.

The explanation seems so simple, so logical and sensible. Such an elementary problem should be easily solved. But the solution is you, and you aren't here.

Clara smiled through her fatigue. She said that she was happy to see me, that she missed her friends, that she longed for a good laugh. She asked about me, and I recited a string of lies, a life made of words that effortlessly slipped from my lips. And suddenly we seemed like two normal people again, two friends enjoying the pleasure of catching up. The power of the illusion was frightening.

"I saw Vasco a few weeks ago," I told her.

Clara cocked her head a few degrees, still smiling.

"He was with some other kids," I went on. "They were up to something."

"What do you mean?"

"There was a homeless guy. They were . . . doing stuff to him. There were so many of them, the man couldn't defend himself."

"What kind of stuff?"

"Talk to him, Clara."

She pressed her lips into a thin, straight line.

"He's a good kid," she said in a whisper.

"I know, but even the good kids do stupid things sometimes. Talk to him."

"It's not easy to talk to Vasco."

"But he'll listen to you. You're his mother."

"Right, Daniel. And that should be enough. There should be some kind of magnetic pull between my words and his heart. But it's gone. It was broken when Almodôvar was arrested, and I don't know what to do. We learn to navigate the world in one way, grow used to certain gestures, accept the power of our own instincts, and halfway through our lives we're addicted to our own perspectives. Then something suddenly changes, and everything we knew how to do so well, so easily, to resolve the simplest problems, becomes useless. How did the world change so much?"

She didn't say that.

You weren't there.

Clara never complains out loud. You're the whiner, not her.

Think what you want, Almodôvar.

Clara was silent, one hand fidgeting on the table between us, her eyes closed, as if her eyelids were stuck together.

"I know it's hard," I said, "but if you don't do it now, then it could get to be too late."

Clara opened her eyes and nodded.

"You're right," she whispered. "You're right. I'll talk to him."

She barely parted her lips—an attempt at a smile.

Then she stood up. She gave me a peck on the cheek and walked away, hugging her arms tight around her chest, her shoulders slumping. I knew then that she would never talk to Vasco. She didn't have the strength.

At Christmas, Mateus and Flor came to spend a week with me. Marta brought them and stayed one night. The four of us sat at the table like old times, as if it weren't a special occasion, none of us wanting to admit that half a year had passed. Mateus told stories, referring to our time together online: "Dad, do you remember that time we played checkers with that Australian guy?" or "Dad, do you remember that time we typed everything without vowels?" He laughed his incredible nine-year-old laugh. We laughed with him, even though it wasn't ideal dinnertime conversation. And every time we all stopped talking at the same time, there was no awkwardness, but a shared sense of anticipation, as if each full moment would guarantee another.

When we put the kids to bed, all my movements lagged slightly behind Marta's. The kids were happy to be at home, back in their own beds; they didn't say it, but it was in their eyes, which were brimming with security, and the way they snuggled into their blankets. It was so sad, Almodôvar. Marta must have felt the same, because when we went into the living room and sat on the sofa, the first thing she said was: "You should come back to Viana with us."

She had said the same thing six months earlier when she realized there was no work for her in Lisbon and decided to leave. I gave her the same answer as before: "If things get too hard, if I can't see any future for us here, I will."

She smiled, as if my words were the solution to everything.

"At least put the apartment up for sale. A buyer might come along. Times are hard, but we could still get lucky."

"This is our home . . ."

"It's just an apartment, Daniel. It's not a lung, it's not an eye."

Then she stretched out on the sofa and nestled her feet in my lap. Her pragmatic approach to life made my heart ache. Even so, I agreed to her suggestion.

We spent the rest of the evening talking about trivial things, my hands cupping her feet, neither of us allowing the conversation to veer toward more serious matters. I really needed it, and I think Marta did too. When we finally got into bed, for a moment the mattress seemed too big for us, as if our bodies had shrunken. She pressed herself against me; I wrapped my arms around her. We were still. We could have made love—we hadn't made love for months—and that would have been the right time, but the prospect had become too scary. Marta fell asleep quickly, while I stayed awake for nearly an hour, staring into the darkness before drifting off.

By then my insomnia no longer bothered me. I had learned to ignore my chronic fatigue, living at night as if it were daytime. I wouldn't just lie in bed waiting for sleep to return: I'd flick on the lights, watch TV, eat, shower, read the paper, clean the house—sometimes I'd even go out for a walk. When I felt sleepy, I'd lie down. It was that, or slowly go insane lying there in the quiet, feeling the hours dividing into infinity.

I slept for a few hours and woke just after three. I didn't move for a long time, for fear of making a noise that would wake Marta and the kids. But it wasn't just the idea of waking them. I was afraid of what they might think if they caught me at four in the morning shaving, washing the dishes, eating scrambled eggs. The man they knew didn't do those things so early in the morning. And I wanted to be the man they knew. It wasn't a new feeling, but it was the first time I felt myself policing my own movements. For some reason, it was at the center of everything: losing my ability to be the same man would be like forgetting how to count to ten, or no longer being able to identify the faces of my own children in a crowd.

I got out of bed slowly, as if the floor were covered in sleeping snakes. Marta remained still, her breathing deep. I went into the living room and turned on the TV. I surfed the channels on mute until I came across some cartoons. No children would be watching TV at that hour; the cartoons were there to comfort sleepless adults. Twenty minutes later, Marta appeared. She stood there for a while, looking at the TV as if she couldn't figure out what I was watching, as if she had never seen a cartoon before in her life. Then she plopped down next to me on the sofa, pressed her back into the cushions, making the upholstery sigh, and with open hands she began to vigorously rub at her eyes and cheeks, as if she were rubbing off her existing face to reveal another one hidden under its surface.

"What's wrong?" I asked.

"Insomnia," she replied simply. But her answer gave me hope.

For the first time since we had been apart I thought: I miss her so much. Why did she have to go?

Six months earlier, she had explained that she was tired of staying at home; she felt empty, sunken in invisible waste—that's how she had put it. She wanted to make money again, to have a job, and her father had a job for her in Viana do Castelo. She concluded by saying, "Here, at this point, I feel like I've disappeared."

But it wasn't true. She may have been unemployed, but her presence was tremendously important. We're used to defining a person by their profession, and when the job is gone, the person disappears with it. That's not right. Marta had always been a whole person; employment is no more than an accessory for her, like a bracelet, or a hairstyle, or a manner of speaking. Regardless, I told her she was right. What's more, I supported her. We never talked about us, our marriage, our forced separation, the distance between us so great we'd have to reconcile it day and night. Because we believed in us, Almodôvar. We had been together for fourteen years, and we still liked each other; why wouldn't we believe? Six months later, sitting beside her, watching cartoons at four in the morning, our separation seemed too absurd to explain logically.

She cuddled up on the sofa and laid her head on my arm. We watched TV together by the light of the cartoons that flickered in the room. Every now and again we'd laugh at the same time. I wondered what she did when we weren't together, the people she'd met, the reasons for her every smile, for her every moment of anguish. She seemed the same. Maybe nothing happened in her life, no memorable conversations, no light, no darkness. Maybe her heart had stopped months ago. But that was so unlikely. We talked almost every day on the phone, it's true, and she told me things about her life in Viana. And yet what she said had no substance, as if nothing she did was that important.

On the other hand, I hadn't told her about Xavier leaving his apartment, the scene in the parking garage, my decision to leave the vacuum cleaner to make room for Ávila, all the money I owed, the job I no longer had. She didn't know that things had gotten even more complicated. She didn't know we were going to lose the house. She didn't know the changes I had to make to the Plan. I could have told her everything at that moment. I could have turned off the TV, taken her hand, and started speaking. She would have understood, hugged me, and told me I wasn't alone, we'd get through it together; she might have kissed me, and then she would have convinced me to go back with her and the kids to Viana. And maybe I would have done it, Almodôvar. Just maybe. So I said nothing.

I woke up again after six. The TV was off, the room just beginning to emerge from the darkness, the shadows losing their depth, and from the outside world came the faint patter of rain. Marta was no longer on the sofa, but I didn't crawl back into bed with her. I stayed still, my eyes open, until my kids got up. At about half past eight, Marta appeared in the kitchen, already showered, dressed as if it was going to be a sunny day. She was smiling and talking, but her eyes didn't rest on anything for more than a moment, as if she didn't want to commit to any object in that space. She drank a mug of coffee with milk and went out. She returned after lunch, loaded her bags into the car, hugged the children, pressed her face to mine for a few seconds, and then she left.

It rained relentlessly for the rest of the week. But that's not why we hardly left the apartment. Flor and Mateus had missed their home, the space and its furniture, and whenever I asked if they wanted to go anywhere, they didn't seem very enthusiastic. I had longed to have them at home, my kids back where they belonged, near me, sharing our daily routines, the reality of it so natural it gave me goose bumps. And the time fucking passed. I knew the week would end and none of it would have been enough. I needed more. I tried to get as close as possible. It wasn't easy; they had changed so much over the past year. Our phone calls and regular visits weren't enough for me to keep up with it all, and much of what we had to share had disappeared.

Mateus lived online. I thought the games, jokes, and videos were his way of feeling close to me. They weren't. He was addicted to them. His world revolved around guys falling off their bikes and surfing dogs and angry birds toppling towers of pigs and kids challenging other kids and other crap that was irresistible to a nine-year-old kid. And when I sat down next to him, we'd speak without taking our eyes off the computer screen, and all our conversations revolved around what was happening on the screen in front of us, with no consideration of past or future. It was so easy, Almodôvar. Laughter came to us so easily. The possibility of life just going on like that forever seemed so strong. I wanted to laugh like that with my son until the end of my life. In short, everything was wrong. One morning, I put his laptop in a closet. I told Mateus that he couldn't spend his days online, that life required more effort from him.

"If you go on like this," I told him, "your muscles are going to atrophy. One day you won't be able to swim or run, or even pick up a pen."

Mateus wouldn't have it. He accused me of dreaming up arguments that made no sense in the real world. He called me a fascist. I asked him if he knew what a fascist was.

"Flor knows," he said.

Then he threw himself on the floor and screamed for a while, as if he were three. Suddenly, he stopped and sat on the sofa, staring at the wall. He stayed like that for the rest of the day, except when he came to the table for lunch. He didn't say a word for eight or nine hours. It was painful for me not to hear his voice. Before dinner, Flor came to me. She spread out the newspaper in front of me.

"It's true, he's always on the computer," she said, "and it's too much. But there are worse things in the world, much worse. Look at today's paper. The word *war* appears fourteen times. *Recession* appears twenty-one times. *Crime* is repeated thirty-seven times. And *poverty* shows up eleven times."

I leafed through the paper. There were words underlined everywhere. I wanted to tell her that if people kept spending so much time online, in twenty years those same words would appear thirty times more frequently—or thirty thousand times.

Instead I just said, "You're right."

Almodôvar, I didn't want to spend the week with my son like that, in that silence. That's why I let him have the laptop back. During dinner, we watched a video of the most incredible goals in the history of soccer. And then, before they went to bed, we played a game online with the sole objective of making a frog eat flies. Mateus's laughter restored an immense sense of normalcy to the house.

That night, I flipped through the newspapers from the past few days. All of them had words underlined—accident, robbery, unemployment, poor, conflict, inflation, dead—a kind of accounting of all that was wrong in this world. That's what Flor had been doing with the papers. She spent so many hours reading: papers, magazines, books on politics, the economy, history, articles online. I don't know where she dug that stuff up. Marta and I never read; we never bought books. Flor absorbed all that information and spoke on the state of the world like a pundit on TV, repeating whole sentences from the newspaper, as if everything about our existence on this planet would fit in the space of fifteen or twenty words. Sometimes it was too easy to forget that she was only thirteen. There was a cynicism in her voice, a tone that was forced, though no less real, as if she knew about not only the present but also the future, and in her mind the future was a swamp in which all of mankind was mired with no hope of escape. I'd watch her mouth move, and it was as if what she said didn't match the movement of her lips.

I did what I thought was best: I stayed up late, sitting at the dinner table, the newspapers from that week spread out before me, and tried to find words that could undo the words Flor had underlined: peace, growth, festivities, discovery, happiness. Almodôvar, the words were there; I found them all. I underlined them all. But in the end, when they were all counted, Flor's words outnumbered mine. Of course, it wasn't definitive; the press has never been a mirror of the world. Their pages have a larger purpose—I understand that. But how do I explain to my thirteen-year-old daughter that conflict, conflict, conflict, peace, conflict, conflict, conflict, conflict, conflict, conflict, conflict, conflict, peace, conflict, conflict, conflict, conflict, conflict, peace, conflict, conflict, conflict, conflict, peace, conflict, conflict, conflict, conflict, conflict, conflict, conflict, conflict, peace, conflict, conflict, conflict, conflict, conflict, peace, conflict is not representative of our reality?

How do you know it isn't?

Because I know.

You have no way of knowing. You'd have to evaluate all the ongoing conflicts in the world. And not just wars or shots exchanged between police and ATM robbers, but fights between couples, kids at school, the hatred some kids develop toward their parents, parents who fill their children full of crap, all the cases in all the courts in all the different countries in the world, all the cases that fail to go to court, the momentary hatred that arises during traffic jams, companies trying to overthrow their competition, skewed partisan disputes, soccer games that end in brutal fan-fights, the constant battles we fight within ourselves, government protests . . . And after you account for it all, as Xavier would say, you'd have to prove that the total is less than the sum of everything good in the world. Maybe you'd be right in the end. Or maybe not.

Fuck you, Almodôvar. I was just trying to protect Flor. My daughter was thirteen and already so jaded. I didn't want that for her. I didn't want her to stop believing that the world could be a good place just because I was unemployed, just because her mother and I had to live apart, just because the newspapers were full of the wrong words.

But that's irrelevant. It was a good week. Any week with my kids is a good week. On the last day, I helped them with the homework they were supposed to complete over the holidays. The first hour was hard; they couldn't concentrate. But I didn't force it, and suddenly there was silence—a good silence, the silence you hear when people are doing something. We worked like that for almost three hours. Our conversations consisted of numbers, verbs in English, names of kings, the digestive system of ruminants. Anyone listening in for a minute wouldn't have been able to understand what we were talking about, yet we understood each other perfectly. I was their father, and they were my kids.

When they left, the first thing I thought was: They are more important to my calculation than I thought. Away from them, my happiness index can't be 8.0. I listened in on the silence, my heart beating on its own. I imagined the days passing before I'd see them again, their image in my mind growing faint. I thought about the impact of their presence on my heart. How much was it all worth? Two points? Three? Maybe. But that would mean that my happiness index would fall to 6.0 or even 5.0. And those values didn't seem real. Look, Almodôvar. I hardly doubted my happiness: I felt it; it existed to the same extent that I existed, like my arm or the smell of my skin. The simple fact of being alive, there and then, was worth half of my happiness. None of this was new to me—I had known it for a long time. So I decided that the absence of my children was equivalent to a 0.9-point decrease in my happiness index. Which put me at **7.1**.

During the week I spent with my kids, Xavier e-mailed and texted three or four times, wanting to know how I was handling the whole vacuum cleaner situation. I didn't reply. He called me in early January. I answered the phone but didn't speak.

"You're mad," he said.

Look, Almodôvar. He says these things, but it's not so much what he says but how he says it, his tone, as if he were a child and I were his father. He knows he screwed up, but he doesn't want to be scolded.

"Fuck you, Xavier."

"We did a good thing."

"I'm going to lose my house, Xavier. That doesn't seem like a good thing to me."

"We saved a man's life."

"Don't be so dramatic. They were just pissing on him."

"They weren't just pissing on him," Xavier whispered.

He paused. I could tell he wanted to speak but didn't want to say anything that would make me angrier.

"Ávila is doing well," he said finally. "He dropped by two days ago. He looked good. Neat hair, trimmed beard, clean clothes. He wasn't drunk. He didn't stay long. He just wanted to thank us. He asked me to tell you that if you need help—anything at all—he'd like to compensate you."

"A thousand euros. I want a thousand euros."

"I doubt he has a thousand euros."

"Then he can't help me."

More silence followed—it was always the same shit on the phone with Xavier. I resolved to count to five and then hang up. I started counting. When I got to five and he hadn't said anything, I kept counting. He spoke again when I reached eight.

"Daniel, are you there?"

"No."

"I've been thinking about that day down there in the parking garage, about those kids. They were recording everything."

"Xavier, that's what kids do these days. They have cameras on their phones. If we had had phones with cameras on them when we were young, we would have done the same."

"I know. But they don't just record. They upload their movies online to prove to the world that their lives are really happening."

"So?"

"So . . . I found it online."

"The video from that day?"

"Yeah . . . those little bastards who pissed on Ávila."

"Are you sure?"

"Of course I'm sure. It's all there. The kids. Ávila. Us."

"Us?"

"It was uploaded last Tuesday. As of today it's gotten four thousand views."

"Send me the link."

We hung up. I sat at the computer. Xavier's e-mail took three minutes to appear in my in-box. The video had a title: *Piss-Soaked Faggot.* It lasted ten minutes and forty-six seconds. If it had been written out, the screenplay would have been as follows:

00:00—Ávila is on the ground, still, his eyes wide as if he already knows what will happen to him in two minutes. Five kids, their faces masked, are gathered around him, trying to pull off his pants.

00:27—Ávila flounders uncontrollably, like a freshly caught fish, holding his breath, on the strength of his most basic instincts.

00:42—A sixth kid appears in the shot, takes two steps, and kicks Ávila in the head. Ávila freezes, wraps his arms around his head, and lies inert on the cement. The kids finish taking off his pants and underwear. One of them throws one of Ávila's shoes toward the camera; the shoe bounces off the top of the van.

1:41—They drag Ávila to the wall and lie him on his side; his shirt is filthy, his ass and legs exposed.

2:05—One of the kids opens his fly, turns to the camera, raises his arms and shakes his hips, and his dick dances as if it had a life of its own. Someone is laughing, maybe the person filming, or someone close to him. The kid with his dick out turns his attention back to Ávila, does nothing for two seconds, and then starts pissing, the arc of it finishing between Ávila's legs. Then the kid shifts the trajectory toward Ávila's buttocks.

(Ávila does nothing, he just lies there like a log, waiting for it all to end, only moving to rub the spot on his head where the kid kicked him.)

2:52—The kid stops peeing. The others applaud. The kid steps back, disappears from the shot.

3:14—Another kid steps up, unbuttons his pants, lets them drop to his ankles, and he starts to piss, a hard stream right at Ávila's bare ass.

Almodôvar, that kid with the shaved head and hoop earring wasn't the only one who peed on our math teacher. Five kids had done the same thing before him. And he might not have been the last if Xavier and I hadn't interrupted their little game.

7:29—Someone cries out, the camera trembles, the image blurs as the shot travels around through space to a car on the other side of the van, a few meters away.

7:52—One of the kids throws a can at the car.

7:58—The car engine revs.

8:00—One of the kids shouts: "Get lost, asshole!"

8:02—The car jerks toward the kids. The kids scatter to the sides, running as if it were a game.

8:05—The car hits the back of the van.

Look, Almodôvar. I knew the scene. I remembered every moment as if I had rehearsed every gesture ad nauseam before the recording started. Except that somehow, it didn't seem possible that the person inside that car chasing those kids was me. And when finally, I—the me in the video—got out of the car and faced the kid with the shaved head (8:26), when I approached Ávila and knelt down to lift him (8:57), it occurred to me that the ending of the video might be different from the ending I experienced in reality.

Someone needs to teach that kid a lesson, I thought. Someone should have gone over to him. Ávila was fine. He could have waited two minutes while I gave the bastard the beating he deserved. I waited for it to happen. The seconds passed, the time bar running out, and then the kid asked, "Want some help?" (9:33), and I was still waiting for me to make a run at him.

But it never happened. I feel the deep anguish and shame of having done nothing. As if Ávila had died that day.

10:32—I set Ávila in the backseat of the car where the vacuum cleaner used to be.

10:38—I look up to the camera, but not directly, for two seconds.

10:45—I get in the car.

10:46—The end.

Besides the title, there was no other description. The username of the person who posted the video was RioNinja, and it was the only video on their profile. In less than four days it had already gotten 4,302 views. Who were these people? How they had found their way to it? I imagined that some had watched the video more than once. Why? And why had that video attracted more interest than our site?

I clicked "Play" again. The video restarted, with Ávila on the ground, the little bastards closing in on him, pulling off his pants. But the content was no longer relevant. I watched the filming. The image hardly trembled; the hand holding the mobile phone had been steady, the shot unmoving as the kids stepped in and out of it, as if they were on a stage. There were no cuts. I tried to calculate exactly where the camera had been located. On the van, of course. But there had been two people with phones, and they had both been filming from the van. Which one of them had put the video online?

Almodôvar, I was trying to figure out if your son had been the cameraman. It's hard to explain, but somehow I managed to understand how it could have happened: suddenly a group of kids starts to piss on a man, and it doesn't bother him immediately. He experiences an adrenaline rush that's impossible to ignore, which temporarily erases any ability to reason; there is no good or evil then, only acts. But the creator of that video was proud of it. Weeks had passed, the rush was over, and yet whoever it was hadn't been able to resist revealing it to the world. That was reprehensible. I thought about Vasco—his reddish curls, his plain T-shirts, his expression always so open. He was one of those people who didn't need to talk much to make friends. Could he have been proud of the video he had recorded in the parking garage? I didn't dare answer the question myself. That's why I went looking for him.

Could you have predicted this, Almodôvar? You in prison, me with no Plan and the time to track down your son to find out if he had lost his mind? You knew Vasco; up until that day you had been a good father, a pillar in his life. But did you know this would happen? Is that why you robbed the gas station? So you could be far away when this day finally came? It probably wouldn't have happened if you had been here. Your silence is your guilt, no matter the solution.

I thought: I'll talk to Vasco, ask him some questions, hear him out, say anything. Nothing too paternalistic or moral, but simply make sure he won't do anything like this again. And then I'd deal with my own life—find some work, pay my mortgage, figure things out with Marta. It was a good plan, and I wrote it all down in my black notebook as if I were signing a contract with myself.

My idea was to bump into Vasco as if by some incredible coincidence, then ask him about that day in the parking garage. I wouldn't neglect its importance, but I didn't want Vasco to think I had sought him out to just talk about that. Which is why I didn't go to your house, or ambush him outside the school gates. Instead, on a Monday afternoon, I waited for school to let out, got in the car, and drove around the streets near the school, passing by all the places where the kids went: the arcade, that café that sells burgers and pork fillets, the shopping center, the park opposite the cemetery. There were kids alone and kids in groups, kids perched on walls and steps, doing nothing, enjoying the fact that the world does not need them yet. There were kids walking, quickly, without having to think about their direction, kids erupting into rehearsed, territorial laughter, like animals pissing on trees, and there were kids who didn't speak, with expressions so grim it seemed impossible that there were human beings behind those eyes. It was hard to distinguish those who were happy from the others, since they all moved so unnaturally in their bodies, as if they were programmed. They all seemed very removed from me. I was able to remember myself at those ages—fifteen, sixteen, seventeen—but if I had wanted to revisit them, I wouldn't have had a clue how to get there. Sometime over the past twenty years I had lost that part of me. Did you lose it too, Almodôvar? I think if anyone could go back to being fifteen, it's you.

I was convinced I'd find Vasco within half an hour. That didn't happen. At about half past six, I stopped the car in front of the arcade. I couldn't just waste gas driving around. I was staking out the place like those detectives in the movies. Kids came and went. From time to time, a group of five or six of them would stop under the streetlamp near the arcade door to smoke and drink beers from the supermarket across the street. They all had backpacks slung over their shoulders, headphones stuck over their ears. Everyone seemed to be standing there together to listen to music—their own music. At just after seven, it already looked like the middle of the night. And it was cold, in the thirties, according to the thermometer in my car. The kids didn't seem fazed by the time or the temperature. They were just there. Inside the car the air stayed warm for almost an hour and then suddenly became cold, and the cold spread to my nose and gnawed at my joints. By eight, Vasco still hadn't appeared. I started the car and went home.

The next day, I went out at the same time. I drove around for forty minutes and then stopped near the park. Despite the cold, there were kids sitting in groups on the benches, talking and laughing, playing with their phones, their breath escaping through their lips in gray puffs, dense and opaque, as if their lungs were on fire. There were three skaters practicing their moves on a nearby wall. One of them, the shortest, could have been a professional, a millionaire, if Portugal were that kind of country, the other two were wasting their time in the wrong sport. A few couples passed hand in hand, their steps synchronized; some kissed on the go with an urgency that could only be explained by their age. None of those kids seemed as if they could have pissed on a man if the occasion presented itself—they were just kids doing kid things. After about an hour, a girl approached the car. She peered through the window and gestured for me to lower it. She wore a denim jacket with a lot of fur on the collar and sleeves, her eyebrow was pierced, and her eyes were rimmed with black eyeliner. She looked about twenty, but it's possible she wasn't a day over fifteen. She had a beautiful face, one that might become more beautiful in time; maybe she'd become one of those women on the street whose beauty is so powerful it's frightening. She spoke in a tone that sounded like she was putting it on.

"You got any weed?" she asked.

Almodôvar, the first thing I thought was: I say yes, I go to Xavier's, buy some grams from him, divide it into ten or fifteen bags, come back here, off-load it to these kids, make enough cash for the week. Shit, I could make a living like that. With Xavier's weed being what it is, the little bastards never would have wanted to smoke anything else; they'd be lifelong customers. It would have been so easy. Only, things still weren't that bad—not yet.

"No, I don't have any weed," I told her.

She smiled. Her smile was ugly, or at least not as pretty as her face.

"You've been sitting there for almost an hour watching us," she said. "If you're not selling weed, then you must be jerking off to us."

Her voice was firm, steady, I remember that much. She wasn't afraid. As if a pedophile masturbating to a bunch of kids wasn't something to be afraid of. Don't you realize, Almodôvar? It didn't bother her at all. How is it possible? What reality does she inhabit where the thought of it didn't make her panic to the bone? I thought of Flor, of course. I thought: She's smarter than that, she knows better than that.

And I wanted to explain myself, but I didn't know where to begin. It should have been easy, a matter of half a dozen sentences, the right words. She would have laughed off the misunderstanding, I would have laughed with her, and I'd tell her it was good she was paying attention, you can't afford to get distracted in today's world, things happen every day, but look, confronting the suspect isn't the best solution, and then I'd offer her a cigarette and light it for her, and we'd become friends, talk about Flor, Mateus, maybe I'd even talk to her about Marta, you. I'd say: I had two friends, one of them was stuck at home for over twelve years and came out once to save our math teacher; the other's in prison. Life threw him a curveball. He ducked, couldn't stand the pressure; it can happen to anyone. You have to be ready, it could happen to you. And then I'd tell her about the incident in the parking garage, talk to her about Vasco. She'd offer to help find him. We'd become a pair of detectives. She'd listen to me like someone who knows that life is only possible if we listen to our elders. It would have been a beautiful story. But I didn't want to explain myself; I was embarrassed. Not because she thought I was a pedophile. It was a panic at the idea of speaking, somehow revealing to her, in my pauses, in my tone, that I was unemployed, excluded from the system, using the world and offering nothing in return. And I know, Almodôvar, that she was only a young girl, but if anyone should understand shame, it's you. So fuck you, you son of a bitch.

"I wasn't doing anything," I stammered.

"I think you were. But never mind."

"I'm looking for someone."

"Who?"

"It's none of your business."

"What happened to that window?"

"It broke."

"You should get a new one."

"And you should go back to your friends."

"Are you sure you don't have any weed?"

"Yes."

"Do you want to buy some?"

"Do you know anyone who's selling?" I laughed.

"Of course." She smiled. "Me."

"You?"

"My brother goes to Morocco every two months. The stuff he gets will make you hoot like an owl."

She reached into her pocket and pulled out a little white bag and dangled it between her fingers. I couldn't see its contents through the plastic, but the smell invaded the cold air in the car, as if weed were growing up through the upholstery.

"Let's do this," she said. "You keep it. On the house. And tomorrow, when you go jerk off to some kids, smoke this shit. It'll be even better."

Then she threw the bag onto my lap and slipped her hand back into her pocket.

"I don't want this."

"Of course you want it," she said, as if she were my mother, as if she understood my deepest needs better than anyone. "I'm here every day at this time," she added. "Come back whenever you want."

She stretched with her hands still stuffed in her coat pockets, and the coat opened as if she had wings. Then she slowly walked away, her sneakers dragging on the wet earth, her head tilted slightly back so the rain could fall on her face. She seemed like someone who was tired after a day's work, someone who can only think about going home, eating dinner, watching their show, falling asleep early, and sleeping without dreaming. She seemed three times her age.

Almodôvar, there's always someone who thinks they're smarter than everyone else. We were all trying to figure out our own lives, navigate the obstacles that got in the way. We had problems hurled at us as if they were stones or rotten fruit. Most of us couldn't even stop to rest, think up solutions. Time was just one problem among many, and all we could do was keep going, walk the path before us in the best way we knew how and hope that in the end there would be some sort of reward, hope that at least there would be an end, at least one ending before the very end. Except there's always someone who tries to take a shortcut. Almodôvar, can't you imagine how much I wanted to get out of that car, go after her, grab her by the arm, give her a shake and a few slaps—not soft ones to startle her, but hard, to hurt her, to feel the sting of her skin across my entire hand, then walk off without ever opening my mouth?

It wouldn't have done any good.

Of course it would have, Almodôvar. I would have felt better, that's for sure. My life wouldn't have become any less complicated, but I would have felt better about it. And besides, that kind of person needs to face some kind of punishment, no matter what kind—it's about balance in the order of the world. In that moment, slapping around that fifteen-year-old kid would have been a comfort to my soul. But I didn't hit her. I started the car and went home.

I went out again the next afternoon. And the next. And the next. I spent over a week looking for your son. I visited all the places I thought he might be, saw the same kids at different times, in different places, always doing the same things: gossiping, smoking, playing with their phones, erupting in bouts of loud and shallow laughter, drinking beers, drinking juices, Cokes, making out, groping each other, looking at nothing, looking at everything, shouting. They had an innate capacity for leisure, for ignoring the responsibilities with which they were burdened just by virtue of being alive. And I grew ashamed of myself, because I was like them. I also sat around wasting time—mine and everyone else's. Maybe we'd be better people, maybe the recession never would have hit, if someone had figured out how to eliminate all those vices of youth.

That's not even fair. They're studying now for the day they'll fill our shoes and understand everything we do.

It's true. But it's not enough. They could give more: more time, more thought, more energy. How many millions of them are there on the planet? Imagine all the hours wasted, the good ideas lost with each text they send.

They need to have fun. They're kids.

Everyone needs to have fun. They need to contribute more.

You can't believe that. You're just pissed.

Maybe. But twenty years from now they'll be pissed too. They need to hear it from someone.

It wouldn't do any good. Think about how we used to be. If someone had told us—

Fuck you, Almodôvar. I was out looking for your son, even though the rest of my life was crumbling to the ground.

What was left of January passed quickly. I didn't go looking for Vasco again. No one answered the e-mails I had sent out with my CV. That last weekend of the month, I was in Viana. Marta was happy for no particular reason. She had missed me, and she hugged me every time we crossed paths in the house, her kisses lengthy and intense, passionate. When I left, I had the feeling that the distance I was imposing on us was a terrible mistake.

In early February, I got a letter from the bank: the mortgage payment was outstanding. But there was nothing more to be done. Every day I spent four or five hours surfing the same job sites, sending out e-mails with my CV and cover letter, requesting interviews, waiting for any answer whatsoever. I had listed the apartment on a handful of real estate sites. Every so often someone would call, show up to see the place, wander the rooms, appraise our things, inspect photos of Marta and the kids; they'd open our closets, ask questions about the neighborhood, transportation, apartment fees. In just over a month I had lowered the price three times, though the house was worth much more—or I had paid much more for it, at least—and the people would seem interested. They seemed to be on the verge of grabbing my hand and exclaiming, "We'll take it!" but then they'd leave and I'd never hear from them again. I opened my Plan to a new page, a blank one, which offered up the concrete possibility of writing something freely, and I gave myself two or three hours to look over the new lines; but in the end the page remained blank, as if none of the words I had learned in my lifetime were right for that space. What more could I have done?

Nothing. You did everything you could.

That's not true.

So what more could you have done?

I don't know, but I didn't do everything. One can always do more.

Daniel, I don't understand why you insist on resolving all your problems through sheer hope.

This isn't just about hope, damn it. It's about having expectations. We did everything right, we gave it our all, we calculated all the steps, we made every effort. Payback is the least we can demand.

But I'm not going to bend over backward seeking explanations for what happened. It was the same for everyone: the lives we had were gone, people who had been around were no longer there, and even so, we woke each day fighting for yesterday, unaware that yesterday is never worth fighting for under any circumstances. So let's move on.

On February 17, my account manager at the bank called. I answered. I could have not answered, but I would have had to face the situation sooner or later. She said we needed to speak as soon as possible. The next day I went to her office. The conversation didn't last longer than twenty minutes. I didn't have the money to pay the mortgage, and I wouldn't have it later. She explained that the bank would be willing to keep the house—*payment in kind* was the term she used—which would cancel a substantial part of what I owed, and I'd only be left with a small balance, a loan reduced to almost nothing. There was a surge of determination in her voice, no trace of sympathy in her tone, and it was obvious that it wasn't the first time she had made this offer, or the second, or the third, or maybe even the tenth—maybe she had even done it that day, a few hours earlier, like an assembly line worker fitting the same two parts together all day long, repeating the motion countless times. And when she finished speaking, I thought: You don't have to do this if you don't want. If you were a decent person, you'd refuse to treat a human being this way; what you're doing is no better than pissing on a bum. Today you'll go home, and I'll be in your head. What you're doing to me will follow you, you won't look at your children without feeling the panic of knowing that one day this same thing could happen to them, someone could sit there across from them, speak to them as if they were infants, explaining the meaning of numbers on a page, pointing to percentages as if they were asleep, and then take away a chunk of their lives. You'll think about this day for the rest of your life. Your remorse will be my small recompense for what you've done to me.

That night I called Marta. The apartment was in my name, but ultimately it was hers too—ours. I explained the situation to her, how there was no more money, the problem with the vacuum cleaners. She listened without asking a single question, her breathing barely perceptible. When I finished, she didn't respond.

"Marta," I said.

"When did you lose your job?"

"I don't know. A month ago?"

"And you're telling me now? I can't do this, Daniel . . ."

"I think I'm going to accept the bank's offer," I said.

I told her we could sell the apartment, but she said it wasn't the same. We'd lose a lot of money.

"I know. If there was any other way . . ."

"There is no other way now, Daniel. You should have discussed this with me a month ago."

"I want to accept their offer."

"And then what?"

"And then I don't know, Marta. I'm sorry."

The next day, I went back to the bank, signed all the paperwork the account manager had prepared, and in less than ten minutes the bank became the owner of my house. We acted as if we were signing a deal that would benefit both parties. We made jokes. I joked that the apartment would be a little small for its new tenant, the account manager laughed, a hearty laugh, and said she hoped we could do business together again soon. We shook hands, and I left with a surreal feeling of accomplishment. That and tremendous relief, Almodôvar. As if that really was the end of a dark period, as if all the problems of the world's economy had been riding on a simple deal between my account manager and me. I could live for weeks, months even, off this relief alone. Everything felt so much lighter. I'm sure you can understand that.

I spent two weeks packing up our life into boxes: toys, bedding, tablecloths, tableware, photographs, papers, letters, paintings. I spoke with Marta ten times a day. She had already been through a lot over the past year, but the divide between us persisted, and I remained unsure of how it would end. She tried to guide me toward a middle ground in such an earnest tone that it gave me goose bumps. She hadn't brought up the matter of the apartment again. And then, one day, she asked, "Have you started looking for a new place?"

I had started looking, in the papers, online. I scoured the neighborhood every day for ads posted in windows, I made phone calls. But I didn't have any money for rent—any rent, not even cheap rent.

"I still haven't found anything," I said.

"Take care of that, Daniel. You don't want to have to stay with Xavier."

Almodôvar, she was proud. She had already asked me countless times to come to Viana with her and the kids, to be a family again, and she didn't want to have to say it again. But I didn't say it either.

"It's going to be okay," I said.

"Of course it will."

A few days later, the apartment was empty. I sold most of our furniture to a nonprofit that gave it away to anyone willing to retrieve it at a warehouse out in Xabregas. All that remained was our dining room table and a china cabinet—both had belonged to my parents—and the bed where Marta and I had slept since our second year together. It all went into João Mota's storage space. I didn't tell him what had happened, just that we were doing some remodeling at home. I also left him twenty-two cardboard boxes filled with anything that wasn't essential at the time. I sold all our appliances at a discount on an auction site. Marta appeared with her father on Saturday morning, and they took away nine boxes of books, CDs, photographs, toys. We hardly spoke about what was happening. We mostly talked about Mateus.

The week before, my son had destroyed my mother-in-law's microwave. He had submerged a lightbulb in a cup of water and then placed the cup in the microwave. He was trying to reenact something he had seen online: supposedly, when the microwave started, the bulb would light up. Mateus claimed he saw it light up before the explosion. Mateus wasn't hurt, but the microwave was wrecked. Marta insinuated that it had been my fault, but when I asked her how that could be, she didn't know how to answer me. But I didn't try to defend myself either. She needed someone to take responsibility for the accident, and I wanted to help her.

Once Marta and her father had gone, all that remained was two suitcases with nearly all my clothing, two pairs of shoes, a towel, a set of bedsheets, a duvet, a bag with toiletries, my laptop, and two notebooks. I loaded everything into my car. Then I got in. I turned the key in the ignition. The engine coughed before it began to purr. My left hand gripped the wheel. My right rested on the gearshift. My feet sought out the pedals. It was as if my body knew something I didn't. And Almodôvar, I didn't know. I could have done anything, gone anywhere. But I didn't. I turned off the engine. That night I slept in the car for the first time, about twenty yards from the building where Marta, Flor, Mateus, and I had lived for all those years.

With the day ahead no more than a possibility, I awoke early, curled up on the backseat, wrapped in my duvet. The glassless window was covered with thick plastic, but the cold still seeped in. I felt good. I had imagined that after a few hours of lying on that seat, my back would twinge and my shoulders would cramp. But my back was light. My whole body was light. As if there were no gravity inside the car. I lay there for half an hour, the light slowly filling the space around me, the world emerging from darkness. The city was right there, people walking by, the sounds of their hurried footsteps vibrating the license plate. It was so easy to be there. I thought: Fuck it, what have I been doing all this time? A house? Why would I want a house? What kind of idiot came up with this garbage about needing a house? No wonder the world was being swallowed into a hole: everyone was buying homes as if there were no alternative. Half the money on the planet was being wasted on bricks and concrete. When had we become so fragile? When had the basis for our existence become so dependent on four walls and a roof? Someone needed to have a word with humanity, explain that the need for a roof is an illusion that is easy enough to overcome, that life can be simpler than that.

Human beings will always live in houses.

Not these houses. Clusters of houses. Rows of houses. Towers of houses. Carpets, heat, aluminum frames, double glazing, wood floors, chairs everywhere, a bathroom for every three hundred square feet, entire kitchens of marble. As if they were kings, Almodôvar. Kings.

You lived like that too.

And electricity. Think about it. Electricity runs through our bellies, our skin, our hearts, our legs. If you have it out for someone, don't get a gun. Just go cut their electricity. Anxiety will instantly hinder their every gesture; three days later, a deep anguish will set in, and after that, they'll die slowly of cold, hunger, boredom.

That's not fair, Daniel. Electricity brought us forward. Our lives have become a thousand times better, a million times better, thanks to electricity.

Fuck off, Almodôvar. You're in no place to talk. One day we'll all be fed lasagna and chocolate mousse through our veins just so we don't have to chew, just so our digestive tract can get a rest. Can you imagine it? And there will be some idiot smiling as he says this new way of eating is an obvious improvement in our quality of life. One day, the life of human beings will be reduced to a 130-year-long sleep, a total absence of physical activity in exchange for absolute comfort; we'll even try to do away with dreams, because nothing is more exhausting than dreaming. Everyone's brains will be as inert as possible, and maybe then we'll all be completely happy.

Daniel, people deserve some comfort.

Maybe. But this kind of comfort has a price that no one ever pays. And you can't talk, you bastard. You're cut off from the world where you are, protected from the elements. You have a bed where you can rest your body, hot water, regular meals—you have no right to talk.

All this because you spent a night in your car? A night doesn't make up for all those years you spent in your apartment with all your comforts.

Thirteen nights, Almodôvar. Thirteen. I'll bet you can't even imagine the feeling of freedom. Around seven in the evening I'd start the car and drive off, alert to the sounds and lights of the city, the movement in the streets. And when I found a place I liked, I'd park, put on my pajamas, and retire to the backseat. I'd sleep on a different street each night, sometimes waking late at night with the inkling that something wasn't right—a noise, shadows, the garbage truck lingering in front of a building—so I'd start the car, drive for fifteen minutes, and stop again in another part of town. It was so simple: *car = home*. I spent most of my time sitting in random cafés reading the paper, doing crossword puzzles. From time to time I'd go to the library, check my e-mail, browse job sites, chat with Flor and Mateus if they were online.

Marta called nearly every day, the worry in her voice apparent, wanting to know how I was holding up, if I needed anything, where I was sleeping. And it was crazy, Almodôvar, but I couldn't even relate to her concern, because for the first time in a long time, things around me seemed right, possible. I didn't tell her I was sleeping in the car. For the first few days I told her I was staying with João Mota. Then, one night, I called and told her I had rented a studio across the river. I had no possibility of resolving my life in the near future; I would be forced to lie to Marta eventually. I preferred to do it as soon as possible, to give Marta's nervous system a rest.

After two weeks of sleeping in the car, I got an interview with a travel agency that specialized in religious trips—Fátima, Santiago de Compostela, Lourdes, Rome, Jerusalem. The whole circuit. The morning of the interview, I stopped by João Mota's and told him that the contractor had shut off my hot water. Uninterested in my story, he didn't ask questions and extended his kindness to me simply because I was a friend. That's how it had always been between us. He was on his way to work and left me alone. I took a shower. I shaved off a few days' worth of beard. I found the clothes with the fewest wrinkles and put them on. I looked in the mirror for a long time; I didn't look like someone who had spent the past few weeks sleeping in a car.

The man who greeted me was young—not a day over thirty—and the son of the agency's owner. As I came to understand, his old man was a devout Catholic, an energetic widower who hadn't set foot in the office since he had lost his wife two years before, now spending half of the year on the road on company tours. The son had been left to run the agency. During the first part of the interview, his eyes darted between me and my CV on the desk as he reeled off a series of questions related to my professional experience, my language skills, my leadership abilities, my ability to perform under pressure. I answered truthfully, making sure not to let on that I was struggling. Afterward, with his eyes half-shut, as if he were reciting something from memory, he asked if I was Catholic. I lied and said I was. Because I was certain they wouldn't want an atheist or a Muslim or a Buddhist guiding groups of Catholics through the naves of the most famous cathedrals on the continent. He grimaced, as if he had just bitten into moldy cheese, and his shoulders sunk.

"I'm sorry," he said, closing the file containing my CV. "That rules out any possible collaboration between us."

"The fact that I'm Catholic?"

"It's been my father's company policy for over thirty-five years. Look, we can't have a Catholic leading twenty-five tourists through St. Peter's Basilica or the Holy Land. It would be like putting someone who is fond of custard tarts in charge of a bakery."

Almodôvar, as the bastard was talking, I could see in his eyes that he didn't believe a word of what he was saying. It was a speech he had memorized, no more than a formality imposed by his father. He liked me, he knew I could become an indispensable part of his team, and he wanted to hire me—I'm sure of it. But not enough to ignore company policy. I considered telling him the truth: I'm not Catholic, I have no beliefs, my only faith is in myself, in the reach of my thoughts and the fruits of my labor. I'd explain the logic behind my lie. But perhaps this would only make matters worse, and he'd think I'd been lying about everything else—or that I was denying my beliefs just to get the job.

And because of moments like these, the world jams up. People let themselves be dictated by their own personal protocols that they've established out of absurdity, their habits so ingrained, their perspectives so skewed that they're addicted to their own logic, and no one is ever willing to step to one side, cede to other ways of looking at things and proceed in new directions; even when reality demands it, even in the absence of alternatives, people would prefer to be stuck than to have to step aside. Imagine where we could be by now. Imagine humanity moving forward, like a wave, never crashing on the shore. Imagine it.

"I'm not Catholic," I heard myself say.

The boy's smile was benevolent. He didn't respond.

"It was a lie," I went on, "not that I'm a liar in general. But I need this job. I know I'd be great."

He kept smiling.

"The recruitment process will still take a few days. Your application will be considered."

Only now *he* was the one who was lying, Almodôvar. It was easy to see. He couldn't bear to tell me the truth, to look me in the eye as he turned me down, to glimpse any trace of pain or anguish across my face. He was that kind of man. He was just waiting for me to leave the office so he could go on with his life, when the remorse that filled his eyes like a thick fog would fade almost instantly, as soon as my presence stopped preventing him from feeling totally satisfied with his life.

When we shook hands, I forced my best smile.

"You'll wish you'd hired me," I said.

He nodded slowly but said nothing. Then he accompanied me to the exit, called the elevator, and waited next to me in silence. When the elevator arrived, he opened the door to let me inside. Perhaps he thought he had redeemed himself with that one gesture. The bastard.

The elevator stopped on two or three floors, and people entered, exited, a sense of purpose in their every gesture. When I reached the street, I ran to the car. I sat behind the wheel. I put the key in the ignition but didn't start the engine. I thought: This is too important to give up on. Plus, I had nothing better to do, so I sat there, looking at the door of the building I had just left. It was a scantly trafficked street, few cars, few people. An hour passed; the afternoon light swelled. A policeman approached, waving me on; I was parked in a loading zone. I didn't lower my window, but made the universal gesture for "a little bit longer," the tip of my index finger and thumb drawn together, separated by a half an inch. His face shrank into an ugly grimace at the sight of it, but then he turned on his heels and went on his way. I didn't see him again. After another hour, the number of cars on the road suddenly increased considerably, as if every street in the city besides that one had just closed. At about half past five, the guy who interviewed me left the building. The light hit him in the eyes, and he stopped to put on his sunglasses. He crossed the street, walked fifty yards along the promenade where I was parked, and entered a car. I started the engine. Thirty seconds later, his car passed mine. I followed him.

Look, Almodôvar. I didn't really know what I was doing. I just knew I had to do something, motion at him from afar, maybe talk to him again. I had been unemployed for almost a year and the guy had a job for me—it was as simple as that.

I followed him, careful not to get too close so he wouldn't see me before the time was right, because I knew there would be a right time, and that when it came, I'd feel it. I don't remember the journey. He drove through the city unhurried, stopping at red lights, making a few turns. I replicated his every move. We must have driven for about eight minutes, certainly no more than ten, when we entered a street with no other cars on it besides ours. I lagged twenty or thirty yards behind him. Two blocks later, he stopped at a red light by a crosswalk. The right time had come, so I stopped on his left.

I looked at him through the transparent plastic that was covering my broken window. I didn't need to nod or gesture—he saw me immediately. He gave me a half smile and stared at me; my face, deformed by the plastic, was familiar to him, but it was as if he couldn't place me. As if our conversation hadn't happened that afternoon, but ten years earlier. I thought: You can shove your job up your ass, motherfucker. I don't need it. I can go on without you. His eyes narrowed slightly the instant he recognized me, and then he nodded to greet me. I gestured for him to lower his window, and he did. A space for communication appeared between us; I could say anything, the potential for getting a job existed, there, at that moment. But I didn't get a chance, Almodôvar.

Three boys crossed the road from right to left, directly in front of our cars. One of them was Vasco. They broke into a run, the walk light having turned red. I honked, and they jumped, even more rushed, none of them turning to locate the source of the noise. An instant later, they had leapt onto the sidewalk. Then, more slowly, they disappeared around the corner.

We got the green light. I turned back toward the guy from the agency. He was still looking in my direction, his expression open to me. But his car was already moving. He gave me a wave and then drove through the crosswalk, pulling ahead of me. I stayed in my lane and made a left.

Did you go after my son?

Of course I went after your son.

What about the job?

Fuck off, Almodôvar. I love Vasco almost as if he were my own son. And the fact that you're a shit-assed coward doesn't change that. The whole scene with Ávila in the parking garage, Vasco on top of the van recording it on his phone, the video online—I couldn't let all that happen in front of my eyes without going after him. Fuck, Almodôvar. It was the right thing to do. Since when do I have to justify my good deeds?

I followed them, Vasco and the two other kids. I spotted them almost immediately, backpacks slung over their shoulders, walking side by side, relaxed, Vasco the shortest of the three. What were they doing? Where were they going? It was nearly six o'clock in the evening. Vasco was about three miles from home, about four from school. Did Clara know where he was?

I followed them for two or three blocks, making sure I didn't get too close, waving at other cars to pass me. One of the kids was carrying a skateboard. At one point he dropped it, hopped on, and balanced on one foot, moving ahead of his friends. He slid down the sidewalk about twenty yards and stopped in front of the door to a building, right next to a drugstore, all without ever getting off the board. By the door to the drugstore, there was a man sitting on a bench reading the newspaper. Vasco and the other kid arrived just after the first. None of the three rang the bell. Instead, the skater kid took out his phone, wrote something, and the three of them stood there, waiting. I stopped my car on the shoulder, put on the blinkers, and got out.

"Vasco," I shouted.

The three kids looked up at me. Your son saw me first, and I could see his body tense, his face contorting into a look of astonishment, as if the two of us encountering each other there at that time were impossible according to the laws of this universe. The other two kids took off up the street, the skateboard coasting toward the drugstore entrance, and in no time they had disappeared between two parked cars.

Do you understand what was happening, Almodôvar? Those kids knew me. They were afraid of me. Of course I can't be certain, but it was likely that those were two of the kids who had pissed on Ávila.

Vasco's instinct was to run with them, but he didn't. He stood there looking at me, waiting for me to say something, his arms limp at his sides, his head cocked slightly to the right. I walked over to him. There was a huge tree overhead, a green canopy stretching out between us and the gloomy late-afternoon sky; the ground was covered with blue and white flowers.

"What are you doing?" I asked, and immediately wished I hadn't—it wasn't the right start to our conversation.

"Nothing," Vasco replied. There was something funny in the way he looked at me, a kind of distrust.

"I wasn't following you," I said. "You walked in front of my car and I stopped."

"I know."

"Have you heard from your dad?"

"No. Have you?"

"No."

And then we fell into a silence, the good kind. It could have been a peaceful end to our conversation. He shoved his hands in his coat pockets and looked around for his friends.

"That day at the parking garage. That was you on top of that van."

He turned to face me, hesitated for a split second, and then his eyes hardened.

"You could have really hurt him," I went on. "Ávila wasn't in such bad shape in the end, but . . ."

"Who is Ávila?"

"Ávila was the guy with no pants. Remember him? That's his name. You know he was your dad's math teacher?"

Vasco's eyes flashed.

"You didn't know, did you? He was our seventh grade teacher. And now he lives on the street. It can happen to anyone. Maybe you don't believe me, but it's true. It can happen to anyone. That's how the world works these days."

Vasco looked around again, except this time he wasn't looking for his friends—he just didn't want to look at me.

"Anyway, Ávila spent a night in the hospital, and the next morning he was probably already getting wasted in a bar along the river. But that doesn't matter. Fuck, Vasco, your friends pissed on him. That's bad. A human being deserves more respect than that. What were you doing there? What were you doing on that van? You're a cool kid. You don't do that kind of shit. Your parents taught you better than that. What would your father do if he knew? The world is already fucked up enough—it doesn't need you to make it worse."

He shook his head; my talk was just another sermon. He had heard it all, maybe in the same words. I was talking to him just like all the other parents, teachers, adults. And that's exactly what I didn't want—to lecture him like an adult. I remember them talking to me like that, the colossal futility of their words, the void they left. So I raised my arms in surrender.

"I'm done," I told him. "But promise me this: if you have any problems, if something goes wrong, if you need to talk, whatever it is, call me. I have time, I can come find you right away, we can talk, and we can find a solution together. Deal?"

Vasco didn't reply.

"Deal?" I repeated.

He opened his mouth to say something, but someone suddenly yelled.

"Fire! Fire!"

I looked around. No one seemed particularly alarmed. A few people slowly retreated. Only one woman ran, dragging two children with her. And there was smoke, black smoke that seemed to come from everywhere at once, dispatched by the spring wind. It entered the space between Vasco and me, then rose and filtered through the green canopy.

"It's your car," said Vasco, as if he were divulging an ancient secret.

I turned to look. It was my car. A thick cloud of smoke meandered through the windows like a fat black worm with multiple heads. There was something burning inside, on the backseat. I remember feeling my body freeze, my muscles plunging deep into a sudden cold, my heart stopping. And then I thought: No, life isn't that much of a bitch. I took four or five steps toward the car.

"Watch out—it could explode!" someone shouted.

And I stopped, my heart pounding erratically through my whole body. Smoke surrounded my face, entered my lungs, burned my chest. I covered my mouth and nose with my sleeve. I tried to peek inside the car, make out what was happening. Through the smoke, I could see my things—clothes, a water bottle, my laptop, toothbrush, toothpaste—but I couldn't see any sign of flames. I was about two yards from the car; I could have just reached the door handle. But my arms were paralyzed with fear. I was sure the car would explode as soon as I opened the door.

I looked back; there were ten or fifteen people on the sidewalk, all of them just standing there, watching my car burn.

"Do something, motherfuckers. Do something!" I screamed.

I walked around the car. There wasn't as much smoke on the other side. I can't explain why, but the sight of it only made me more anxious. I had lost control over my movements. I reached out and tapped the window hard, as if the car were a sleeping beast. Then, on impulse, I opened the back door. Smoke tumbled out in my direction. I recoiled and fell backward onto the road, my hands covering my face.

And an instant later there was a man beside me, crouching, bent over me, protecting his head from the smoke. It was the man who had been sitting by the door of the drugstore. He let out a grunt and took a few steps toward the car. There was a bucket hanging from his hand, his arm pulled downward with the weight of it. He took two more steps until he was very close to the car, his torso disappearing in the smoke. Then he raised the bucket with both hands and dumped the water into the car.

Almodôvar, I didn't see it, but I can imagine how the water doused the backseat, immediately soaking the black upholstery, the billions of fabric particles beginning their process of rotting, the intense smell of burnt acrylic forever seared into the space. It was where I slept. It was a catastrophe.

The man dropped the bucket and stuffed himself into the backseat. He emerged holding a tree branch, three feet long, its green leaves scorched—some completely consumed—by an invisible fire, their stems still smoldering. The man dragged the branch across the road and let it fall a few yards from me.

"It was green," he exclaimed, wiping sweat from his brow. "The branch was green. It didn't burn, but it made for a hell of a lot of smoke."

Then he held out his hand to help me up.

Look, Almodôvar. The bastard thought I had been lucky. And why did he think it was luck? The branch had been green: it burned without catching fire, and the car didn't explode. But the inside of my car—my house, my kingdom—had been destroyed by the smoke and the water he had thrown onto the seat. Not to mention the fact that the smoke had infiltrated all my things. Seriously, how could he say I had been lucky? I should have picked up the branch, lit it again, dragged it across the sidewalk and into his drugstore, left it there to smolder. And when a black cloud filled the entire store, when the bastard felt his blood freeze in his veins with the panic of watching his life being reduced to ashes, the smell of burning coal forever infused into the air of his drugstore, then perhaps he'd reconsider his words.

And the people on the street were still looking at me as the car continued to steam, some filming it with their phones. Vasco was not where I had left him. I didn't even look; I knew he was gone. A policeman approached. He wore a serious expression, the muscles around his eyes tense. He asked who owned the car. I raised my hand.

"What happened?"

"There was a smoking branch in the car, and that man put it out."

"Who put it there?" the policeman asked.

The man who put out the fire said nothing. I shrugged and shook my head. I thought: It was those kids—Vasco's friends.

"I don't know," I said. "I didn't see anything. Before I knew it the car was already smoking."

"Want to call a tow truck?" he asked.

I walked to the car. I opened the door. I got in and sat at the wheel. The air was warm. The smell of burnt plastic was overwhelming. I looked in the back: the right side of the seat gaped to reveal the foam filling, worm-eaten and melted and wet like an animal's wound.

Everything was black: the upholstery, the roof, the floor, the plastic trim on the doors, the windows. I remember thinking: This should be enough to allow me to kill someone.

The policeman stuck his head in the car, his hand resting on the door, which was still ajar. I said something, I don't remember what. I wanted to get out of there. I put the key in the ignition and turned it. The engine started. I waited a few seconds, wondering whether it would explode. Then I looked at the policeman. He peered into the backseat and winced. Then he looked back at me and nodded. He closed my door and the one in the back. Then he took two steps away. I drove off.

Almodôvar, as I was driving no place in particular, I tried to be pragmatic. I was high on a cliff, a black sea below me, and all I wanted to do was jump in headfirst, my body taut and straight, to dive as deep as possible, to lose myself, to let myself be taken by the currents, to bemoan my bad luck for all eternity. Only I couldn't. It was seven thirty, and the sun had dipped below the horizon, the temperature dropping twenty degrees with it. The urgent matter of finding a place to spend the night absorbed all my thoughts. The car was no longer an option—I could smell the toxic gases accumulating in the air around me. And I couldn't call anyone for help. It wasn't out of shame. I just didn't want to stop believing that I could do it on my own, that I alone was enough, that I had what it took to face adversity.

My first thought was to go home. I still had the keys, and the bank wouldn't have sold the house so quickly—surely the rooms would have been empty. It would only be for one night. I'd go in, rest, ponder the situation. Had I been evicted? Was I homeless? Early the next morning, when it was still dark, I'd leave, and no one would ever know. But when I got there, my key didn't fit the lock. My first thought was that maybe it had all been a dream, that maybe I had never lived there at all. But the bastards had changed the lock. As if they had known some kids would light my car on fire and I'd have no choice but to take refuge in the very house I had sold them.

I tried all the keys on my ring in the hopes that one might work. This, yes, would have been luck. None of them opened the door. But it was then, as I was looking through my keys, that I had another idea. There were six keys in my hand, and two were from the agency. Almodôvar, the year before I had been laid off from the travel agency where I had worked for all those years, but I had never handed in the keys to my office. It had been an oversight on my part, but then again, no one ever asked for them. I remembered the last time my old boss had called me, maybe two months before, to tell me about how much he and his wife had been enjoying his early retirement. He had mentioned that the office was still for rent. It all fell into place.

I got in the car, an overwhelming rush of excitement spreading under my skin as I zipped through the city. That one little victory was enough for me to keep believing that at least part of the universe was on my side, if only for a moment. I turned on the radio, and I sang a song I had never heard before. Loudly. And then, suddenly, I thought: They must have changed the lock—that's why they didn't ask for the keys. Still, it was worth a try. Especially since I had run out of options.

I double-parked across the street from the building and sat there, still. It was almost nine in the evening. The wide glass door was closed, although the entryway remained lit. I looked up to the fifth floor windows: they were dark. The floor seemed to be vacant. I sat there for ten minutes or so. During that time, three people exited and none entered; the building was emptying out for the evening. The street was full, the city unaware that night had fallen. People were out for dinner, going to the movies. They were strolling, tourists, couples, groups of three, four, five people walking in all directions. And so many cars. As if everyone needed a car to get anywhere. Everyone seemed so busy. They marched into the restaurants as if they were solving the national debt crisis, as if their presence in that place, at that time, were essential for the survival of the species. And they seemed happy, secure in all their gestures, absurdly certain that the next day would come. Were they capable of imagining that, inside that car, I was waiting for the perfect moment to trespass on private property? If they weren't, their failure was unthinkable, unacceptable. Their ignorance was, in so many words, perverse.

I started the car, drove over to the next block, and parked. I sorted through everything in the trunk and then stuffed some clothes into a backpack along with my toiletry bag and my computer.

I walked into the building and called the elevator. When the doors opened, there was a man inside wearing a gray suit, the top button of his shirt undone, his tie loose around his neck, a black bag over his shoulder. I thought: Run—he'll never catch me.

But he just said, "Good night."

"Good night," I replied.

Then I was in. The doors closed, and the man disappeared from view. I studied my reflection in the mirror: my blue suit, my combed hair, a five o'clock shadow filling out my face. I looked like someone who had spent the day sitting behind a desk, staring at a computer screen, serious and dedicated and competent.

The elevator brought me to the fifth floor. Before I stepped out, I pressed the button for the first floor, and when the door closed at my back, the elevator descended. I didn't turn on the light. I felt for the key in the dark and then tried to unlock the door. I turned it, once, twice, three, four times. When the door finally opened, I quickly slipped inside and closed myself in with four turns of the key.

The space—five partitioned offices, two meeting rooms, two bathrooms, a lounge—was dark. I was still for a minute. It felt as if the lights would suddenly flick on and my former colleagues would jump out and yell, "Surprise!" But they didn't. I walked along the corridor, peered into the offices. The blinds were up, and the green, red, and blue lights of the city leapt through the windows. The desks and filing cabinets were all in their places, as if they didn't know the company no longer existed. But there was nothing else—no papers, no folders, no computers or printers. I ran my hand over a desk and felt a thin carpeting of dust. No one had occupied that space since the agency had closed; it had probably been months since anyone had entered.

I went to my old office. I closed the door and crawled on my hands and knees through the darkness until I was under my old desk, finding just enough room for my body and little else. I left my bag within arm's reach and programmed my phone to wake me up at 5:50 in the morning. Then I lay down on the worn carpet.

It was a rough night, my sleep fraught with the fear of being discovered, one long wait for a hint of daylight so I could leave that place as quickly as possible.

8.9

Almodôvar, remember: I never gave up. I never thought: Okay, this is it—it's over. That would have been too easy; I would have been one among many. And it's true, I was living on nothing, with no ground left to stand on. Even so, I was focused—focused on being focused.

I can't explain it. I simply woke up in the morning and shaved, got dressed, knotted my tie, smiled into the mirror. Like I'd always done.

That night—the night your son's friends lit my car on fire, the night I slept in my old office at the agency where I had worked all those years—wasn't the only one I spent in that office. I remember leaving sometime before five thirty in the morning, exhausted after hours of panic and the physical sensation of dangling at the end of my own rope. I got in the car—the burnt smell making me impossibly nauseated, exacerbated by the simple fact that I hadn't eaten in over twenty-four hours—and spent a few hours driving around Lisbon. The city seemed small, as if it were possible to be on all the streets at the same time. Then I rented the cheapest room I could find at a sinister little hotel near Cais do Sodré. I spent two days there that still seem like years. Nothing happened. I slept little, ate sparingly, leafed through my Plan a few times, but I couldn't find a way to carry it out. I remember thinking: This doesn't make sense; it can't be right. My life is worth more than this. And I know, Almodôvar, that justice is just a concept, and like anything else conceived by man, it has its shortcomings and absurdities and never applies as we think it should. Even so.

Anyway, after two nights in that miserable little room, I did the math. Every night I spent there would cost me eight euros. The four hundred euros I had left would afford me fifty nights. But I still needed to buy food, do my laundry, and pay for gas. Not to mention the sixty-three euros I had to pay to the bank each month. I could have stayed at the pension for a few more nights, of course, perhaps a week or two, but that would have only delayed the inevitable. So I went back to the empty office.

The office became a home in just a few days. It's remarkable how we adapt to places, create a relationship with our environment, create resources where they don't exist. Is that what you did, Almodôvar? Do you feel at home in there, in your cell? I didn't even have to try: the space was suddenly organized, my things stowed away in a closet with brochures on practically every tourist destination on the planet. I swept the floors and made a comfortable bed under my old desk out of pads from the conference room chairs. And I learned to find my way around in the dark, to do all my living when the other companies were closed; I had my own routine, a kind of life. There was no hot water, no bathtub, but I quickly got used to washing myself with cold water as I hunched over the sink. I did have electricity—who knows why it hadn't been cut off, except that maybe they had been expecting to rent the property any day. And I had Internet. One of the companies in the building, a Catholic book publisher, hadn't put a password on their wireless Internet, and I managed to get a reasonable signal in the bathroom, close to the window. So I dragged over Mr. Medeiros's old leather swivel chair that reclined until it was practically level as a bed, and I spent the worst hours of my insomnia there.

As my fear lessened, it gave way to the occasional worry of being found there, asleep, or walking the halls in my underwear, or shaving in the bathroom. I thought of what I might say: I used to work here; I came looking for some stuff I forgot.

After a few weeks, the excuse evolved: I used to work here, I still have the key, and I have no place to sleep.

And then: I have no place to sleep.

And then: Fuck you, motherfuckers, I have no place to sleep.

And then: Ha, ha, ha, ha, ha, ha, ha, ha, ha.

It's true, Almodôvar: I had no place to sleep.

You could have asked for help.

No, I couldn't have.

You could have stayed with Marta in Viana. All you had to do was call her and tell her the truth. She would have let you come; the two of you could have taken on the world side by side, maybe figured things out between you, maybe everything would have been like old times.

I thought about that. It was a possibility, and I weighed it. But I always had the feeling that I had other options to resort to before that one.

You could have talked to Xavier. There are rooms in his house he hasn't entered for years. He would have liked it if you had stayed with him. You could have watched him, looked after him.

It wouldn't have worked. The sadness in that house would have killed me. I'm not invincible.

You could have asked him for money. He has money, an inheritance stashed away in a bank account he hasn't touched for years.

Almodôvar, you have to understand: I wanted to believe that I could get out of the situation on my own. It was very important to me.

I know. You could have robbed a gas station, ended up here, kept me company. We could have spent our time shooting the shit.

Fuck off, Almodôvar.

You could have made a request on our site. Maybe someone would have popped up to give you a hand.

You don't understand.

Asking for help is not the end of the world. Everyone asks for help, Daniel.

You didn't.

It's true. So you and I are more alike than we thought.

I didn't rob a gas station.

You trespassed on private property. It's the same shit, Daniel. The only difference is you didn't get caught.

You're wrong.

Suddenly you're the paragon of virtue.

What's that supposed to mean?

I said it in your language.

Are you mad at me?

Go fill someone else's ears with your shit.

Dude, you only exist in a locked cell that no one else can enter; you've absented yourself from the world, submerged yourself in a permanent solitude. I can only hear you because I'm imagining you. You can't be mad at me.

What? Nothing to say?

Go fuck yourself and your silences, Almodôvar. You can say what you want, cloak your spirit in fantasies to justify your actions—or lack thereof. Because the difference between us is real and it's as wide as the sea. I didn't just disappear, motherfucker. That's the difference. I'm still around. And believe me: I wanted to disappear, throw myself into the void, tranquilize my body, my mind, live inside myself—it would have been so nice to live inside myself—be so still I could forget I existed. But it doesn't work that way; you can't just turn your back on life. It's not right—it's just not right. If that's your decision, you might as well go lie down on the train tracks. Maybe I can understand why a person would consider handling things that way, but your decision—your decision to sit there in your cell, turning away visitors all this time, out of sight from the world, with no way of knowing if things are okay—is like choosing to lie down on the train tracks every goddamned morning. I didn't leave, Almodôvar, and because I didn't leave, your son is alive. At least thank me for that.

Daniel, I won't thank you for anything. Imagine me thanking you if you want, but I won't do it.

You motherfucker, I was fine sleeping in the car with the whole city as my home; it was a good start, something I could build from, my expenses reduced to practically nothing besides food and gas. No more responsibilities. And I was sleeping well. Did I mention that, Almodôvar? Did I tell you that during those two weeks in the car my insomnia declared a truce? I was sleeping five, six, sometimes seven hours straight, and slowly my arms and legs began to feel lighter, the haze over my eyes dissipated, my spirit became a clear blue day. And then your son's friends stuck a burning branch in my car. Look. I could have reported Vasco, and through him the police could have found the little shits who did it; maybe I would have gotten some kind of compensation. It's not like I didn't need the money. But I didn't do it. I didn't want to make problems for Vasco—with the police or with those delinquents he called his friends.

It's true: the office wasn't mine. But I wasn't hurting anyone. The space had been vacant for a year, and no one was losing any money because of me. Plus, it was only temporary. I wanted to get out of there as soon as possible.

You didn't leave once you found work.

I spent my days on the street, wandering here and there, sitting in cafés, the library, a garden, if the weather was good. Rarely was I at the office when the other companies were open. I'd leave early and return after eight in the evening. From time to time, I'd come across someone else, and we'd exchange brief greetings; sometimes I'd have to share the elevator. I was just waiting to be found out, for one of them to call the police. But it didn't happen. I usually spent the mornings in a café down the street, a café whose virtues included free Internet. I'd arrive shortly after nine. I'd order a coffee. Then I'd read the paper that was always out on the counter. I'd open my laptop, read my e-mail, search the job sites, take some notes, gather contacts for agencies, hotels, museums, tourism associations, city councils—any place that might have some interest in someone with my profile. I'd send half a dozen e-mails, cover letters, my CV. At eleven I'd order another coffee. Around half past noon, the tables would begin to fill up for lunch, and I'd leave. And on one morning like all the others, someone offered me a job.

I sat down at the table farthest from the door and turned on my laptop. Mateus was online. But he shouldn't have been: he had classes in the morning. We hadn't spoken for several days.

Are you there? I wrote.

Yeah

Why are you home?

I have a fever ☺

I remembered how, as a child, a baby in his bassinet, he never cried when he had a fever, not even a whimper, nothing; he'd hardly move, as if he didn't have the strength to fight. Marta and I would always suffer in silence, terrified at the thought that he might not survive. I'll carry that anguish inside of me forever. For five seconds, I fought the urge to get in the car and drive across the country to be with my son until his fever subsided.

What are you doing? I asked.

Studying Siddhartha Gautama.

Who?

The Buddha.

What Buddha?

There is only one Buddha.

For a school project?

No.

????

I found some videos online. Some man was talking about the path to happiness. He mentioned Siddhartha. I wanted to learn.

Almodôvar, it took me a minute to work through my shock and answer; my stomach had turned to ice. Who did that man think he was, putting ideas into my son's head? Those people. Twenty years ago, they were locked away in their homes, lurking in remote corners of the globe, speaking—maybe even shouting—but their voices didn't have the strength to penetrate the walls. The Internet has changed everything now, given them the means to spread their facile philosophies, to leave them sitting around within everybody's reach. But they've done nothing to deserve this access to people, and their ideas are the same crap that couldn't pass through the old filters created by human intelligence, schools, newspapers, books. The Internet has rules about copyright violations and pedophilia, but there's nothing to stop some blowhard from spouting off about the path to happiness. No one seems to care about the repercussions. Do these people realize there are nine-year-olds listening to them?

Are you trying to become a Buddhist? I wrote.

No. I want to be happier ☺

His answer gave me a pain at the base of my skull.

You're already happy, I replied.

I know, but I want to be even happier.

????

Everyone in my grade is happier than I am.

How do you know?

They answered the question.

What question?

The question about being satisfied with life. The one you asked me.

That was a stupid question.

They answered and everyone was happier than me. The lowest was an 8.5. Three people said 10.

That's impossible. No one can be completely happy. They're lying.

Siddhartha says it's possible.

I didn't know what to say to that. I reclined in the chair, interlaced my fingers behind my head, and stared at the screen. I wanted to go find a Buddhist and force him to rate his satisfaction with life in front of Mateus. The answer would be so ridiculous, so conclusive. I spent a long time searching for the right words. I used to be good at it—appeasing my children's doubts with a reply that made them feel safe enough to reach a conclusion on their own. But something had changed. Because the only response that came to my mind was that Siddhartha was an asshole who never had a serious problem in his life; he had more free time than he knew what to do with, so he sat around dreaming up theories. Shit, Almodôvar, if a Buddhist had walked into the café right then, I would have strangled him.

But it was then, as I stared at the screen and read that sentence—*Siddhartha says it's possible*—that the voices of two men at the table behind me intersected with my own thoughts. It wasn't so much what they were saying, but the tone of the conversation: there was an uneasiness in the way they spoke, along with an almost childlike enthusiasm, as if they were about to jump from a plane in free fall. I didn't turn to look at them; I just listened. They were counting out loud, together, as if it were a game. They were counting money, multiplying it by days: one hundred euros times thirty was forty-six hundred and something. And along with the figures, they were reciting names of drugs, a long list of drugs. Suddenly, they fell silent. I imagined them sitting face-to-face, the table between them piled high with bills and pillboxes. Thirty seconds passed.

Then one of them said, "We'll need a car."

"We will need someone to drive the car," the other one added.

Almodôvar, I knew it immediately. I didn't need to hear any more. It was a job; they had a job for me.

Let's chat later, I wrote to Mateus, then snapped my laptop shut.

I turned in my seat. One of the men was facing me; I could see the other's profile. They were young, twenty-five, maybe younger. The one facing me had a long, thick beard, very blonde, almost yellow, though the hair on his head was brown. The other was wearing glasses with lenses so thick his eyes seemed to be floating. They shared a likeness without sharing any features; I thought they might be cousins. There were two glasses of water on the table, two cups, and a notebook open to a page covered in scrawled numbers, tables, and lists. I waited for them to look at me. They didn't. So I said, "I can drive a car."

They looked up at me with a trace of surprise and confusion, as if I had spoken to them in some exotic language.

They needed a driver. I knew how to drive.

They exchanged glances and looked back at me, smiling imperceptibly, and waited.

I went on: "I've been a licensed driver for eighteen years, and I have an impeccable sense of direction. And I have a car. You also need a car. I have a car."

But they kept staring at me in silence, as if I were in the process of telling a joke, as if all they had to do was wait for me to finish talking to start laughing. And all I thought was, We're wasting precious time, I could already be sitting behind the wheel, driving you where you want to go, I could be working by now, making money, it's this kind of hesitation that slows down the world; decide, idiots.

"Do you need a driver?" I asked, looking at the man who was facing me.

There was a flash of surprise across his face—until then he hadn't realized I was serious.

"Yes," he replied finally.

"I can be your driver."

"Have you ever worked as a driver?" asked the other man.

"No. I worked for years at a travel agency that closed last year. But I'm unemployed now."

"Unemployed?"

"Yeah. But I want to work. I really want to work. And if you need a driver, I can be a driver."

They exchanged looks again, their heads slightly cocked in the same way, mirroring one another. I stayed quiet, gave them time.

"What do you think?" asked the guy with the glasses.

"I don't know. Maybe we should interview more people."

"Let's get this out of the way now."

"He's not even a professional driver."

"Who cares? He looks like a good guy."

"He's unemployed."

"He's well dressed, clean-shaven."

"Let's not rush this. We haven't even decided how much we can pay."

"We don't have to pay much. The dude is unemployed—he'll take anything."

Look, Almodôvar. I'm not just imagining a hypothetical conversation between them about hiring me. They were talking like this in front of me, as if I wasn't even there, shamelessly, with no filters and a frightening sincerity. The bastards. I thought about getting up and leaving. I had never considered becoming a driver—or a waiter or a supermarket cashier, or a garbageman. I wasn't looking to throw myself at the first opportunity that crossed my path. I could have looked more. Maybe finding work as a driver wasn't as hard as getting a job as a travel agent.

"Make me an offer," I interjected.

The man with the yellow beard looked at me. He lifted his hand and said, "One moment, please."

"I have a car."

"One moment, please."

It was a game, Almodôvar. It was war. There we were, in the middle of the café, in a face-off, holding our breath, each waiting for the other to make their move. In my head, people at the other tables were breathlessly hanging on our every gesture, our every look, the air between us swelling with a silence that couldn't sustain itself for long. And I was willing to fight to the end. I had nothing left to lose; the job was too important.

I studied the bearded guy for a few seconds. Then I said, "Your partner is right: I am unemployed, I'll accept anything. Make me an offer."

Ten seconds passed. Then they made a proposal. I accepted immediately, without negotiating, without giving a second thought to what they offered me: four hours of work, six days a week, at 4.20 euros per hour, plus gas—maintenance of the car was on me—to deliver drugs to people's houses between half past three and seven thirty in the afternoon.

They weren't cousins, but brothers. They owned a pharmacy on the same street as the office where I slept. That is, their father owned the pharmacy—they had both studied business administration. The youngest, the guy with the glasses, was finishing a master's degree in marketing, but neither of them knew a thing about pharmacology. They didn't work in the pharmacy, but they went there almost every day. They had big plans for the business. They wanted to implement a series of marketing strategies, develop parallel services, remodel the space, reduce costs by streamlining. They spoke of the pharmacy as if it were a multinational. As we walked there, they explained that their father had lost control of the business, that the world was changing with each new day, but the old man still managed his stock as if it were the '80s, willfully ignoring the existence of the Internet. He wouldn't hear of investing in a new logo for the pharmacy—the current one, a radiant cross rising over a mountain, was nearly twenty-five years old. They had been trying to convince their father to make home deliveries for almost a year, and he had resisted for months; until January, when another drugstore popped up just down the street, and sales immediately slumped. When they introduced me to their father, the old man looked at me askance and laughed through closed lips, his chest slightly rising. His name was Arnaldo Sacadura. His appearance was contradictory: on the one hand, he had very little hair left, his hands trembled, and he had a rather pronounced humpback that caused him to stoop; on the other hand, he moved like a ten-year-old boy. He said nothing and waved me away, along with his children, as if we were flies.

"You're all nuts," he snapped, receding behind the counter.

They weren't nuts. But for them, life was easy, a place where everything was within reach. For them, work and money had never been essential, and everything was a question of will. They had started out ahead of most of the rest of us, the family business already cemented, hard to ruin in spite of adversity. They reminded me of you, Almodôvar. You could have been like them. If your father hadn't left you the shoe store in such bad shape, the building in such disrepair, you could have been just like them.

I started working a week later. I'd spend the first month gaining experience, not only as a delivery person, but also getting used to the whole idea of it. They printed two thousand flyers advertising the new service and a promotional offer: the first delivery would be free, and each subsequent delivery would be subject to a fee of 2.50 euros. I spent two mornings leaving flyers on café tables, stuffing them into mailboxes, pinning them behind windshield wipers. During rush hour, I'd stand at the entrance to the metro, an arm outstretched into a crowd heaving in all directions, waiting for someone to grab the paper in my hand.

And it worked. The two brothers were right: people were willing to pay just so they didn't have to leave their houses to buy medicine or diapers, or condoms, or anti–stretch mark cream, or the pill. (Since when did putting on your shoes, getting into the elevator, and walking two or three blocks become so hard? Since when was that worth 2.50 euros?) Somehow, the country had not yet sunk as low as we thought. Or maybe it had—maybe everything was already submerged and people just didn't want to know.

The phone never stopped ringing from day one. I'd wait on a stool at the counter, where Dr. Sacadura or his assistants would prepare the orders in an airtight bag—three or four of them at a time, sometimes more. And then I'd leave, holding the bag with both hands, keeping it level, as if I were holding a cake, or some soup, and I'd walk out to the car. The car was parked around the corner, so that neither Dr. Sacadura, or his children, or the assistant pharmacists, would ever see it. I didn't want them to know I was making deliveries in a car full of dents, with a cracked windshield, the passenger side window covered with plastic and an interior charred black, foul with the odor of decomposing material.

Almodôvar, maybe in there, in your refuge of cowards, you can't imagine the satisfaction of having a job after a year of looking for one. And besides that, I was doing a good thing. I was the bearer of salvation, of relief; I was an angel. You should have seen the gratitude on the customers' faces when they opened their doors. Some of them looked so fallen, wrapped in blankets, leaning against the wall to stay on their feet, people with all kinds of ailments. My work gave me an incredible feeling that lingered for hours and somehow neutralized all the evil around me. And the hours passed so quickly; suddenly it would be dark and my shift would end, even though I could have persisted into the early hours, exhaustion never even entering my body. Every day I'd talk to Dr. Sacadura and suggest we extend our delivery hours; I explained how we'd all benefit—the pharmacy, me, the customers.

But he'd just shrug and mutter, "Calm down, we need to take it slow."

All I wanted was to grab him by the neck, shove him against the wall, and shake him awake. Calm down? Incredible things were happening, the world around us was beginning to move again, a path had reappeared, and all we had to do was put one foot in front of the other and travel it—it was that easy. But the old bastard wanted calm, so we couldn't do it, Almodôvar. We could never dig ourselves out of the mud.

At the beginning of my third week, I called Xavier. I was excited; he could hear it in my voice.

"What's up?"

"Sorry I didn't answer your messages."

"I sent you twenty-seven e-mails," he said.

"I've been busy. I need to ask you something."

"You could have answered me."

"I was busy, Xavier."

"Did you at least open the e-mails?"

"Of course I did," I replied, though I hadn't opened one of Xavier's e-mails in over three months.

"So you saw the videos?"

"Mmmm."

"Did you see them or not?"

"Yeah."

"It's a load of shit."

"It is. It is a load of shit," I echoed.

But I didn't know what he was talking about. There was an apprehension in his voice: he was drawing out his words, pausing between them, as if he had just discovered that Hitler was still alive, and he didn't know how to live with the information. Only I was too excited to care about Xavier's problems.

"There's nothing we can do," he said.

"We can talk about this later. I need to ask you something. Do you still have that happiness index with all the different countries?"

"Yeah."

"I need you to tell me the country where the average happiness index is **8.9**."

"8.9?"

"8.9."

"Who do you know with an 8.9?"

"What do you care?"

"Is it you?"

"It doesn't matter who it is."

"It is you," said Xavier. And he let out a sarcastic sigh. "You know that's very unlikely, don't you? You've miscalculated."

"You and your calculations. Fuck you, Xavier. Tell me the country."

"There is no country where the happiness index is 8.9."

"There isn't?"

"The highest is 8.5. Costa Rica."

I tried to recall the list of countries. I had somehow imagined that the highest score was a 10, but I suppose that was about as possible as boarding a spaceship and flying to the end of the universe.

"There's no one with an 8.9?"

"Of course there is. But those people are rare. I don't know anyone who's that happy. To tell you the truth, I don't want to. But the numbers are just averages. Hang on."

He was silent for a moment. I could hear him rummaging through papers. I had no desire to hear what he was going to say. You know how Xavier is—the conversation was already getting too technical.

"Here it is," he said. "Costa Rica. The standard deviation is 1.71. Not so big. Still, one can say with some confidence that there are probably people in Costa Rica with a happiness index of 8.9. But in terms of a national average, 8.5 is the best you can do on this planet. And if you think about it, that's not bad at all. I'm sure that the Costa Ricans who are happier than 8.5 feel right at home among everyone else. If I had an 8.9 like you, I'd move to Costa Rica."

"I don't want to move to Costa Rica."

Xavier let out a steely chuckle.

"Then your happiness index isn't 8.9."

"That's what you say."

"How did you get that number?"

"I thought about it."

"Did you use a pen?"

"I don't need a pen to think, Xavier."

"Yes, you do. To calculate something as all-encompassing and complicated as a human being's happiness, you need a tremendous quantity of information—numbers, memories, calculations, tables, emotions, desires, and so forth—that your brain could never process without the aid of a pen and paper. Not to mention a calculator. Or a computer."

"I don't know why I keep calling you."

"8.9 isn't your number, you're just deluding yourself. Though I admit, that fact in itself is relevant. Your desire to be happy already bumps you up a few decimal points. But 8.9? No way."

"You're a fucking hypocrite, Xavier."

"No, Daniel. You are. You don't have a clue about happiness and you call me up asking me what 8.9 means, which country it is."

"I understand more about happiness than you, you bastard."

"No. You don't. The fact that your desire to be happy is greater than mine doesn't mean you understand more about happiness."

"Fuck you, Xavier."

"I just wish you were more honest with yourself."

"Fuck you, Xavier."

"What about the videos?"

"What videos?"

"Fuck you, Daniel. The videos I sent you. The kids and the homeless people."

"What about them?"

"What are we going to do?"

"I don't know."

"Can I at least ask you a favor? Could you visit Ávila?"

"Why? Did something happen to him?"

"No. But I think it could."

"He's a grown man, Xavier. Have you spoken to him?"

"I haven't heard from him in a while. We used to talk on the phone. Sometimes I'd call him on his cell, or at the boardinghouse where he usually sleeps. He hasn't shown up there for a few weeks . . . I have no idea where he spends the night."

"Xavier, I don't have time for this. Things are starting to happen again. I have to stay focused. I can't run around searching for Ávila."

"What if they piss on him again?"

"They won't."

"How do you know?"

"They just won't. That day in the parking garage was a one-off."

"You didn't watch the videos."

"What?"

"You didn't watch the videos, Daniel."

"Of course I did."

"Go watch the videos and then we'll talk."

"Look. I'll go find Ávila, talk to him, make sure he's okay, give him a snack. I'll let you know as soon as I have news."

"Go watch the videos and then we'll talk, motherfucker."

"He's going to die soon anyway," I said, but only after I hung up. Almodôvar, Xavier is a sponge. Try as we might to keep our distance from him, there's something in his voice—the words, the silences—that sucks us in, consumes us, keeps us around. His anguish pours out of the confines of his body and floods everything and everyone around him.

He was right.

About what?

You've never been 89 percent satisfied with your life—especially not when you were separated from Marta and your kids, sleeping under a desk in an office that was no longer yours, and working as a delivery boy for a pharmacy.

The prospect of a future is reason enough to be happy.

Maybe that's true according to some logic. But you haven't thought it through. Your optimism is remarkable, but still.

Fuck you, Almodôvar, you're not one to—

Did you go see Ávila?

I went. But not because Xavier asked me to.

After I spoke with Xavier I went to the pharmacy, did my job—I still put my work first—and only when I got back to the office around eight did I open my computer. I sat down, stretched out my legs across the toilet and rested the laptop in my lap. I started to open Xavier's e-mails, looking for the ones that linked to the videos.

I didn't want to watch it. I had no intention of getting involved. I didn't want to be that guy who was trying to save the world every week. I had my own life to save. Of course if saving the world came with a six-figure salary and an attractive benefits package, I'd be doing it all the time—but it doesn't.

Except I was still thinking about Vasco. I hadn't tried to find him, nor had I seen him since the day his friends lit my car on fire. As far as I knew, your son had been on the loose for the past month. I didn't want to watch the videos. I just wanted to know if the username of the person who put them online was the same as the one that posted the video of the kids pissing on Ávila.

Xavier's e-mail from February 23 contained a link to a video sharing site I'd never heard of. The page opened to a video titled *MiT—Part 2*; it had been uploaded there in August of the year before under the username "kingmike." I thought: I'll give this thirty seconds, then I'll turn this shit off once and for all and go save my own life.

I clicked "Play." The video didn't start; it was password protected.

I went back to Xavier's e-mail. It only said: *Another video.* I opened an e-mail from three days earlier. It said: *Did you see what I sent you yesterday?* I opened the e-mail he had sent me the day before. Xavier had written: *I was up all night working on this. The password is* anybody. *Watch it and then call me.* And he linked to a video on the same site titled *Man in Trash—Part 1.*

I repeat: I didn't want to have anything to do with this shit, this confusion, these anonymous videos, passwords, living as if I were in a detective movie with a murderer on the run, scattered clues that were all somehow connected, hunches becoming obvious as soon as they're confirmed. Fuck it, this is real life, and we have so much more to do; we have to fight against the affliction of knowing that the future hasn't yet been written, that anything can happen and not all of it depends on us.

I entered the password. When the video started, I minimized the page so I could only hear the sound.

Voice 1 (whispering): He's awake. Look—he's moving.

Voice 2: Cut it out, help me . . . here . . . pull this under him . . . it won't . . . it won't . . . it won't go . . .

Voice 1: 'Kay fine. 'Kay fine. Shit . . .

Voice 3 (shouting): Dude is up!

Voice 1: Fuck. Run!

I maximized the page again. The image took a few seconds to fill the screen.

There was a man writhing on the ground, his arms flailing in all directions like a fan made of snakes, and his voice matched his movements, a powerless, rage-filled babble. His head was hanging down, as if he could no longer sustain the weight of it. He seemed drunk. Or drugged. Or both. He was wearing a yellow Windbreaker and denim shorts—no shoes. His hair and beard framed his face like a mane. He was trying to crawl, but his legs were tied together, the rope tight around his ankles, the other end tied to a post. Then someone appeared in the shot on the right, stopping about two yards from the man. It was a boy. His mouth and nose were covered by a scarf, but I immediately recognized him: it was Vasco.

Shit.

I know. I'm so sorry, Almodôvar.

Voice 1 (the kid who was filming): Watch out.

The man grunted and reached for Vasco, who stood still, staring at him. It was like a bad zombie movie.

Then another kid, his face uncovered, appeared in the shot, dragging a garbage can behind him. I can't be sure, but it looked like the one who had been pissing on Ávila when we showed up at the parking garage: he was skinny, with a shaved head and a thick earring in one ear.

Vasco and the other boy held the garbage can and slowly tipped it over onto the man on the ground. The man squirmed away like a caterpillar. But when the garbage began to fall on him, he just stopped and cringed, waiting for it to end.

The garbage can was empty in under a second. And the man on the ground had become indiscernible under the pile of garbage; he was just in it . . . somewhere.

They dropped the garbage can on the ground, and Vasco leaned over the man and shouted, "Fuck you, you fucking drunk."

The other kid kicked the man's legs. The kid who was filming let out a nervous laugh.

Then the screen went black.

And I felt my eyes flood with hot tears, Almodôvar, an immense sadness, and I could hear your son's angry voice echoing in my head, ingrained in my memory forever. It was impossible to reconcile. How could Vasco bring himself to dismiss a human being like that? Imagine the hatred he must have been harboring to be able to say a thing like that. There's no acceptable explanation for what he did. Shit, you should have been with us—with him. None of this would have happened if you had been there. It makes me so sad.

The world didn't need it. What those kids were doing was horrific. Look. Every day, billions of people wake up, go out, cross paths, exchange glances, touches, words, and everyone is constantly trying to make sure it all goes okay, aware that we're all in this together; if we weren't, it would be impossible for anyone to survive. But a scene like that—three kids, a garbage can, a tied-up drunk, a camera. The negative energy generated by that one moment could be enough to undo everyone else's progress.

There were multiple videos: Xavier had found six, but there could have been more. I didn't watch the others—I didn't want to absorb such dark energy. At around three in the morning, my insomnia invaded my thoughts, and I decided to call Xavier. He was awake—Xavier is always awake. I asked him what was in the other videos.

"Kids, drunks, kids beating drunks, berating them, dragging them by the legs, stripping off their clothes, covering them in garbage, pissing on them, spitting on them, poking them with sticks tipped with flaming balls of newspaper, tying them up, insulting them, suffocating them with a mop. There's a little of everything."

"Always the same kids?" I asked.

"There are at least four or five repeat offenders."

"Do you recognize any of them?"

"From the parking garage?"

"From there, or anywhere else."

"I recognize three from the parking garage. That's it. I don't leave my apartment, Daniel. Why? Did you recognize anyone?"

"No," I lied. "I don't think so."

"We have to do something."

"No, no we don't."

"Let's go to the police."

"They're kids, Xavier."

"They're men, Daniel."

We hung up.

The fact that Xavier hadn't recognized Vasco in the other videos didn't mean he wasn't in them. Maybe Xavier didn't remember your son. How long had it been since he had last seen him? I tried to remember when you might have visited Xavier and brought Vasco with you. If it ever happened, I never knew about it. I never watched the other videos. I had already seen enough. I thought: I'll talk to him, but not now. I needed time, Almodôvar. There was a nausea forming deep in my throat, something close to terror, at the idea of intervening, getting in the middle of it all. I couldn't make a move until that feeling passed.

But I went to see Ávila—the least I could do—just to make sure that he was still alive. I found him without difficulty in a place Xavier had mentioned. He was leaning against the bar between two old men, the three of them watching the TV on the wall. Cycling was on, thirty or forty men on bicycles pedaling up a hill with great effort. None of the men watching spoke, as if they couldn't fathom what the men on bikes were doing, as if they couldn't find the right words to describe something so extraordinary. I tapped Ávila on the shoulder; he turned and smiled when he saw me, but he didn't recognize me. He was too drunk. We sat at a table.

"Xavier is worried about you," I said.

"He's a good boy, that Xavier. He should get out more."

He said it with such a straight face, I couldn't tell if it was a joke. Still, I laughed.

We were standing just under the TV. The other two men lowered their gazes to our level, their expressions lost in the haze from the white light on the ceiling. It was never daytime in there.

"Are you okay?" I asked.

Ávila blew out a sigh and, with trembling hands, mimed tightening an imaginary tie around his neck. He said nothing.

"Are those kids still bothering you?"

"What kids?"

"The kids from the parking garage."

"Oh that. I forgot about that. What can you do? Take it one day at a time, right?"

He had phrased it as a question, but wasn't expecting an answer. He looked up at the bartender—a fat man, completely bald, his elbows resting on the counter, his chin resting in his hands, eyes on the television—and ordered two glasses of white wine. The man didn't move.

"I'll serve you when you've paid for the three you've already drunk."

"I'll pay you when I open my wallet. But it's still early," Ávila answered.

Then he turned to me with an empty, static look, his mouth sunken into a pathetic smile, his head slowly swaying as if it were on a rope. The bastard wanted me to step up and offer to buy him his next glass of wine. It wasn't enough that I had saved his life.

Look, Almodôvar: it was all wrong. Ávila wasn't a victim; he was just another leech living off the system, the mercy of other people, the justice in our society. Some kids pissed on him. And then what? It was nothing compared to what he had been doing to us for years: drinking obscene amounts of wine, giving blow jobs to married guys in exchange for a pittance he doesn't even pay taxes on, living off Xavier's money and God knows who else's. He had been pissing on all of us for years. When did it become acceptable to just give up? We were better than that, our spirits a tremendous force, the physical world never enough to trample our will. Look at us now. The issue isn't about everyone fighting their own battles. The issue is the number of people who don't bother to fight at all.

"Do you know why they did that?" I asked him.

"Well, they're kids," said Ávila, sounding very academic. He fell silent for a few seconds, and when at last he spoke, his voice was like foam dissolving in every syllable: "I know how kids are . . . I watched a lot of them grow up to do stupid things . . . things that would shock the devil . . . if someone gave them a button to blow up the world, they wouldn't hesitate . . . and now look . . . they're men . . . they're women . . . they live among us . . . they're part of all this . . ."

"They're not on the right path."

"There is no right path . . . you should know that . . . and besides, they'll get back on track . . . they always do . . . or almost always . . . but when they do . . . they'll be people . . . like you . . . and like me . . ."

I laughed, Almodôvar. A loud, sincere deep laugh. The nerve of that guy, to believe that he and I were the same kind of people, unaware of the distance between us, the countless levels separating our existences.

"But," I replied, "the ones who don't grow up to be people like me will continue to go around pissing on you."

"It was just bad luck."

"It wasn't bad luck. It was going to happen sooner or later. Believe me, it wasn't bad luck. If Xavier and I hadn't shown up in time . . ."

"Thank you."

"Your gratitude is worthless as long as you're still here, as long as you haven't learned your lesson."

His eyes wavered. I thought he might cry. But he didn't. It's just that he couldn't keep his eyes open—he was nodding off.

"The next time, we won't be there to save you," I said threateningly.

He nodded again, an almost involuntary movement. We were silent. A few minutes passed. I felt the chair's hardness, the sweat on my shirt. The heat inside that bar was incredible. No wonder Ávila and the other old men spent the day throwing back glasses of icy white wine—to cool their bodies, numb their senses, cast spells against other spells. Suddenly, with apathy still in their eyes, the two old men at the counter started clapping at the television. Ávila instinctively joined them. I leaned in and looked up at the screen: ten or twelve riders had fallen over on top of one another into a puzzle of bodies and bikes that spread across the asphalt. The old men continued to clap for almost a minute, the time it took for the cyclists to stand up, untangle their bikes, and speed off again. I looked at Ávila. He wasn't clapping anymore. He sat up very straight, his head falling forward, his eyes closed. It was eleven thirty in the morning, but inside the bar, time was irrelevant—it wasn't among the dimensions.

Maybe I should have stayed and hoped that Ávila would wake up; maybe he still had something to tell me, something that would convince me that he was making progress—even if he was being reckless about it—seeking out paths and not giving up. But I left. Ávila could roast himself alive in the heat of that tavern. It wasn't my problem.

That day, I was almost twenty minutes late for work, though I can't remember why.

"This is unacceptable, Daniel," Dr. Sacadura said when I arrived.

"I know. But I've never been late before. It won't happen again."

"I'm not talking about that. I am talking about your car."

"What?"

"I saw you this morning. Is that what you use to make deliveries?"

"It is my car, Dr. Sacadura."

"It's not a car, Daniel. It's a wreck."

"Did someone complain?"

"I'm complaining."

"I'll get the car to the shop as soon as I can."

"As soon as you can? Which is when?"

"I can't give you a concrete date."

"This week?"

"That might be too soon."

"This month?"

"I don't know. As soon as I can."

"That might be too late."

This is it, Almodôvar. This is how we become weaker and slower: we lose our sense of direction, allow ourselves to be distracted by bullshit. I was doing a good job, making deliveries in record time, working late, impeccably managing the prescriptions and payments, not to mention the irresistible smile I always prepared before I knocked on anyone's door. But the bastard decided to pick on my only weakness. It wasn't that someone had been dissatisfied with the service, or that my car had caused a drop in orders—he was just giving me a hard time for the hell of it. And that's how the world falls apart, Almodôvar. That's how it starts.

The first two hours were hard: I made nine deliveries, six of them to chronically ill patients. With the exception of an eighty-year-old woman—who opened the door to me in jeans and an Algarve Beach T-shirt with a simple expression on her face as if she had just arrived in the world—everyone seemed haunted by some secret or imminent threat, as if they were being held hostage in their own homes by a stranger in hiding and had been forbidden to speak. I'm not sure if the people who opened the door and paid me were the patients themselves, but it's possible they weren't. Except for the eighty-year-old woman. She herself told me she was very ill with pancreatic cancer, pointing to the place where the tumor had settled and running a hand over her T-shirt as if she were petting an animal. On my way back to the pharmacy, Marta called me.

"You have to come this weekend," she said, her voice restrained, her calm forced.

Almodôvar, Marta had stopped asking questions about my finances or my job search—she knew I was making deliveries for a pharmacy, but she didn't know the details. We almost never spoke about us, or the future. But I hadn't seen my children for three months, and she was getting worried. The month before, she had hinted that my absence was starting to affect Mateus and Flor, and urged me to visit them as soon as possible. A few days later, she mentioned it again, suggesting that the kids spend a weekend with me. I told her it would be impossible, and when she asked why, I just said that things were complicated, that my new place was in no condition for visitors. She wasn't convinced, but she didn't insist. Over the next few weeks, we repeated the conversation several times, and it became a kind of game, the ball bouncing from one side of the court to the other, with me always on the defensive, clearly losing my patience. And I wanted so badly to go, Almodôvar. My eyes burned with my children's pain. But I was living on almost nothing. When I started working at the pharmacy, I was already two months behind on the mortgage for the house that was no longer mine, and I still needed 150 euros to settle it. The trip to Viana alone would cost me almost half that.

"I have to work this weekend," I replied.

"I don't care, Daniel. Figure it out. You have to come. Things aren't going well."

"What happened?"

"What happened is that I got home and your nine-year-old son had shaved his head—and I'm not talking about a buzz cut, which might even look okay with his baby face. He's bald, Daniel. He used one of my razors; a friend from school helped him."

"Did you ask why he did it?"

"He said he wanted to convert to Buddhism and that it's part of the process."

I remembered the conversation I had had with Mateus the morning I got the job with the pharmacy. He hadn't mentioned Buddhism again.

"He wants to be happier," I said.

"I don't follow."

"He wants to be a Buddhist because he thinks it will make him happier."

"He said that?"

"Yeah."

"When?"

"About a month ago."

"And you didn't tell me?"

"I didn't think it was that important."

"Your son tells you he's not happy and you don't think—"

"Mateus never said he wasn't happy. Actually, he said he was happy. Very happy. But he wanted more—he wanted to be one hundred percent happy."

"What did you tell him?"

"I explained that no one can be one hundred percent happy."

"Why would you say that, Daniel?"

"It's the truth. No one is one hundred percent happy. There's always something that messes up the numbers."

"What numbers, Daniel? What truth? I have no idea what you're saying. And even if I did, Mateus is nine years old, and he doesn't need to hear about what is and isn't possible in this world."

She was so right, Almodôvar. So I just said, "His hair will grow."

"No wonder Flor doesn't want to study anymore," Marta said, and sighed.

"What are you talking about?"

"She told me she discussed it with you."

"I don't remember that conversation."

"She says it's not worth it."

"What does she mean 'it's not worth it'? She's at the top of her class. She always has been. She could become a researcher and find the cure for death if she put her mind to it."

"Her words were, 'In the future we'll all be slaves,'" Marta replied.

"Is she awake?"

"Yeah."

"Put her on the phone."

Marta called Flor's name, but not too loudly, as if she were right there, a few yards away. But it took at least half a minute for Flor to speak. I thought about what I'd say to her, my fatherly speech—how could she even consider not studying? She had every option in the world; she could do anything and everything she wanted with an absolute guarantee of success. I was deeply convinced of this.

"Can you explain to me what's going on?" I asked.

"Sure."

Flor has this ability to control her voice so that her tone never wavers, whatever the situation; she believes so strongly in the sheer value of her words that she doesn't see the need for intonation.

"So tell me, you're going to stop studying and do what, exactly? Get a job?"

"I'm not going to stop studying. I just won't study as much. It's not worth it."

"Of course it's worth it, Flor."

"Why?"

"Why? Because everything you learn now will help you solve problems later, problems with your work, your family, your head. You'll have more options, you'll be more equipped to deal with difficult situations."

"That's not true. There are millions of people around the world who studied a lot and now they're unemployed, or unhappy, or angry, or alone."

"But there are also millions of people who did study, who worked hard to get ahead, and because of that they have good lives."

"Maybe that's true. But the world is changing, Dad. Ten years from now no one will have a good life . . . unless they're Chinese."

"Chinese?"

"The Chinese are going to take over everything. We'll have no choice but to obey them. We're going to become slaves to the Chinese."

"Where did you hear that?"

"People."

"I'm coming to Viana. We can discuss this when I get there."

"We're already discussing it."

Flor got off the phone. Marta got back on the line.

"So?" she said.

"So what?"

"Can I count on you this weekend?"

"I can't, Marta. I can't even think about it. Next weekend. You have my word. I'll be there next weekend."

"What if they do something stupid, Daniel?"

"They won't. They'll be fine."

"I'm not so sure about that. I really wanted to believe that they were fine. But believing isn't enough, is it? Is that how you handle it? Do you convince yourself, force yourself to believe that they're still fine? Do you just eliminate all the grim possibilities from your imagination?"

A guy does what he can to keep from losing his mind.

You're one cold-blooded son of a bitch, Almodôvar, a reptile.

You don't visit your own kids for months and I'm—

But we spoke every day; I knew what was happening in their lives.

But you didn't see them.

I couldn't. I didn't have any money. It was understandable.

Of course you could have. You could've asked Marta for money, or Xavier, or even Clara.

That's true. But I thought: One more week and I get paid; I'll wait one more week, and then I can see my kids.

So what happened the next weekend? Did you go see your kids?

Fuck you, Almodôvar. You have no clue what you're saying. And that ironic tone of voice is highly unnecessary.

That week flew by. I was so focused. I tried not to think about Vasco or Xavier. I hardly felt the days; my only goal was to get through them with my spirit intact. Whenever I spoke to Marta, she'd sum up the state of things in a few sentences, and I'd reaffirm my promise to be there in a few days; she said nothing, deeply distrustful of my words. And I thought: What happened? She knows me. We lived together for over a third of our lives. She knows what kind of person I am, what I'm capable of. What changed?

My plan was to catch the first train to Viana on Saturday morning, arriving in time for lunch, and spend two days with Marta and my kids, returning to Lisbon on Monday morning. Almodôvar, it seemed so simple. But it never happened.

That day, the phone rang very early, just after six. I was awake, dressed, ready to go. A number flashed across the screen—no name. I thought: It's a job. But it was Saturday, and no one ever phoned on a Saturday for work. So I answered and heard air, a loud, long burst of wind. And then, after the wind, someone spoke.

"Daniel?"

"Speaking."

"It's Vasco. Almodôvar's son."

"Did something happen to your dad?"

"No. I don't know . . . you said I could call you."

"I did?"

"That day . . . you said if I ever needed help, I could call you."

"Where are you?"

"I don't know. On a beach."

"A beach? Which beach?"

"I don't know. On the Costa de Caparica. Can you come get me?"

Can you believe it, Almodôvar? It was your son. I immediately thought: I won't do it. Let the kid figure it out for himself. I have to solve my own life.

"Call your mother," I said. "I'll call if you want."

"I already called her. She's not picking up."

And he began to cry. The son of a bitch began to cry.

"Vasco, listen. Vasco, stop it and listen to me. Go find a café or a restaurant. Sit down and call your mother again. When she answers, explain everything and she'll pick you up. I can't help you."

"There is a restaurant . . . I can see it from here, but—"

"Go there. It's early, but it might be open. And if not, someone will come along eventually."

For a moment there was nothing.

"Vasco? Are you there?"

"I can't."

"You can't what?"

"Go to the restaurant. Walk there."

"You can't walk?"

"I have glass in my feet and . . . blood and . . ."

"Shit, Vasco."

Almodôvar, are you listening to this? Do you even understand what was happening? Your son couldn't walk—and he was fucking over my life. The fact that you weren't there that morning meant my life was fucked. People ask for help without stopping to think about the implications, just assuming that someone will offer whatever they have. And if we don't, if we refuse, we're heartless bastards.

"Where are you, Vasco?" I asked. "Which beach?"

"I'm on the Costa de Caparica, but I don't know the name of the beach."

"Can you hold out until I get there?"

"Yeah. I think so."

"So hold out."

Almodôvar, I thought: I can do this. I'll skip the morning train, get in the car with a suitcase, and in less than fifteen minutes I'll be over the bridge and on the other side of the Tagus River; I can get to Caparica before seven, look for the kid, hopefully find him fast, be back in Lisbon before nine, drop him off at home, dash to the station, catch the nine o'clock train.

So you went?

Of course I went.

Thank you.

Go fuck yourself, motherfucker.

As I drove through the city, I tried calling Clara, but there was no answer; I sent her three texts. I didn't want her to worry, but then again,

I did. When I reached the bridge, I called Vasco and told him to try to find out what beach he was on, the name of the restaurant; I asked if he could spot any sign, plaque, or landmark.

Five minutes later I called him again. He answered with a grunt, as if he were an animal trying to speak like a person. I couldn't make out every word, but I gathered that he was dragging himself across the sand to the restaurant.

"Are you far?" I asked.

"Yeah."

"Can you crawl there?"

"I don't think so. There's glass in my hands and knees."

"Seriously? Fuck, Vasco. Fuck."

Again, silence.

"Give me something. Do you see any buildings?"

"No, no buildings."

"So what do you see?"

"The restaurant is . . . white and blue . . . and there's a flagpole without a flag . . . and a wooden walkway."

"Okay, got it," I said.

He had just described every restaurant on the Costa de Caparica.

I sped up. When I reached the next town, I didn't stop; if he didn't see any buildings, it meant he was on one of the beaches farther down the coast. I reached the first beach just after seven. There were two cars and an RV in the parking lot. I parked, got out of the car, ran across the walkway to the restaurant, and looked out over the sand, the rough sea, the sun just peeking out over the water, the still-dim horizon. There was a young man running along the beach, a woman sitting cross-legged close to the surf, staring tranquilly into the waves, and two surfers warming up. I scanned the beach. I didn't see him. I called his name.

"Can you see anyone else where you are?"

"No. There's no one."

We hung up. I ran to the car and drove to the next beach. I crossed the wooden walkway to the restaurant and looked out over the sand. There was a woman in her sixties walking barefoot, shoes in hand. I got back in the car. The next beach was empty, the stretch of sand between the dunes and the water seemed as if no human had ever set foot there. I imagined Vasco lying there, covered in sand thrown at him by the wind, camouflaged, invisible. I stood there trying to spot him for a few minutes. Then I called his name.

"With your back to the sea, is the restaurant to your right or left?"

"My left."

I scanned that side of the beach. He wasn't there. I went on to the next beach, but he wasn't there either. And then I drove on, stopping at every last beach looking for your son. Around eight, I called him again.

"Are you sure you're on the Costa de Caparica?"

"I think so."

"But are you sure?"

"No."

"Fuck, Vasco."

I remember thinking: What if I can't find him? I could spend all day driving from beach to beach along the coast of Portugal. That wasn't an option, Almodôvar. I didn't know when, but at some point I'd have to give up, turn back, and leave him there—wherever he was.

Then I stopped the car in a parking lot and followed a wooden walkway that forked after fifty yards. I went to the left. I walked another hundred yards and reached the beach. The restaurant was closed—it may have been abandoned. I looked at the beach. Someone was lying about two hundred yards from the restaurant. Whoever it was didn't move. It could have been anyone; it could have even been clothes left by a swimmer. In front of the restaurant, facing the sea, there was a large, sloping balcony. I went up the stairs and approached the railing to get a better view.

"Vasco! Vasco! Vasco!" I shouted.

The person in the sand remained motionless.

I called him on the phone.

The person finally stirred and brought his hand to his ear.

"Daniel?"

"Did you hear me scream your name?"

The person in the sand lifted his head, then sat up and turned toward me. It was him.

"Sorry," he said. "I fell asleep."

"Didn't you want someone to save you?"

"Of course."

"It doesn't seem like it."

I hung up and walked over to him. He didn't move as he watched me approach.

Almodôvar, if you don't have the heart, then don't listen to what I'm about to tell you. Your son was a wreck. He was barefoot; his feet were all cut up, shards of glass still glinting in his flesh, which was encrusted with blood and sand. More blood stained his pants at the knees, his palms; his shirt was torn. And his face, Almodôvar. His face had gone completely white, his lips purple, his dark eyes hollow, as if he had been dead for hours.

There was nothing around except for the black circle of what had been a bonfire, an overturned beach chair, and, a little farther down, a pathway of glass—twenty or thirty broken beer bottles—two yards of shards gleaming in the sun that pointed in the direction of the sea. Do you follow me, Almodôvar? Your son, our little Vasco, that clever boy you raised, dropped a handful of neurons, decided to play the ascetic, and fucked up his feet.

I took off my coat and gave it to him so he could warm up; he may have been on the verge of hypothermia. As I helped him up, he groaned once and then fell silent, swallowing his pain. I asked him if he knew where his shoes were, and he said he wasn't sure, but that he may have tossed them into the sea.

"Why?" I asked.

He shrugged.

I supported him under one arm to help him along. But whenever he touched his feet—especially his right foot—to the ground, he let out a cry and collapsed to his knees. So I hoisted him over my shoulder and carried him to the car. I laid him across the backseat on the blanket covering the burn hole. When I gave him water, he drank more than half the bottle, nearly a liter, and as he drank I called Clara again.

"Your mother isn't picking up the phone."

"I know. She's working."

I thought: Fuckfuckfuckfuckfuck.

I got into the car and drove back to Lisbon. By the time we reached the bridge, Vasco was already sleeping. It was after nine in the morning. I did the math. I wouldn't make the nine thirty train now, or the one at ten, but the twelve o'clock was still in reach.

When we reached Lisbon, I drove straight to the hospital. I parked the car in one of the lots, quite far from the emergency room entrance. I shook Vasco. He woke up and immediately grimaced with pain. I helped him out of the car, hoisted him over my shoulder again, and carried him to the emergency room.

The waiting room was packed, and a woman burdened with heavy bags stood up so Vasco could sit. He shrank into the chair, keeping the bottoms of his feet off the floor, and closed his eyes. An old woman—her right cheek swollen and black as if she had been hit with a frying pan—looked at Vasco, then glared at me with indignation, as if I were to blame for the state of your son. I sat on the only empty chair, three rows behind Vasco. I sent one message to Clara to tell her what was going on and another to Marta to explain my delay; neither of them responded.

After an hour passed, I knew I wouldn't make it to the station by noon. I thought maybe I could catch the two o'clock.

They called Vasco and brought out a wheelchair. I lifted him into the seat. He was asleep and didn't stir. I pushed the chair into the screening room. A nurse shook him by the arm. He didn't move. Then she looked at me and asked what he had.

"He has glass in his feet, knees, and hands."

"Not that," said the nurse. "What did he take? Why isn't he waking up?"

"I think he was drinking. He's probably drunk."

The nurse got up and pulled a flashlight from the pocket of her blue shirt.

"Hold his head," she instructed.

I did what she asked. She leaned over and shined her flashlight into Vasco's eyes, as if she were trying to see into his brain. Suddenly, she looked up at me.

"Was he just drinking or did he take something?"

"Something like what?"

"Drugs?"

"I don't know."

She didn't give me time to explain. She inserted herself between me and the chair and pushed Vasco through some double doors.

Another hour passed, and no one came to explain what was happening. I started to think, to rehash my every move that morning. Could I have made it to the beach any sooner? Of course I could have. And what if I had? Maybe it would have made a difference, maybe the situation wouldn't have gotten so bad. Was it my fault? Fuck, no. But what if I had talked to him that day they burned my car? What if I had left it to smoke and explode? Took the time to tell him that things weren't so bad, or that they were bad, but that they could still turn around, that . . . Fuck it. No matter how you see it, I wasn't to blame. Do you get it, Almodôvar? I wasn't the one to blame. I couldn't be expected to go around plugging up all the holes you left behind.

I spoke to a nurse. She didn't bother to look up, but she said she'd try to find out what had happened. Forty minutes later, she appeared.

"They pumped his stomach. He's awake now."

"What about the glass?"

"I don't know anything about the glass."

"Can I see him?"

"Yes. I'll take you. Wait here, and I'll come get you."

Another half hour passed. I'd never make it to the station for the two o'clock.

My phone rang. It was Clara.

"How is he?" she asked, gasping for air.

"I don't know. They still won't let me see him."

"I'm on my way."

The nurse appeared, sucking on a lozenge, one cheek rounder than the other.

"I'm sorry," she said. "I took a lunch break. I hadn't eaten anything since eight in the morning."

It was one thirty. We entered an endless corridor—over a hundred yards long. The wall was lined with patients on stretchers. Vasco was one of them, near an abandoned counter. He was awake, confused. He looked terrible, as if he had actually died and had just been revived. His feet, hands, and knees were wrapped in bandages. Above him there was an IV bag running into a vein in his left arm. He only noticed me when I stopped next to him. The nurse told me to wait there for a doctor and walked away. Vasco closed his eyes. We were silent for a few minutes. Then Vasco spoke. You know what he said, Almodôvar?

He said, "Please don't tell my dad."

Wait. No. That's not how it went. First he asked, "Am I going to die?"

"No," I answered.

Then he said, "Please don't tell my dad."

We were quiet again. Ten minutes later a doctor showed up studying a chart.

"Barbiturates," he said. "The dose wasn't excessive, but with the alcohol, it was enough to knock him out. It could have been much worse."

He said it slowly and looked at me with a certain severity, as if *worse* were a clinical term.

"When can he leave?"

"He can leave now."

"Now?"

"Yes, now. There's no reason for him to spend the night here. His condition is stable; the worst is over. He needs rest, that's all."

"I think he should stay."

"There's no reason for that," he said, and walked away.

With the help of a nurse, I lifted Vasco into a wheelchair. Clara called. She was already at the hospital. We met her at the entrance.

She saw your son, Almodôvar, and knelt in front of the chair to hug him. Vasco flung up his arms to protect his hands. She cried for a minute, clutching him. Then she wiped away her tears, stood up, and studied him in silence, as if she'd somehow come to understand everything that had happened. Then she turned to me.

"Thank you, Daniel."

"You don't have to thank me. You guys know you can count on me."

"Even so, thank you. I don't want to think about what might have happened if you hadn't gone looking for him."

"Then don't. He's fine now. He needs to rest. Tomorrow he'll be like new."

She looked at her son as if she were trying to discern whether what I had said was even possible.

"Can you walk?" I asked.

Vasco shook his head.

Clara stared at him for a long time, motionless, her arms limp at her sides, her lips pressed tightly together. Then she turned back to me.

"Daniel, I have to get back to work. Can you can take him home?"

"The clinic is open on Saturday?" I asked.

"No. I do home nursing for an old lady, eighty-seven; she can barely get out of bed and needs someone to take care of her. I cover evenings and weekends."

I looked at Vasco and tried to imagine him at home alone every night. It was somehow impossible to imagine; I knew it would affect the rest of his life.

"Can you take him home?" Clara asked again.

I checked the time. It was two in the afternoon, and the next train left at seven.

"Sure," I replied.

"Can you stay there with him?"

"I can stay until six thirty. Then I have to leave. I'm going to Viana today."

She nodded. "Thanks."

When we arrived at your house, I helped Vasco strip off his torn, damp, and dirty clothes. He looked exhausted. Even if his hands hadn't been bandaged, he still couldn't have managed to put on his pajamas alone. I wiped away the rest of the sand and blood clinging to his hair. Then I helped him lie down. He fell asleep immediately.

I sat on the sofa and called Marta. I told her the whole story, minute by minute, every detail, so she'd understand that none of it was my fault.

"I'm waiting for Clara," I explained. "I'll leave as soon as she gets here. I'll be there by eleven."

It seemed like a simple promise, Almodôvar. I couldn't imagine that Clara wouldn't show up.

I waited nearly three hours and then called her.

"Daniel, I can't leave until someone comes to cover me," she explained. "The woman can't be alone."

"When is someone coming?"

"I don't know. Her daughter lives in Setúbal. She said she'd try to call the nurse who works the day shift during the week."

"I have to leave, Clara. And Vasco can't be alone either."

"I know. But this is my job. I can't lose this job. And I can't leave this woman alone. If something happens, I'm responsible."

"But this is your child, Clara. And I have to leave."

"I know," she repeated. "I'll be there as soon as I can."

I waited, still believing it was possible to make it to Viana; Clara would come and I would fly through the city and jump on the last train just in time.

At 6:40, I called Clara again.

"I'm leaving," I told her. "I have to leave now, and Vasco is going to be here alone for a few hours until you get here. When are you coming?"

"I don't know, Daniel. I haven't heard anything. But go ahead and go. I'll be there as soon as I can."

Almodôvar, just so you know, Clara didn't come home until Monday. But your son wasn't alone all that time. I stayed with him.

DJIBOUTI, EGYPT, MONGOLIA, NIGERIA, PORTUGAL, ROMANIA: 5.7

Almodôvar, at this point in my story, perhaps you need a recap of what actually happened. So here it is.

In the spring of 1966, your father, the young Andalusian son of a shoemaker, nocturnal and restless in nature, given to hopping over the border to chase Portuguese women in full flight—I believe those were his words—found himself in Lisbon, lying on a cold, hard cot in a cramped closet of a hotel by the river, where the whores conducted their business. He was in a bad way, with a high fever that had come on in the middle of a drunken escapade. He didn't know anyone in town—at least no one he could turn to in a pinch. And it never crossed his mind to call his father in Seville for help. He spent hours drifting in and out of a thick delirium, surviving thanks to the pills he always carried in his wallet and a resilience that, it seems to me, you didn't have the fortune to inherit. During his second day of fever, to ensure he wouldn't die indebted to anyone—his reputation as an honest man had always been his collateral—he went down to reception and paid for the five nights he had spent at the hotel plus three more: the time he believed it would take for the fever to win out over his body.

I know the story, Daniel.

I know you know. But I want to remind you.

Your father paid and started up the stairs to his room, but as he reached the third step, he was suddenly overcome by a dizzy spell. He couldn't withstand the shock of it and collapsed as if he were made of sand. He couldn't get up. The boy at the reception desk that day was an honest type, and with some of the money your father had paid him, he got a taxi to take your father to the hospital.

It was the beginning of pneumonia. Your father was hospitalized for ten days. Despite the fever that refused to relent, despite the room he shared with seven other men suffering from all manner of ailments, and despite the fact that he had no idea how he might return to Spain—his remaining money would barely get him across the Tagus River—those days in the hospital were not bad ones. He met your mother, a diligent nurse who seldom smiled and devoted more time to him than necessary, helping him translate his Spanish pickup lines into Portuguese. He fell in love with her, and she let herself fall in love with him. How could those have been bad days? They were the start of everything.

They married five months later, on a day of heavy rain. There was that photograph at your parents' house on the three-legged table, over by the phone: your father looks like the happiest man in the universe; your mother, still unsmiling, rests her head on his shoulder with the look of someone who deeply believes in all that is right in the world. And then came the shoe store. It seems that your father, in the midst of the storm that was his youth, learned something of your grandfather's craft. Plus, your mother was always levelheaded enough to calm her husband's impulses. They were a perfect couple, infallible, at least for many years. You had a privileged childhood as the shoe store owner's son, the kid who showed up to school each month with new shoes, who traveled two or three times a year to Italy, France, Argentina, accompanying his father to the biggest shoe expos on the planet. And despite all your advantages, you weren't a jerk. On the contrary: you were so cool, everyone liked you; I was so proud to be your friend, walk alongside you through the school hallways, eat lunch with you, go to your house.

You had a lot of faith in that shoe store; you believed it would last forever. You used to repeat what your father always said: No one wants to walk barefoot. Then your father got sick, and you ran to take that six-month course in sales and management. You learned all the buzzwords you needed to be a good salesman, all the established marketing techniques, more advanced approaches to finance, as if that shoe store was a multimillion-euro business. In your head, perhaps it was. Somehow, you inherited your dad's unshakable faith in that store. And the day they started building the shopping center five streets away, you all laughed it off over dinner through mouthfuls of your mother's meatloaf. You thought that a shopping center would bring more business to the neighborhood, that everyone would win. Your naiveté was disarming. Or maybe you knew perfectly well what would happen but just couldn't let go of your faith in the business.

What a slow death—too slow. You'd been in business for nearly two decades. In the final years, after your father died, you laid off all your employees and manned the store alone—a thankless task. But you never complained, not at all. Somehow, life continued to delight you. And you managed to find time for all of us: Clara, Vasco, your mother, Xavier, me, your group of dedicated friends, always there for anyone who needed it.

Then you had the idea for the site. You got Xavier and me on board. You had invested all your money in it—although we didn't know it at the time. It was supposed to be your salvation. But not only that: a site where people could go to help each other would be your legacy to the world, your philosophy of life offered to society on a scale that had been unthinkable before the Internet. But the site didn't work out, and you went and robbed a gas station. Then you had the nerve to get yourself caught and thrown in jail.

The shoe store closed—did you know it closed? Even though you weren't in much debt, Clara couldn't keep the business going. I don't know if she had to declare bankruptcy. I know that the windows are papered over and the shelves are empty. I don't know what happened to the shoes that remained. In any case, your family missed the money the store brought in—no matter how little it may have been. Clara started doing double shifts at the clinic. Then, once she realized she'd never be able to pay her bills, she got another job on nights and weekends as a hospice nurse for an old lady who hardly left her bed: Clara helped her with everyday tasks, bathed her, managed her medications, and kept her company. When she left the clinic, she'd run home to eat dinner with Vasco and by nine she'd be sitting next to the old lady's bed, the two of them listening to some Catholic radio program. She only slept at home one or two nights a week.

And that's how your son was left to his own devices, how he got involved with the wrong people—it happens to a lot of teenagers. And that's also how, without any adult supervision, your son made a human wreck of himself on the Costa de Caparica. He called his mother, and when she didn't answer, he called me. Then it was just a matter of cause and effect: because of the cuts in his feet, Vasco couldn't walk, and because of the cuts in the hands, he couldn't eat or go to the bathroom. In other words, he couldn't be alone. Clara couldn't take care of him because she was too busy taking care of an old woman who was clinging to life by a thread. And I already happened to be there, so I stayed. And because of that, I couldn't go to Viana to see Marta and my kids.

Almodôvar, can you see the thread running through all these events over the past forty years? It seems so simple, so straightforward. If, at any time, you had stopped to look up, you could have easily seen what was coming. You could have easily stopped the chain reaction in time. And then we might have been saved. Except you didn't.

That Saturday, at your house, as Vasco slept and daylight quickly drained out of the apartment, I called Marta and told her what had happened. I was indignant: the injustice of the situation, Clara's negligence, you and your senseless absence, Vasco's stupidity. I wanted us to be on the same side. And it wasn't hard: my indignation was real. I wanted to feel her support, but when she finally spoke, it was only to ask about Vasco. I told her what the doctor at the hospital had said, trying to use all the clinical terms I remembered, thinking they'd surely justify why I wasn't in Viana. She was quiet.

"Are you mad?" I asked.

"Yeah," she said.

"At me?"

"I don't want to have this conversation now, Daniel."

"I love you."

"I know."

For the first time, I admitted to myself that things between Marta and me might have already ended long before without either of us having realized it.

Around nine, I opened the fridge. It was empty. But I found twenty or thirty premade meals in the freezer. I heated up a vegetarian lasagna, which I ate standing up, leaning against the kitchen counter. When I finished dinner, I went to see Vasco. Your son slept as if he would never wake up. I placed a hand on his forehead; he had a fever. He didn't seem to be aware of my presence and hardly moved when I slipped two pills into his mouth—a painkiller and a fever reducer—and gave him some water so he could swallow them. I spread out a blanket on the carpet next to his bed, lay down, and covered myself with a duvet I found in your bedroom closet. I slept in fits and starts and woke up more exhausted than I had been when I went to sleep.

Early the next morning, Clara called. She said she was still alone with the old lady, but that someone might come to replace her so she could get home for dinner.

That Sunday lasted forever. I didn't want to be there; you were everywhere in that house, Almodôvar, and I wanted to move on, leave you behind. I turned on the TV. I flicked through the channels without stopping on any of them; none of it seemed to matter, or maybe I had forgotten how to watch TV. I called Marta. Flor answered. I told her I was sorry I hadn't come to Viana.

"It's us who should be there with you," she said with a laugh.

Almodôvar, she wasn't mad at me. Or maybe she was and didn't want to tell me. My daughter has an ability to be at peace with the world that I had always wanted for myself. Flor never desires what she doesn't have; she doesn't mourn her losses. She knows life is long enough that, in the end, everything becomes worth it.

Vasco slept until six in the evening. When he woke up, I fed him some cod with cream sauce and another painkiller. I took him in my arms to the bathroom, helped him pull down his pants, and sat him on the toilet. Then I wiped him. Neither of us said a word. When I laid him back down on the bed, he fell asleep within minutes.

Clara arrived just after eight that evening. She looked terrible, her face sunken, her eyes hollow. She gave me a hug and thanked me. She clung to me for a long time, as if she might fall asleep standing there, her forehead resting on my shoulder, her bag hanging from her hand. I wanted to tell her that the situation had gotten out of hand, that her son was adrift in the world and had lost his sense of right and wrong, that the scene on the beach could have been even worse, that she had to talk to him, spend time with him, show him the way. But she turned and went into Vasco's room. She sat down on the edge of the bed and just looked at him. After a minute, she lay down beside him, snuggling into his pillow. I was standing in the door and, before she closed her eyes, she asked me to wake her around ten. I watched them for an instant. I thought: She'll never talk to him; as long as Almodôvar is gone, she'll never have the strength to talk any sense into this child. It wasn't her fault.

I woke her at ten. She kissed Vasco's forehead and slowly rose. As soon as she reached the hall, she spoke: "I need you to stay another night. Can you stay?"

"Where are you going?"

"I have to get back to work," she said. "Can you stay?"

"Sure."

"Tell him I was here."

She thanked me and left.

Vasco woke up shortly after. There was a terror in his expression, as if he didn't recognize his own room. But he looked better, refreshed; his fever had subsided. He told me he was hungry again and I heated up paella. I helped him sit up in bed and positioned the plate in his lap. As I spoon-fed him, we talked. We talked about you. I told him about that night you and I jumped the zoo walls and visited all those animals in the dark, the chimpanzee that shook your hand through the bars, the cockatoos that erupted into gibberish when they felt us approach, our terror when we mistook two guards for bears on the loose. He smiled for a second, and after a long silence he said, "What do you think will happen when my father gets out of jail?"

I thought: We'll all die a little.

But I just said, "When he gets out, we'll have a party. Then life will go on."

He nodded for a long time, as if he wanted to believe me but couldn't.

"Your mother was here," I said. "She slept next to you for a while."

"Yeah, but then she left," Vasco muttered.

"Don't be like that. She's doing her best."

"Well, her best isn't good enough."

"That's not fair. It's all on her until your dad comes back. The house. The bills. You."

"Me?"

"You. And if you're not happy with things, you could consider helping her. You're turning sixteen, right? You're old enough to work. It might just keep you out of trouble."

Almodôvar, your son turned his head away, but I kept feeding him. We were silent until he finished eating.

"Do you want to tell me what happened on that beach?" I asked.

"No."

"Whose idea was it to walk barefoot on glass?"

"It was a bet."

"A bet." I laughed. "Did you win, at least?"

He raised his arms to show me the bandages on his hands.

"What do you think?" he asked.

"I think you're smarter than that. Shit, Vasco, what were you doing on the Costa de Caparica coast with those assholes?"

"They're my friends."

"Are they the same friends who were with you that day in the parking garage?"

He didn't answer, so I went on.

"I don't understand, Vasco. Why would you want to be friends with those guys? You go around beating people up. I don't get it."

"I was on top of the van. You saw—I didn't hit anyone."

"Maybe not then, but I saw the other videos. Fuck, Vasco, you did some crazy shit. The least you can do is be man enough to admit it."

Almodôvar, your son's eyes trembled as he tried not to cry. He was about to speak, but I didn't let him.

"You didn't used to be like this, Vasco. But now, because of those friends of yours, you're beating up on defenseless men. They've turned you into that kind of person. I get it: you're angry, your dad is gone, your mom is never home, life got a lot harder. But nothing justifies what you're doing to those guys."

"We don't just go around making trouble. We're friends . . ."

"Shit, Vasco, they're not your friends. They left you on the beach. They left you there with your hands and feet in shreds, in the cold."

He shrugged. I could have said so much, Almodôvar. I could have recited a whole speech about what real friends are, and I could have told him about us—me, you, Xavier—about trust and respect and shit like that.

But instead I just said, "Sons of bitches."

He laughed, a short huff through the nose.

And after more silence, he said, "They're pissed at me."

"Why?"

"I took something that belonged to them . . . and they found out."

"What?"

"It doesn't matter."

"Of course it does. What?"

"Money."

"How much money, Vasco?"

"About three hundred euros."

"Three hundred euros? I thought they were your friends. You can't steal from your friends. How did you steal three hundred euros?"

"I stole it from a guy who sells pills to kids in school—I took it out of his wallet."

"Perfect. Your mother's going to love this. Not to mention your father."

"Don't—you can't tell them."

"We'll see about that. So now what?"

"Now he wants his money back."

"Is that why they left you on the beach?"

"Yeah."

"Vasco, give them the money and forget about these people."

"I can't. I spent it."

"On what?"

"I bought a cell phone and a portable game console."

"Fuck, are you serious? This whole country is going down the toilet; everyone's struggling to stay afloat, it's a daily struggle, and there's no justice for many of us. Then you get your hands on three hundred euros that aren't even yours, and the first thing you do is buy a phone? People like you are the reason the world has sunk so low. Do you know how long three hundred euros can last some people? Months. You could have solved all your mother's problems with that kind of money."

He didn't answer. He just stared at me with a helpless look on his face.

"I can't help you," I said. "Sorry. Even if I wanted to. My life hasn't been that easy lately. I don't have that kind of money."

He nodded.

"Sell the phone and the console. Online. At school. Sell them fast and give those guys their money back. And then get your shit together. Focus. Life is more important than you think. If your father were here—"

"But he's not."

"No, he isn't. But I am. And you're going to figure your shit out, Vasco. I don't want to hear about you getting into any more trouble. The world and the people in it deserve more respect from you."

Almodôvar, your son suddenly seemed so small to me, a child who had just learned to walk. There was nothing more I could say; he had to learn for himself. So I shut up and left the room, gave him some time and space so my words could sink in.

Around one in the morning, his fever came back. I gave him some pills, water, a cracker. He asked me to sleep in his room, so I stayed.

The next morning, Clara appeared early, before eight, to stay with her son. It was Monday, but she had asked for a day off at the clinic.

She was so tired she hardly spoke. Still, her presence filled your house with an air of hope that hadn't been there before.

When I said good-bye to Vasco, I didn't mention our conversation from the night before. He gave me an unsettled, almost embarrassed look. We stayed like that for a moment. Then I left.

The following Friday, after my four-hour shift, I got in the car and drove the 250 miles to Viana do Castelo. It was an extravagance, of course; the train ride would have cost half of what I paid in gas and tolls. But there were no more trains to Viana, and I didn't want to wait another night. I wanted Marta to believe in me again, to know that I was doing everything I could for us, that I wasn't drifting away, that she and the kids were as important to me as ever. During the week, we hadn't discussed the possibility of a weekend visit, and it was only when I was sixty miles outside of Lisbon did I text her to say I was on my way. I knew she was expecting something from me, a word that would resolve everything, a patient look that would restore her confidence that the world—or at least our world—still had a solution. But Almodôvar, I was so tired; I didn't want to solve anything. I just wanted to be with them, laugh with them, touch them; I just wanted to feel normal again.

I reached Viana shortly after midnight. Marta was waiting up for me. She led me into the kitchen and kissed me slowly on the lips, as if she had rehearsed that very moment. I thought that perhaps her anger had passed, that we could rebuild ourselves on that kiss alone. Mateus appeared, groggy with sleep. His head was still shaved, but some fuzz was starting to grow back. He hugged me around the waist, burying his face in my chest. Without a word, he sat down at the kitchen table, opened his laptop, and played around for a few minutes, his eyes glued to the screen. Then he said, "Good night."

He went back to bed. Marta explained that he had been playing an online game in real time for the past few weeks; the game consisted of managing a virtual aviary. At any time of day or night, he had to be available to control an ever-increasing population of chickens, ducks, and turkeys; oversee egg production; and haggle over the sale of poultry and eggs—all so that the business could run smoothly. He had put in about eighty hours and was in sixteenth place out of more than 120,000 players; he owned thirty-two aviaries and more than two million birds. He had created powerful alliances with some of the strongest players, and his production had begun to dictate the price of eggs on the virtual market. As Marta spoke, I felt my heart tremble, as if my son had just jumped into a sea of enormous waves.

The next morning, I found Flor in the courtyard in front of my in-laws' building, lying on a lounge chair and reading a book called *(Something) in a Haystack*. She smiled at me but didn't get up, and I bent down and kissed her on the forehead. I sat beside her on the ground. We talked: my work at the pharmacy, the six-car accident her Portuguese teacher was in, her new haircut, how much she missed the heat, the wind in Viana do Castelo, all the good friends she had made in so short a time. All in all it seemed like a lot. Then I pointed to the book resting on her lap.

"What are you reading?"

"A novel."

"What about your newspapers?"

"I stopped reading newspapers. I stopped reading anything that's real."

"Why?"

"Because I know how it ends."

"How does it end?"

"Badly."

Almodôvar, she was only thirteen, but that's exactly what scared me. All I wanted to do was say something to prove her wrong. But being there with her, hearing her voice, was too nice, and I didn't want to ruin it. Later that day, Marta told me that the week before, Flor barely opened her schoolbooks; the year was coming to a close and her final grades might be in jeopardy.

When I mentioned it to Flor, she just said, “If it’s that important to you, I’ll pull off good grades on my exams. But it won’t change anything.”

That’s what I wanted to hear. But it also wasn’t.

After dinner, Mateus opened his laptop and took me on a full tour of one of his aviaries. There was an almost pedantic pride in the way he recited all the statistics about his multimillion-euro company, his largest transactions, his production peaks. After almost an hour, I touched my cheek to his head.

“I like your hair like that, all scratchy.”

He stopped playing on the computer and looked at me.

“But it’s not enough,” he said, and sighed.

“It’s not enough for what?”

“To be a Buddhist. To be happier.”

“What’s missing?”

“A ton. I started reading a blog about it. It’s complicated. I’ll tell you when I know more.”

“Deal,” I said.

But I didn’t tell him what I was thinking, which was that he should forget about Buddhism and happiness, that he was still a child, and that children don’t have to be thinking about those things—they just have to live each day as if they had just been born, that everything is good: happiness and sadness, anger and love. Everything counts for something.

Marta didn’t kiss me again for the rest of the weekend. It wasn’t as if she was avoiding me or still angry—she simply didn’t kiss me. Sunday night in bed, after we had turned out the lights, she broke the silence as if she were reading from a script in the dark.

“We can’t go on like this,” she said.

I let a few seconds pass as the sound of our breathing filled the darkness.

"No, we can't."

And we were silent again. I thought about what to say next; I had to give her something—I wanted to give her something. But Marta spoke first: "I don't know which one of us screwed up. But this doesn't make sense anymore. I thought we could overcome this. I thought we were stronger than all this, but the truth is, it just stopped making sense."

"What doesn't make sense?"

"Us. Me. You. At least like this, the way we are: me here with the kids, you in Lisbon, months between visits."

"I know, you're right. But it won't be like this forever. Once I find a decent job, everything will change. We'll buy another house, or rent—whatever we want—and you'll move back to Lisbon, and the four of us will be together again. When I find a job—"

"And when will that happen, Daniel?"

"I don't know. It's just a matter of waiting; things are changing."

"Things are not changing. Don't you watch the news? Everything is getting even worse."

"I know, but I won't be unemployed forever. I was good at what I did; someone's going to notice."

"You could come to Viana, find work here. At least we'd be together."

Almodôvar, I felt the air thinning around us. She no longer believed we could ever go back to the lives we had before.

"I could," I replied. "But if there's no work for me in Lisbon, there will be even less work here."

"You could find work in another sector."

"Marta, my job is who I am, and I have no desire to change that."

"You're a delivery boy for a pharmacy, Daniel."

"You know it's temporary."

"Fine. Sorry. But promise me you'll at least think about it."

I couldn't bring myself to say yes aloud, so I just nodded. I'm not sure if she saw me. Then I hugged her. She didn't move. She fell asleep almost immediately. I stayed awake for three hours without moving, until Marta woke up. Then we made love. In the darkness of dawn, everything seemed easier.

The next day, after lunch, I got in the car and drove back to Lisbon.

Almodôvar, I didn't need to think about it. What I had said to Marta about my job being who I am was true, but I was willing to set it aside in a second to be with her and my children.

In that case, why didn't you promise to think about it, Daniel?

For her the solution was obvious: she no longer believed. But I did; I still had hope. I wanted her to understand that. I wanted her to know that moving to Viana would mean giving up all hope. That she was asking me to make a tremendous sacrifice.

You're a fool, Daniel. Your hope has been wearing you down for years and you can't even see it.

My hope, Almodôvar, is the only thing that keeps me from dying; even so, I was willing to give up on the idea that Marta would regain hers. That Monday, I arrived in Lisbon with a new plan: I'd work at the pharmacy until the end of the month, settle things with Dr. Sacadura, load up the car, drive to Viana do Castelo, and try to find a job there. It was simple. In the meantime, I'd continue to sleep in the office, spend my days at cafés, libraries, gardens, supermarkets. Almodôvar, I still haven't told you about all the hours I spent in supermarkets, pushing a cart around, filling it with shampoos, cleaning products, imported cheeses, wines, canned foods, frozen shrimp, as if I had a home and a family to maintain. I spent hours looking at packaging, reading labels, deciding what to choose, selecting the best cuts of meat, the freshest fish, the ripest fruit, making small talk with employees, smiling at the other customers, and then, suddenly, I'd push the cart full of hundreds of euros of products into a random aisle and abandon it there without actually buying anything. It's what I had to do to feel normal.

But as I was saying: I had three weeks to kill in Lisbon before heading to Viana do Castelo. I still hadn't made any promises to Marta; I hadn't even told her about my plan. I didn't want her to have any expectations. But the truth is that I had made my decision. Then something happened that made me reconsider.

Almodôvar, a few days after I got back from Viana, I received a call from a recruiter who had been trying to place me for over a year. Through them I had already been on four unsuccessful job interviews. The first thing the woman on the other end asked was if I was still looking for work. I said yes. And I thought: It's finally happening. The position in question hadn't been filled in more than a decade; it was with a company in the tourism sector that was looking for someone competitive and motivated and dynamic; they were offering a stimulating work environment and a very enticing salary. The recruiter mentioned my profile, my qualifications, and my professional experience, praised the fact that I speak three languages besides Portuguese, and expressed her hesitation about my level of computer literacy. She asked me three or four questions about my professional aspirations, and in the end added something about how I might be an ideal candidate for the position in question. I asked her the name of the company.

"At this stage of the recruitment process, I can't tell you anything else," she replied.

Then she briefly summarized the responsibilities: creation and implementation of tour packages, sales team coordination, digital content management, participation in company strategy on a consulting basis.

"Are you interested?" she asked.

"Of course I'm interested."

She said they'd more closely evaluate my profile, and in a week they'd let me know if I had made it to the next round, which consisted of an interview with someone from human resources at the company in question.

Finally, some good news.

Almodôvar, it was nothing. It could have been the start of something, it's true, but at that moment, it was still nothing. Plus, I had heard that kind of thing before. Do you have any idea how many of those phone calls I had received in the previous year? You know how many times I had to answer questions about my professional ambitions?

But there was the prospect of an interview. And they were recruiting. It was good.

Almodôvar, these companies are always recruiting. Even if they don't have any openings. It costs them nothing to interview candidates, find out what kind of people are out there looking for work, without ever actually hiring anyone. It's not that different from what I was doing at the supermarkets.

So it wasn't that significant?

No.

But you said it made you rethink moving to Viana.

It wasn't significant, Almodôvar, but it was something. And, in my mind, I couldn't let it go. How could I? That's not what we were taught. Think about it. Forty years ago, this country was nothing, suffocating under a dictatorship, and the rest of the world wouldn't even acknowledge that we were dying. After we saved ourselves, life started to make sense again. We joined the rest of the planet. They gave us a hand, pulled us up, put some faith in us, told us they believed we could do it. And why shouldn't they have believed? Suddenly, everything began to happen: the words *training*, *investment*, and *development* were everywhere; the country filled with unprecedented wealth that hadn't been seen in several centuries. Maybe we weren't prepared to manage this wealth, but it still made us feel so good, so confident. And they told us that the future would be made from that moment onward, that things would get even better. They didn't know what they were talking about, but then again, we didn't know that they didn't know. So we learned to believe, bought cars and houses, put our kids through school, exchanged our money for stocks and bonds; we built a new country because the old one would mean nothing in the future. The human spirit is so malleable, Almodôvar: it only took four decades for us to believe that the fate of humanity is permanent evolution, that the future will always be a better place than the present. I so wanted to think the job prospect was nothing, a false lead. But I couldn't. So I decided to leave Lisbon only after I found out whether I had made it to the next round of the recruitment process.

This was on a Friday. I waited the entire week for the recruiter to call me back. She didn't. Still, I told the pharmacy I'd be leaving at the end of the month. Old Dr. Sacadura looked at me, obviously displeased, and said, "I knew these deliveries would be nothing but trouble." He didn't speak to me again until my last day of work, as if I had been the ruin of his entire business.

I packed all my stuff into a suitcase and a box, except for my daily essentials. And I was ready to leave. If the recruiter called, I'd go on the interview, load up the car, and drive away.

The woman didn't call that week—but Xavier did. We hadn't spoken in over a month, but as soon as I answered he blurted out, "Someone needs help, Daniel."

"Hi, Xavier."

"There's someone who needs help, Daniel."

"Just one?"

"Fuck off, Daniel. It's a woman. In Switzerland."

"A woman in Switzerland? How do you know?"

"She said so on the site."

"On our site?"

"She needs someone to help her visit her brother in the hospital."

"Calm down, Xavier. When did she write in?"

"Four days ago. But I just saw it today."

"And it's not a prank?"

"Of course not, Daniel. Why would someone pull a prank like that?"

"I don't know . . . Did anyone respond?"

"No. No one."

"How many views did it get?"

"Thirty-seven."

"Is the message in Portuguese?"

"Portuguese and French."

"But she's in Switzerland?"

"That's what her profile says. The request too."

"Do we have any other users in Switzerland?"

"No. So?" Xavier asked.

"So what?"

"What do we do?"

"We do nothing, Xavier. Hopefully someone will reach out."

"What if no one does?"

"Let's just wait and see."

"The chances that no one will reply are very high, Daniel."

"If no one answers, there's nothing we can do. Xavier, we built this bridge to allow people to reach each other; we created a path that didn't exist before. But if people decide not to use it, we can't make them."

"So what will happen to this woman?"

"I don't know. But at least we gave her a chance."

"We raised her hopes for something that will never happen."

"You don't know that. Let's wait and see. Shit, Xavier, it's how the world works. Just wait a while. Just wait," I said.

When we hung up, I got on my computer and went to the site. The woman's message was the only activity from the past ten days. It read:

* * *

My name is Doroteia Marques. I'm French, born to Portuguese parents. I'm 68, and I've lived in Geneva, Switzerland, since I was 33. I've been a paraplegic for six years.

I've had a good life. My happy childhood memories give me strength: our two-story house on the outskirts of Paris, my two brothers, one older than me, the other younger. I married a man who loved me, who always treated me well and took care of me when I needed it. He died young, but somehow I learned to live in the empty space he left behind. For forty years, I was a geography teacher, first in a high school in Montpellier, then at an academy here in Geneva. I studied; I learned languages. I traveled the world a few times. I was always very shy, though I did make a few friends—unlike my husband, who could make lifelong friendships in the line at the post office. My lack of friends was never cause for regret; on the contrary, I like being alone. I'm at peace with my dearly departed—my parents, my younger brother, my husband, some friends—which is important at my age. Paraplegia left me in a wheelchair, unable to leave the house alone, though luckily I'm too resilient a spirit to lose my enthusiasm for life because of it. I have the Internet, my books, and my cats. That's enough for me.

I'm writing because of my brother. He lives in Marseille with his wife and his eldest son. He owns a karaoke bar. On the morning of May 16 (three days ago), he, my sister-in-law, and my nephew closed the bar and got into the car to go home. They had an accident; a drunk driver hit them head-on. The driver of the other car died on impact, along with my sister-in-law. My nephew died a few minutes later in the ambulance. My brother went to the hospital. He's still there. The doctors say he could die too.

I want to go see him. I want to go see my brother. I don't know whether he'll die, but I want to see him before something happens. But I can't. I can't travel alone, with my wheelchair, from Geneva to Marseille. I need help. If anyone could help me, I'd be eternally grateful.

Are you happy now, Almodôvar? After all, someone was actually using the site to get help. Maybe your idea really was great. Does this woman's anguish make you happy?

Don't be ridiculous, Daniel. What happened? Did someone offer to take her to see her brother?

Wait, Almodôvar. There's something I have to tell you first. That week, Vasco also called me.

He was in trouble. The kid whose money he had stolen had been harassing him for two days straight with a combination of threats, silence, and screaming. Clara had gone back to work and still hadn't noticed, but she'd find out eventually.

"Have you got the money?" I asked.

"I have part of it. It's hard when I can't leave the house. I managed to sell the phone, but not the console."

"Give him what you have. Say you'll pay him the rest later."

"I tried. But he says he wants it all now. He says he's coming over here, Daniel."

"Vasco, he can't enter your house."

"I know. But he says he's going to wait on the street until I come out. And I'll have to come out one day."

"Shit. How short are you?"

"A hundred and eighty euros."

Almodôvar, there are those moments when life can grind us down and we don't even notice. We really want to do the right thing, even if it makes us lose our footing. I didn't have 180 euros in my account—I probably didn't have half that.

"I'll lend you the money."

"Seriously?"

"Seriously. But you have to promise me that you won't run around with those kids anymore."

"I promise."

"And I want to go with you. When you return the money, I want to be there."

Silence.

"Vasco?"

"Fine. You can come."

The next morning, I spoke to Dr. Sacadura and told him that he was right: I couldn't keep driving my car in its deplorable state, and I'd be willing to address it immediately, but I'd need an advance. He was checking a list of orders and didn't look up when he replied.

"Now that you're leaving you want to fix your car?"

I didn't answer. I just waited. He kept working in silence for almost a minute. Then, without another word, he got up and went to the cash register. He pulled out two hundred euros in twenties and put them in my hand as if I had forced him to do it, as if he were the victim of a robbery.

Vasco had agreed to meet the kid that same day after lunch. I picked him up at your place. He still had bandages on his hands and was having trouble walking—it took a long time to cover the twenty yards between the door of your apartment building and my car. But he seemed excited; he looked like a kid again, with his shorts and baseball cap and the backpack slung over his shoulder, a determined look on his face. He pretended he was going to dive into the car through the broken window.

"Like in that movie!" he exclaimed.

He sat down beside me and took off his cap. I asked where we were going. And then he said, "Remember the street where you found me that day? Where they burned your car?"

"How could I forget?"

"It's there."

"What's there?"

"An apartment on the fourth floor of the building."

Almodôvar, according to Vasco, the apartment belonged to a German who had moved to Portugal almost ten years before because she wanted more sunshine in her life. Word had it there were a few photographs in a bedroom dresser drawer showing a woman in her early forties—tall, big-boned, with very short black hair, a minuscule smile, and huge breasts spilling over her low neckline. She gave high school and college students German lessons in her home, and the boys liked her because of her breasts, which brushed against them when she leaned over to correct their work, causing the kids to get up in the middle of the lesson and jerk off in her bathroom . . . You get the picture. And then, one day, a kid excused himself, reached into his pocket to hide his erection, and closed the bathroom door. When he returned, the German was on the floor, motionless, staring into infinity, her chair overturned. She was dead. It was a heart attack or something, Vasco didn't know. The kid called the police and then called his parents. But you want to know what he did when he was waiting for someone to come? He knelt beside the corpse, unbuttoned her blouse, unclasped her bra, and squeezed her breasts as he jerked off again on the spot. Kids are capable of anything. Then he put her apartment keys in his backpack. The police arrived. The kid made his statements, the corpse was carted away, and the apartment remained uninhabited, with all the German's things in it. The kid went back three months later to make sure they hadn't changed the lock, and then gave the key to two brothers who lived on his street in exchange for a surfboard.

According to Vasco, the two brothers first entered the German's apartment sometime the year before. At first, they only went there from time to time, after school, with their girlfriends, or to play PlayStation with their friends, smoke joints, drink beers, throw parties. No one ever came to claim the property: no relatives, no bank. When bills came in the mail, they'd all chip in to pay them. And look, Almodôvar, the building was old, the remaining apartments were almost all empty, and most of them needed major work. There was just one old man who lived on the top floor, but he rarely left the house. They could come and go as they pleased, make all the noise they wanted; there was no one to stop them. That place was a dream for any fifteen-year-old kid. And for a kid like Vasco, with his father in prison, his mother always working, and problems in school, the place must have seemed like the last refuge on earth. It was in this apartment, Almodôvar, where your son had spent most afternoons until just a few days before. It was where he had been all those weeks I spent scouring the streets for him.

We parked in the same spot where my car had been when the kids had tried to set it on fire. It was a quiet street, with just a few stores, a car repair shop on the next block, an apartment building right next to the drugstore, with a man sitting by the door reading the paper—the same man who had put out the fire in my car. Above us, those trees, enormous and green. And beyond the trees, the deep-blue sky of spring.

"How do you know someone will be there?" I asked.

"Someone's always there," Vasco replied.

"Are you guys running some sort of operation up there?"

"What kind of operation?"

"A weed nursery? Trafficking?"

"Of course not."

"What do you mean *of course not*? You said yourself the money you stole was from selling drugs."

"Yeah, that guy sells drugs. But not here. In clubs."

"Do you guys keep any weapons?"

"You don't get it. It's actually pretty chill. It's just a bunch of kids who want to hang out without any adults on their backs."

"Chill?"

Vasco shrugged. "Let me go up first. If they're okay with you, I'll give you a call and you can come up too."

"Don't even think about it. I'm going with you."

"They'll be pissed."

"They're already pissed."

We entered the building. Dampness was everywhere: in the air, in the sunken stairs, in the gaping walls. We climbed quickly, taking the stairs two or three at a time, our footsteps hardly making a sound. On the third floor landing there were two bikes parked next to a ficus tree that was withering from lack of sunlight. Besides the bikes, there was nothing else to suggest the presence of teenagers in the building.

When Vasco rang the bell, I felt my shoulders tremble. Almodôvar, until then I hadn't even realized that I was scared. Thirty seconds later, the door opened to reveal a tall, fat boy with long bangs, his face pitted with acne, wearing a T-shirt with Homer Simpson sitting on the couch in his underwear, drinking a can of Duff. He was big: he could have crushed your son and me in a matter of minutes. He looked at Vasco and smiled.

"You are so fucked," he said.

Then he suddenly saw me and stopped laughing.

"What's this guy doing here?" he asked.

"Puto, this is Daniel. Daniel, this is Puto," Vasco said.

"You brought your dad here?"

"He's not my dad," said Vasco. "Get out of the way."

As if he harbored supernatural strength, Vasco pushed Puto aside with a sweep of his hand and stepped past him into the apartment. I followed him inside through the narrow space between Puto's body and the doorjamb. Vasco looked at me and whispered, "Aníbal's not going to like this."

Almodôvar, that kid with the bison body was harmless; he probably wasn't older than fourteen or fifteen.

The entryway was tiny and crammed with clothes, broken skateboards, an old monitor, a supermarket cart. It smelled of marijuana—not like smoke, but the cool and sweet smell of a plant growing somewhere inside. Maybe Vasco had lied about not growing weed. The walls were covered in graffiti, orders, messages, random words; the same was true for the stucco ceilings and the tile floors—the apartment was practically a book. There was music playing softly, a swift beat pulsing through a symphony of synthesizers.

Can you imagine your son in a place like this, Almodôvar?

I walked behind Vasco. Puto followed me. We entered a room. In the middle of the floor were the remains of a fire, gray charcoal and pieces of wood still smoldering; the ceiling above was completely black. The only furniture was a huge sofa and a china cabinet with no doors. There was a flat-screen TV hanging from a rope tied to a curtain rod. It was on split screen, a figure on each side wearing shorts and boxing gloves. Two kids stood side by side in front of the screen, vigorously punching at the air. On the screen, the figures mirrored their every movement, although they lacked the same fury and momentum.

Their backs were to the door, and when we entered, they didn't notice. We stood silently behind them until the game ended and one of the kids raised his arms and bellowed in victory, hopping from one foot to the other as if he were a real boxer celebrating in the ring. It was in the middle of this celebration that he turned, saw us, and suddenly stopped, struggling to catch his breath. Almodôvar, he was the kid who had been pissing on Ávila that morning in the parking garage. When he recognized me, his eyes widened. The other kid saw us too. He was black, an insipid fluff growing along his upper lip and overly prominent jaw. He was bent over, his hands on his knees, gasping as if he might cough up his lungs.

"Fuck . . . who . . . is this guy?" he managed to say.

Vasco told him my name. And then he added, "He's my friend."

The kids laughed. The winner of the fight dropped onto the sofa.

"Well, if he's your friend, he's our friend," he exclaimed.

The others laughed again.

"I have the money, Aníbal," said Vasco.

"Well, let's see—"

"Vasco," I interrupted, "give him the money and let's go."

Aníbal pointed a finger in my direction.

"Dude, you can't just walk in here and start giving orders. This isn't your house."

I raised my hands to say I didn't want trouble. Aníbal asked Vasco to sit next to him on the sofa. Vasco sat.

Almodôvar, in my mind, the plan was to enter, say hello, put the money on the table, and leave. A matter of two minutes, maybe less. I went there believing that my presence—an adult, a man—would intimidate a bunch of kids, no matter how crazy they were, and that Vasco would be free to do as he pleased with me at his side. I was wrong, Almodôvar.

"Shit happens," Aníbal began. "You saw the money, and the money spoke to you like a girl calling your name from the other side of the street, so you went over there to talk to her and before you knew it, you were kissing; then you decided to take her home and be with her forever. I get it. Fuck, believe me, I get it. It's happened to me. Only you have to be careful, man. You have to be careful because the chick might already have a man. And if her man finds out you took her home, then you're fucked. And before you know it, it's nighttime and you're alone on the beach; it's dark and cold and your feet are all cut up, and you have to drag yourself out of there, just to keep from dying in the cold."

Beside me, Puto was occupied with rolling a joint and laughed without taking his eyes off the pile of weed.

"You were . . . mad wack," stammered the black kid. He had gone back to punching at the air between him and the TV.

"Fuck, next time just don't take shit if you don't know what it is," Puto said.

Aníbal laughed. So did Vasco.

"Vasco," I said, "give them the money and let's go."

"I understand your problem," Aníbal went on. "But I need you to understand mine."

"I understand," said Vasco.

"I'm not sure you do."

"Sure I understand. And I'm sorry. I shouldn't have done what I did."

Almodôvar, I don't know if you can believe this, but after all that had happened, your son didn't want those kids to stay angry with him; he still wanted to be their friend.

"Well, if you understand," said Aníbal, "then you know it's not enough to return the money you took. You have to give me more."

For a second, Vasco looked up at me. I didn't know if he wanted me to get us out of there, or if he wanted me to leave and let him stay. Then he reached into his backpack and took out the envelope with Aníbal's three hundred euros.

"It's all there. But I can't give you more, because I don't have it."

Aníbal took the money and put one foot up on the sofa. Then he hiked up his pants to his knees and stuffed the bills into his sock.

"I know you don't have more. If you did, you wouldn't have stolen it from me. But maybe you can make it up to me some other way?"

Aníbal looked at me as he said this, a conciliatory smile on his face, as if he expected me to back him up.

"Come on, Vasco, let's go," I said.

Vasco didn't move; he just sat there, waiting.

"Help me sell the rest of my pills at your school and we'll be even."

"Fuck off," I cried. "Enough already."

Puto passed the joint he had rolled to Aníbal, who held it as if it were a pen and he were poised to write with its glowing nib. Almodôvar, my presence in that apartment had no effect whatsoever; they weren't afraid of me—they weren't even embarrassed.

Aníbal took a long hit off the joint. He held the smoke in his chest, sucking back his words: "You could make some money that way. You know you need it."

Vasco nodded; I pulled him up by the arm.

"Let's go," I said.

"I don't need an answer now. Think about it," said Aníbal, his voice suddenly soft, almost musical. He wasn't going to hurt us. At least not that day. He just wanted to present his proposal. It was business.

A cloud of smoke hovered around Puto, and inside the cloud the world was no longer the same. Nor was it the same inside that apartment. There in that room, the most incredible things seemed possible. These kids' every move was powered by a momentum that made them seem invincible. Laughing seemed so easy. Maybe even happiness was easy. Because for them, time didn't exist as a continuum—it was every instant they were alive that mattered. For them, life passed one second at a time. Vasco had every reason to want to be there.

Even so, when I left the room, your son followed me; maybe he didn't want to disappoint me, or maybe he was planning to return later. And just as we were making our way to the door, another door opened at the other end of the hallway. It was a bathroom; I could hear a toilet flushing. Then a man staggered out.

It was Ávila, Almodôvar. It was that son of a bitch Ávila, totally shit-faced, trying to button his pants, his fingers tripping over each other.

He saw us. He raised a hand to greet us and steadied himself against the wall with the other. His pants slipped down to his ankles. He stared at his feet as if he were trying to understand what had just happened. It could have been a comedy scene from one of those high school graduation movies they play on Sunday afternoons. But it wasn't. It wasn't a tragedy, though, either. It depends on how we look at it, Almodôvar. We look at the world and decide whether to laugh or cry. The world is only good or bad when someone's looking. If there's no one to look, the world is just the world. So we left.

You left Ávila behind?

No. He chose to stay.

He was drunk. You know the kids took him there to do something to him.

It wasn't my responsibility.

You could have done something.

I did. I lost a vacuum that cost me a lot of money and a job to save a man who never wanted to be saved.

It wasn't enough.

It will never be enough. We can always do more. We know there are people dying of hunger, of diseases that can be treated with simple medications, of cold, heat, anguish. But we do nothing. And why? Because we have our own lives to live. And that's not necessarily a bad thing.

Fuck you, Daniel. You could have at least called the police.

What about Vasco, Almodôvar? You still don't get it. If those kids found out I had told the police about that apartment, things would have gotten ugly for him. Not to mention the fact that your son is in those videos beating up on homeless guys.

I left the apartment with Vasco. You should be grateful for that.

When I dropped off your son at home, I told him he couldn't go back to that apartment, that he couldn't hang out with those guys again. He nodded without conviction; it was still too early to tell if he would listen to me. As he climbed out of the car, I grabbed his arm.

"And sell that console fast. You owe me some money."

He laughed; I laughed.

* * *

That night, as I lay down under my old desk, I reconsidered my level of satisfaction with life.

I thought: It's obviously not 8.9.

Then I thought: 7.5? No.

4.5? Maybe—but maybe not yet.

Xavier was right: happiness is an equation of multiple factors that have to be carefully weighed. So I thought about:

being apart from my kids;
missing Marta;
you in prison, refusing to speak;
my empty days;
sending out dozens of résumés;
all my failed job interviews;
living in my old office;
sleeping under my old desk;
spending four hours a day delivering drugs;
the money I didn't have;
the life I didn't have;
the possibility of a call from that recruitment agency;
the decision to go to Viana that I put off for so long;
my unconditional hope for the future;
me, you, and Xavier and the memories that bind us forever;
my certainty that Xavier would give up one day;
the nights I hadn't slept;
all the changing parts of my body;
my aches and pains;
the strength I need just to laugh;
my eventual death;
the death of my parents long before their time;
the whole world slowly crumbling;
growing old with Marta;

my children's children;
my blood constantly traveling through my veins;
every one of my thirty-eight years;
Vasco in those videos;
Flor's contempt for her own abilities;
Mateus and his virtual aviary;
the sun;
Marta's body, naked, on mine;
my need to do what's right;
all my mistakes.

There was more, of course; the list is never complete. But it was a start. I assigned values and weights to all of them. I added it all up. It came to 5.7. My new number was **5.7**. I wasn't pleased: it was too low; it didn't seem to represent me. I redid the math, tried to configure the values for a higher result. But there wasn't much room for change.

I called Xavier.

"Still no news," he answered bitterly.

"News?"

"About the woman in Switzerland. No one answered. Tomorrow it will have been ten days since her brother's accident, Daniel. Time is running out. Maybe he already died. I can't stop thinking about her; every morning I wake up to find that no one has offered to help her."

"Xavier, it's not our responsibility."

"Of course it is, Daniel. Without our site, she wouldn't even have the hope. This woman's hope is our responsibility."

"Whatever, Xavier. I need to ask you something."

"What?"

"That happiness table. Can you can send it to me?"

"Do you have a new number?"

"That's none of your business."

"Are you inching closer to 10?"

"Can you just send me the table?"

Three minutes later, an e-mail arrived with the table. I ran my finger down the numbers on the screen to find mine. Almodôvar, there were five countries where the average happiness index was 5.7: Djibouti, Egypt, Mongolia, Nigeria, Portugal, and Romania. Isn't that ironic? Portugal. My level of satisfaction with life was the same as the average in my own country. I thought of the people I know, my friends, Marta, my kids; I tried to conjure the faces of the people I see every day, the words we exchange. These people are only 57 percent satisfied with their lives. That was bad. Did they even know it? Did they even know they could be happier? Did they know how real it was? Were they trying to be happier? Did they have a plan? They must have had a plan. I'm sure we could climb the table without too much effort, maybe to 6.0. And if we really tried, I just know we could climb to 7.0 in a few years. I'm sure of it. 7.0 is already pretty respectable. But 5.7? 5.7 doesn't reflect a very high level of satisfaction with life. 5.7 reflects our level of dissatisfaction with life.

That weekend Marta called. Mateus and Flor would start summer vacation the following week, and she wanted them to come stay with me for a week or two. She was busy at the café, and my in-laws couldn't watch them.

"They're grown," I said. "They can be alone. Flor is responsible."

"Maybe. But only for a few days."

"I have a job too."

"But you only work four hours a day. They can be alone for four hours a day. And they need to be with you, Daniel. They miss you a lot."

Almodôvar, I said yes. Because even though Marta didn't know it yet, it was likely I'd already be in Viana by then. The recruiter still hadn't called, and I was ready to go.

* * *

But the recruiter called on Monday.

"You made it to the next round," she said.

"What does that involve?"

"An interview here at our offices with someone from the company's human resources."

"When?"

"We don't know yet. I'll call you when we have a date."

When we hung up, I thought: She thinks I have all the time in the world, that I can just hang around and wait.

I got an e-mail from Xavier. Actually, the e-mail wasn't for me, but Doroteia Marques, the French woman in Switzerland who needed help visiting her brother in the hospital. Xavier had cc'd me. The e-mail was short and formal. In it, Xavier identified himself as a site administrator, as if it were standard procedure for an administrator to write whenever someone asks for help. He began by congratulating her for her courage in asking for help; then, in the same sentence he asked about her brother, sending him best wishes for a speedy recovery. He ended by warning her of the possibility that no one would respond to her request.

I called Xavier.

"What is this?"

"She has to know this might not go anywhere."

"She knows, Xavier. It's life. Not everyone is afraid of living, like you. Besides, we're not supposed to interfere unless it's serious."

"This is serious. If it wasn't for our website, she'd just be home crying. But now she has hope. And when she finally realizes that no one will help her, it's going to be horrible."

"That's not our fault."

"It's all our fault . . . We could go help her."

"We?"

"We."

"You're insane. She lives in Switzerland. Do you want to go to Switzerland? You won't even cross the street."

"But if I did, would you come with me?"

"I refuse to have this conversation. It's not going to happen."

"If you came with me, I think I would go."

"Even if I wanted to, Xavier, I don't have the money to go to Switzerland. I don't even think my car would make the trip."

"What if I put up the money? And a car?"

"Fuck off, Xavier. Don't start with your ideas."

We hung up.

An hour later, Doroteia Marques responded to Xavier's e-mail. She said that her brother's condition was serious but stable, that he had always been tough, and she had no reason to give up hope that someone would take her to Marseille. Her words were simple, secure; I could imagine she had written them with a smile on her face.

The recruiter called again on Thursday.

"Can you be here tomorrow morning for the interview?" she asked.

"Before I answer that, I need you to tell me one thing," I said. "Is my application being considered seriously?"

"As seriously as what?"

"Is there an actual chance I could get this job? Or is the company just fishing?"

Almodôvar, I knew what I was asking; I had read everything there was to read about recruitment processes.

"Of course you're being considered seriously."

"Show me."

"I don't understand."

"Give me some assurance that I'm not just a puppet filling an empty space between the real actors on the stage."

She was silent for a few seconds; I thought she might have hung up.

Then she finally spoke. "You have considerable experience designing tour packages, far more than the other candidates. And it's a key requirement for the job. Does that work?"

"It does."

We scheduled the interview for ten o'clock the next day, she gave me the address, and we hung up.

I got an e-mail from Xavier on Friday before the interview. It said: *I got a car and a driver. The cost of the trip is on me. We can leave in three days.*

I didn't answer. My kids were coming on Sunday night. I still didn't know what to do with them. Above all, I didn't know how I'd explain to them that my new home was my old office. It wasn't an easy situation. Going off to Switzerland wasn't an option.

I arrived at the recruitment agency about thirty minutes before the appointed time. There were four other people waiting in a windowless room with chairs pushed against the walls and a short little coffee table in the center full of magazines. The room was cold, as if they didn't want us to get too comfortable. The four people waiting included three women and one man; they were dressed as if they were prepared to sign a million-euro business deal, all of them absorbed in their smartphones. When I entered, they greeted me without looking up. When they called one of the women, the man wished her good luck, but she didn't answer. Shortly after that, I fell asleep. It was a good sleep, long—at least it seemed long. I don't remember dreaming. It was almost as if I had fainted: all my senses suddenly stilled.

When I woke up, the room was empty. A girl was calling my name. I rose and followed her to a small room with a conference table that swallowed up most of the space. Three people were sitting on one side of the table: one woman and two men. The woman stood to greet me; she was diligent yet relaxed, with an incredible smile—beautiful, open, and alive. She was the same woman with whom I had spoken on the phone, and it didn't seem possible that her smile could coexist with the formal tone she had used during our conversations. I sat in the empty chair facing them.

The interview lasted twenty minutes. One of the men—the youngest, very dark skinned, with gelled hair—led the conversation, while the other spoke only twice, to ask me questions that had nothing to do with the job but about my children, my hobbies, my childhood, my opinion on the state of the country. The woman said nothing throughout the interview. The man with the gelled hair asked about my professional experience, my various responsibilities at the travel agency, my dismissal, my ambitions; he asked me to evaluate my career and then asked me to state my best and worst qualities; he asked me to explain my three most important projects; and finally he asked about my expectations regarding the recruitment process. Shit, Almodôvar, I had already heard the same questions during other interviews. The answers I gave were the same ones I had prepared more than a year before when I had started my job search. I recited them word for word, almost like poetry. They were the best answers I had. I didn't know of any better way to sell my work, my skills. The interviewers were very friendly—the standard treatment. In the end, they recited some requirements that the ideal candidate would have to meet: experience creating and developing tours, leadership skills, project management, willingness to travel. But they never indicated what kind of business it was or the salary, and they didn't specify the job title. The three of them suddenly rose at the same time—their coordination was surreal—and said they'd call with their final decision that week. They seemed enthusiastic.

I wanted so badly to tell them it wouldn't be possible, that I'd be gone by the following week, that my life would be elsewhere. But I couldn't—I had to know if these people believed in me. I needed to know that I hadn't been mistaken, that my decision to stay in Lisbon alone for over a year was not as ridiculous as it was beginning to seem.

* * *

Later that afternoon, before my final shift at the pharmacy, I dropped by the office to change out of my interview clothes and into something more comfortable. During that month I had gradually stopped caring about the hours I kept at the office. It hadn't been a conscious choice: as the office became my home, I simply started coming and going as I pleased.

When I got off the elevator, I noticed that the office door was open a crack. And immediately after that I heard the echo of voices overlapping in that high-ceilinged space, lively conversation, collective laughter. Almodôvar, there were people in my home. I thought about everything I had there. The suitcase and the box with most of my things were stored in a closet, well hidden among other boxes. But other things were out in plain view. I tried to remember if I had tidied them up that morning as I usually did—though not always, because every now and then I'd leave certain things out: the pads on the floor under the desk, clothing on a chair, my toothbrush in a glass in the bathroom. I wondered if any of them would go overlooked by the people who were in there now. I thought about what might happen if one of those people found a sock or an open can of tuna or my nail clippers.

Who were they, Daniel?

I don't know. The former owners, maybe, or the new ones. Maybe they were homeless like me and needed a place to sleep. I don't know. I didn't get closer to hear what they were saying. I didn't wait for them to leave so I could see their faces. I stood in front of the door for about five seconds, then got back into the elevator and left.

You left your things behind?

No. I went to the pharmacy and did my job. It was my last day, though it seemed like any other day. Old Dr. Sacadura said good-bye to me as if he was going to see me the next day. Later, around midnight, I hung around in the street near the office building for a long time, staring up at the fifth-floor windows, watching for someone to appear, a sign of movement, a light. There was nothing. Around one thirty, I entered the building and took the stairs up to the space. I pressed my ear to the door: total silence. I inserted my key into the lock and opened the door. Then I extended an arm into the darkness and felt for the light switch. When the hallway lit up, I stood there for a few seconds, prepared to flee if someone suddenly appeared from one of the offices. But no one did, so I went in.

I didn't stay for more than ten minutes. I found my suitcase and my box. I gathered my clothes and a pair of shoes, a toiletry bag, my notebook with the Plan, my duvet and pillow; I stuffed the clothes in the suitcase and everything else in a sports bag I'd found a few weeks before in one of the closets. I put everything in the elevator, using the box to keep the elevator from closing, then went back inside to make sure I hadn't forgotten anything. After I had scoured the place, I locked the door and took the elevator down. Out on the street, I piled the suitcase and sports bag on top of the box and walked to the next block, where I had left my car. On the way there, I passed a garbage can. I put everything on the ground, opened the garbage can, and threw the office keys inside.

It was just after two in the morning, but it was June, and the air was warm. So I drove to the river and parked as close as I could to the water's edge. A warm breeze wafted through the broken window. That night, I went back to sleeping in my car.

The next day, a Saturday, I woke up early to visit you in prison. It was something I did from time to time, especially in the first months after you were arrested. I'd appear without warning during visiting hours, ask them to call you, and wait. But they'd always say you didn't want to see me, so I'd leave. I did it so many times. It wasn't out of stubbornness, though I realized almost immediately you'd never see me. But I knew it was the only way you'd know I was still on your side—that I hadn't abandoned you . . . You're a son of a bitch, you know that, Almodôvar?

In any case, that particular Saturday I inexplicably believed that you'd finally see me, that we could talk. That day, more than any other day since you had been arrested, it would have been so nice to talk to you. But as always, they told me you weren't accepting visitors.

Look, Almodôvar, I was suspended between my past and future lives. I had nothing keeping me in Lisbon, but there I was, waiting for a call from a company that may or may not have wanted to hire me—and I still hadn't decided if I wanted the job. But it would only be a matter of days. I had waited for so long; I could wait a little longer. My only real problem was my kids, who were arriving the next day.

After I left the prison, I went to Xavier's.

He opened the door, studied me for a few seconds, then smiled. He was wearing denim cutoffs and no shirt, revealing his overlapping tattoos.

"So you're in?"

Almodôvar, he thought I was there to go with him to Switzerland.

"I need a favor," I said.

"What?"

"Can I stay here with my kids for a few days?"

"What happened to your house?"

"The bank took it."

"Seriously?"

"Seriously. It's just for a few days until we move to Viana do Castelo."

"You're moving away?"

"Things aren't working here, Xavier. Marta and the kids are there; there's no reason for me to stay in Lisbon. Can we sleep at your place for a few nights?"

He said nothing and motioned for me to follow him down the hall to a stark room with a white sofa covered in stains and a tall bookcase with empty shelves.

“Will this do?” Xavier asked.

“Of course.”

“Wait here,” he said, and left the room.

I sat down on the sofa. It felt unusually comfortable. And it wasn’t the sofa itself. It was being there, with Xavier. I thought: Why didn’t I do this before?

Xavier appeared, dragging a huge mattress; he pushed it sideways through the door, then let it fall on the floor in front of the sofa.

“Mateus and Flor can sleep here,” he said. “Where are they?”

“They’re coming tomorrow.”

Xavier sat down beside me on the sofa. We didn’t speak for a while. I leaned my head back and closed my eyes. The silence, Almodôvar. The silence between Xavier and me was so powerful, like a balm, a memory that would persist forever, beyond death, a confirmation that our friendship had been real, and that in spite of everything, we were still the same people.

Then Xavier said, “We have to go to Switzerland. We have to help that woman.”

“Why, Xavier?” I whispered, my eyes still closed.

“She’s not to blame for our incompetence, Daniel. Because of our website, she’s harboring the false hope that she could see her brother again before he dies, but what she doesn’t know is that our site doesn’t work. I can’t figure out why. We should have taken it down a long time ago, but we didn’t, and now this happened. We have to go to her, Daniel. I’d go alone, but I can’t. You have to come with me.”

He was right, Almodôvar. It was the right thing to do. So I said, “Fine. Let’s go.”

As soon as I heard myself say those words, everything seemed possible; life suddenly made sense. I could sense a wave of happiness overtaking me at an incredible speed; it was an almost supernatural feeling. And there was a calming conviction that the trip would solve everything, that after the trip, nothing would ever be the same.

We planned it all right there, sitting on the sofa, my eyes closed, Xavier rolling a cigarette. We addressed any issues that arose as if we could solve anything just by talking it out.

For example, I said, "We'll need money for gas, tolls, overnight stays, and food."

And Xavier replied, "I have my inheritance from my grandfather. It's been sitting in the bank for ten years. I haven't touched it; I had no reason to. It's not much, but I think it will be enough."

Then I asked, "What about the car? We need a car."

And Xavier said, "I took care of that. Remember that guy who wrote in offering a nine-seater van? I wrote to him. He's driving us."

See, Almodôvar? The world's not such a hard place, after all.

Xavier suggested that we leave the next day. But I couldn't; my kids were coming.

"Fine then. Monday," said Xavier.

I didn't respond right away. Mateus and Flor were coming to Lisbon, and I couldn't just leave. But then I thought: Fine, let them come with us. Plus, they should see this act of kindness. The woman needs our help, her brother is dying, and we're going to travel fifteen hundred miles to help her. They have to come.

And then, as if I were fitting the final piece into a puzzle, I thought: Vasco. The van has nine seats. He has to see this.

CROATIA, ESTONIA, SOUTH KOREA, UZBEKISTAN: 6.0

We couldn't leave on Monday. Vasco needed an authorization signed by Clara to cross the border with me, and she couldn't prepare it until just after lunch that day. It wasn't hard to convince her. I think she was actually relieved that he'd be off her hands for a few days; she didn't know what to do with him now that his summer break was starting, and she was afraid he'd get into trouble again. Xavier wanted to go without Vasco. He'd exchanged a few e-mails with Doroteia Marques and learned that her brother hadn't died yet, but that his condition was highly unstable; it was imperative that we leave as soon as possible, and Vasco wasn't an indispensable part of the mission. I let Xavier explain himself, and when he finished, I said that I wouldn't go without your son, period.

We left on Tuesday just before six in the morning: me, Xavier, Mateus, Flor, Vasco, and Alípio, the driver of the nine-seater van. And even though I was still so angry at you, Almodôvar, I couldn't help but think you should be there with us. You had conceived of the site, it had been your idea to help people, and your presence would have lent more meaning to the trip. Besides, maybe you could have foreseen what would happen next. Because I couldn't.

Almodôvar, I planned that trip as if I were back at my old job at the agency. I calculated the distances, the van's mileage, and the price of gas in each country we'd cross; I'd traced the route in order to avoid toll roads, booked rooms in hotels for the three nights we'd spend on the road, and made a list with some points of interest we could visit if we had time. Look, I was prepared. I can't explain it, but suddenly my mind was empty. Maybe reality was just as empty, maybe our mission to help Doroteia Marques visit her brother in the hospital was the only thing I had left to do in life. It would be a rite of passage, and at the end of it I'd have learned everything I needed to know to solve all of life's problems.

I can't say if the others in the van felt the same. Perhaps Xavier did, though he was so scared for the first few hours, I can't tell you what was going through his head. The night before I had tried to explain to the kids what we were doing. Flor wondered why we had to go to Switzerland, why no one else could do it. I told her I didn't know, but there was no one else, so we had to do it ourselves. She said nothing, unsatisfied with my answer. Mateus didn't ask many questions about Doroteia Marques or her brother; he was more curious about Switzerland and France and the distance of each leg of the trip. There was a pragmatism in his questions that frightened me, especially since I was sure he had inherited it from me.

Vasco had said nothing. After dinner he found me alone in the kitchen and paid back the money he owed me. I wanted to ask how he had sold the console and whether he had gone back to that German lady's apartment, if he was still hanging around with Aníbal and the others. But at the same time, I wanted him to feel that he could trust me. I told him he should be proud of what we were about to do.

He just smiled and asked, "Have you told my dad about the woman in Switzerland?"

Even if we had tried, I told him, you wouldn't have seen us.

"It would make him happy to know we're doing this," said Vasco.

Maybe in my mind Vasco occupied your place in that van. I don't know.

In any case, I believed that once the kids met Doroteia Marques, when she entered the van and shared her story, when they saw her arrive at the hospital, maybe they'd realize the importance of that trip.

And then there was Alípio. He was a short, fat man in his sixties who was always gnawing on an unlit cigar, and he had an incredible willingness to talk about everything. Just after we hit the road, he started talking about other road trips he had made with his wife in the years immediately following their wedding almost thirty years before—to Italy, Czechoslovakia, Germany, Sweden, Belgium, Ireland, back when Europe was a different place. I sat next to him, and even though he was speaking to everyone, I may have been the only one who was paying attention.

He said he had been an accountant in a shoe factory on the outskirts of Matosinhos for nearly forty years. After the company was taken over by a German group, they transferred production to Poland, and the factory closed. Over a hundred people were laid off, including Alípio. But it wasn't the end of the world, he said: he had only been a few years from retirement, and the early break did him some good. Plus, he was never entirely without a job. His wife worked in the cafeteria at a Porto high school and suggested he start a service to take kids to school in his van. It was a 1984 Toyota with nearly 150,000 miles on it, but it looked like it had just left the lot. Alípio bought it almost new from a friend in financial straits in the early 1990s and then only used it for occasional weekend and holiday excursions. Plus, he bragged, he got it inspected yearly, kept it covered during the long periods it was parked on the street, and washed it regularly—the works.

The student transportation business worked for three years; his van was full most months of the year. And he liked it, working an hour and a half each morning and again in the afternoon; listening to the kids' conversations, their laughter, did him good. Then things got bad for everyone, and the parents began to cut back on Alípio's services. Within a year, he only had two or three students left, barely enough business to cover gas and maintenance. In short, Alípio's story is like so many others that it's not even worth telling. He and his wife lived on very little—her small paychecks, his meager retirement pension—making every euro count.

When I asked him how he had found our site, he said he didn't remember, but that it certainly was one of the wonders of the Internet. Then I asked him why he was there, driving three thousand miles to help someone he had never met.

"I like to stay busy," he replied.

I thanked him for his availability and said we had been counting on people like him when we decided to create the site, but back then we hadn't known how rare those people were—my way of saying I thought he was extraordinary.

He just said, "I'm the one who should be thanking you."

As soon as we got in the van, Xavier took two pills—I don't know what—and almost instantly fell asleep for seven or eight hours, until long after we had passed Valladolid. It's possible he was trying to sleep for the entire trip. I'm sure it had crossed his mind to give up and stay in Lisbon, though he never said it aloud. The bastard was panicked; I get it. But I had other things to think about; Xavier's shit would have to wait. He could take the whole bottle of pills for all I cared. And besides, this had all been his idea. A man has to live up to his own ideas.

Flor and Mateus were sitting in the back. From time to time I'd turn to look at them, wondering what they were thinking. I wanted to know if they had any doubts about what we were doing, what kinds of questions were on their minds. Flor had her headphones on, her feet up on the seat, and an open book resting on her knees. I looked at her, and she, without taking her eyes off the page, stuck her tongue out at me.

Mateus was resting his elbow against the window, his chin in the crook of his arm, his eyes on the most distant point of the landscape as if there weren't a single thought in his head. He stayed like that for a long time. I knew what he was doing. The day before, he had told me a true Buddhist should free himself of desire, on the premise that desire causes pain. I told him that, on the other hand, desire is what makes us human.

"I don't want to be a human being," he replied. "I want to be happy."

So my son was conflicted: it was a battle between him and desire, especially the desire to play his aviary management game. Up until that point, he had lost several battles; along his journey, he'd lose many more. We were close to the border with Spain when he asked me for his laptop. I passed it to him, and he opened it up on his lap. An arc of heartbreak appeared over his eyes, something close to fury. He was silent for a minute before erupting.

"This computer doesn't have Internet?"

Vasco was sitting in the middle seat, next to Xavier, reading a music magazine; he laughed out loud but didn't look up from the magazine.

I told Mateus that there was no wireless signal in the car.

"You never told me that!" he shouted, as if I had tricked him on purpose.

"I didn't think it mattered."

"Does anyone here have a phone with a Wi-Fi signal?" he asked.

No one did.

Mateus began to cry. It was contained, quiet, yet his despair saturated the space. We stayed silent, waiting. For a second, Alípio diverted his eyes from the road to look at me.

Then Vasco said, "If you want to play a game on my console you can."

He pulled a console from his backpack and passed it over the seat to Mateus. Mateus stopped crying, an almost mechanical reflex.

Vasco turned back to the front and I looked at him, into his eyes, trying to understand.

"I thought you sold the console," I said.

"No," he replied.

"Why not?"

"It wasn't necessary."

"Where did you get the money?"

"It doesn't matter."

"You're a shit, Vasco."

"Dad!" Flor shouted.

I faced forward again and stared at the road. Your bastard of a son lied to me, Almodôvar.

At least Mateus calmed down. I couldn't see the game they played for the next three hours, passing the console between them over the seats, but from the few words they exchanged, I knew that it was about Chinese and American soldiers in World War III, and that blood splattered whenever anyone took a bullet or was stabbed, and I knew that in certain situations, it was acceptable to shoot at civilians who found themselves in the line of fire. They immersed themselves in that alternate reality for hundreds of miles, Mateus's desires temporarily satisfied.

In Spain, we stopped at a travel center. It was eleven in the morning and the air was already too hot, as if the ground under our feet might burst into flames. Xavier was still asleep. Mateus didn't want to get out of the car; he had just encountered a squad of Afghan mercenaries. Alípio filled up the tank. I got out of the van and told Vasco to get out too. We walked up to the entrance of the cafeteria.

"Where did you get the money?"

"I already said. It doesn't concern you."

"Of course it does. I went to that apartment with you. I know what goes on there. Did you start selling drugs?"

"Daniel—"

"Did you?"

"You don't understand . . . the guys weren't going to leave me alone unless I agreed . . ."

"I do understand, Vasco. It's easier to cheat than to play with the cards in your hand. Fuck."

"It was only this once to shut them up. I won't do it again."

"That's a lie."

"It's not a lie, believe me."

"Sorry, but I can't."

Almodôvar, when I said those words I felt so sad. As if I was giving up on your son. But it was true: I couldn't see a way out for him.

I entered the cafeteria. The air-conditioning hit me with a welcome pain. Flor appeared at my side. We bought bottled water and ham-and-cheese sandwiches for everyone, plus a coffee for me. We sat at a table by the window, the daylight streaming through the glass almost palpable. I looked at Flor, her hesitant movements, her face so sincere. I asked if she was okay.

She took off her left headphone and said, "Of course."

"We're doing a good thing," I said.

"I know."

"This woman needs help, and we're going to help her. We're doing a good thing."

"I know."

"That's why we made the site," I went on. "But no one else wanted to help."

"I know," Flor repeated, turning her head to look out the window, squinting in the light. She stayed that way for almost a minute. Then she said, "What happens the next time someone asks for help on the site?"

"What do you mean?"

"Are you going to help them too?"

"I don't know. We can't help everyone."

"But if you could, would you help everyone?"

I looked at her, Almodôvar, and I knew it was one of those times a parent has to decide whether to tell it like it is, or tell it like it should be.

"I don't think so," I answered with a laugh. "I'd need a break now and then. Helping people can be exhausting."

She laughed too. Maybe she knew what I meant, but I'm not sure.

We went back to the van. Alípio was behind the wheel again. Vasco had jumped into Flor's place in the back next to Mateus. So Flor sat next to Xavier. I asked Alípio if he wanted me to drive.

"No way," he said. "Only I drive this van."

And he started the engine. I laughed. Almodôvar, everyone—even the most thoughtful and intelligent people—has at least one nonsensical idea in their head among the billions of other ideas. Apparently, for Alípio, it had to do with his van.

"We're driving almost three thousand miles in five days," I said. "You're going to have to let me drive at some point."

"I like to drive."

"That has nothing to do with it, Alípio."

"Don't worry. I can handle it."

"It's ten hours of driving per day. No one can handle that. It's dangerous. And we have kids on board."

"You knew that was my condition," he said. He paused to smile and then added, "I explained everything to your friend over the phone."

"I know. He told me. But I didn't know it was nonnegotiable. A trip this long can't have a rule like that."

"This one does."

"What happens if you get tired?"

"I won't."

"Everyone gets tired."

"If I get tired we'll pull over."

I didn't want to fight with him, Almodôvar. Without his help we never could have made the trip. So I set it aside for the time being.

We passed around the bag with the sandwiches, which eventually came to rest in Xavier's lap. Alípio announced that it was the best sandwich he had tasted in twenty years. He was itching to praise the virtues of Spanish ham, but no one gave him a prompt to proceed. We ate in silence, and when we finished, we were quiet. We made it nearly two hundred miles in a good, comfortable silence. We had few tolls to stop for, and Alípio drove fast, the speedometer always over sixty miles per hour. I realized Xavier was awake when I heard him rustling in the bag for his sandwich. I turned, and he looked up at me like he was drowning and no one could possibly save him. Still, his fear seemed like it was under control. When he was done eating, he took two more pills. Ten miles later, he was asleep again.

Then suddenly, Mateus said, "What happened?"

"It ran out of battery," said Vasco. "Hang on."

He pulled his bag into his lap and fished around inside.

"Shit," he whispered.

"What?" asked Mateus.

"Hang on."

"What? What happened?"

"Hang on."

He fished around in the bag some more, an anxious rustling.

I turned around.

"What's wrong?" I asked.

"Shit."

"Vasco, stop it. Tell us."

"What happened?" asked Mateus.

"I forgot the backup. And the charger."

"What?" Mateus cried.

"Do you remember putting them in your bag?" I asked.

"I don't know. I think so. I'm not sure. It was all in a smaller bag. It isn't here."

"It's not the end of the world," I said.

Mateus whimpered. Flor turned to face the backseat and took her brother's hand. "Have you checked everywhere?" she asked Vasco.

"Yes, I checked everywhere," he said, making a face at her and grunting like a pig.

"I can lend you a book," said Flor. "I brought three."

"Don't be an idiot," said Vasco. And he pulled the same face again.

"Vasco," I said. "Enough."

The sound of tires on pavement suddenly filled the cabin, and we rode in their roar for over a hundred miles. From time to time, I looked back over my shoulder. Mateus remained serious, Flor still holding his hand. Vasco was lying back in the seat, his hands clenched against his brow, as if he were trying to bend time. Suddenly it occurred to me that we might not make it to the hospital in Marseille in time, that maybe Doroteia Marques's brother would die before they got to see each other one last time.

It was after seven when we crossed into France. Daylight was disappearing behind us. I looked over at Alípio, who had become a silhouette, his face shaped by shadows, his hands vigorously gripping the wheel as if it were a musical instrument. I asked if he was tired.

"Just of the silence," he said. "I hope you guys have more energy tomorrow."

We had been traveling for over thirteen hours. And yet, all we had experienced was the inside of that van and the bathrooms at four gas stations. We hadn't spoken to anyone, and we hadn't seen more than some roads and fields, hills and villages. It could have been anywhere in the world.

I felt someone touch my shoulder. It was Xavier, awake again, looking exhausted, as if he hadn't slept in weeks.

"We have to stop," he said. "I've had enough, Daniel."

I told him I had booked three rooms in a hotel near Bayonne, twenty or thirty miles ahead.

He pursed his lips and exhaled hard through his nose.

"This isn't easy for me," he said with a sigh.

"Relax, Xavier."

"That doesn't help."

"Then open the door and jump out."

"Dad!" shouted Flor. "Don't talk like that."

I looked at her: her head was bowed, she was biting her lower lip, but she didn't seem angry—just sad, or disappointed. Then I looked at the others: Vasco had fallen asleep, and Mateus was on his knees facing backward, looking at the road through the rear window.

Flor pointed to Xavier's arm, the dozens of overlapping tattoos that climbed up from his knuckles and disappeared beneath his T-shirt sleeve, covering every last inch of his skin. Flor traced the red circle near his elbow.

"What's this one?"

Xavier rolled his arm inward and admired it, as if he hadn't seen it for a long time or didn't even remember what it was. Then he answered, "It's a planet."

"What planet?" asked Flor.

"I don't know the name."

"What does it mean?"

"It's me," he said. "It's me thousands of years from now."

Can you believe it, Almodôvar? I know the guy's an artist, but even so. Think about it: if we all thought about the same kind of shit Xavier spends his time on, the world would have ended ages ago.

For the next twenty minutes, Flor and Xavier discussed the tattoos on his arm, Xavier assigning them indecipherable meanings. For example: a small black spider in a bottle on the inside of his wrist represented the way humanity thinks of itself; a bare tree on fire was the first idea of the first man to walk the earth; an eye with the number 3 in the middle was desire in its most primitive form; a naked woman wrapped in herself was God, if God existed; an alphabet that wrapped twice around his forearm represented the weakness of human beings.

In the meantime, Vasco woke up. He and Mateus were leaning over the seat, listening to Xavier. Mateus pointed to the eye with the number 3.

"I'm trying not to feel desire," Mateus said.

Xavier looked at Mateus for a few seconds. Then he raised his hand and they high-fived with an absolute understanding between the two of them that I envied with all my heart.

Xavier continued with his explanations. As he spoke, Flor hummed harmonious interjections with an almost exaggerated admiration.

"And this?" she asked. "What's this?"

I turned my head. Her finger was pointing to a small circle of uninked skin in the middle of all the tattoos, a kind of island. I didn't know there was a blank space left on Xavier's arm.

"This is the future," he said.

"There's nothing in the future," said Flor.

"Exactly," Xavier replied. "There's nothing."

"Xavier!" I said. "Stop feeding the kids your nonsense."

Xavier crossed his arms across his chest and turned to look out the window.

"Let him talk, Dad," said Mateus.

It was the first time he had spoken to me after nearly six hours of silence.

"We're here," chimed Alípio.

We pulled into a parking lot with small beds of shrubs and trees, and four or five cars dotting the spaces. The hotel was a three-story building with peeling paint. Alípio parked near the entrance, and we hopped out, and the ground seemed to rise as if we were on a raft on the high seas. I opened the back, and we all retrieved our luggage.

At the front desk, they gave us the keys to our rooms: one for Mateus, Flor, and me; one for Xavier and Vasco; and another for Alípio. We took the elevator to the third floor.

Vasco said, “I’m getting a tattoo when we get back.”

“Me too,” said Flor.

“Me too,” said Mateus.

“Me too,” joked Alípio.

I thought: This trip was a mistake.

Alípio and I got into the van and drove the three miles to Bayonne, where we found a pizzeria, bought three pizzas, and brought them back to the hotel. In our room, Vasco and Mateus were lying belly-down on one of the beds with the laptop in front of them. Vasco avoided my eyes.

“Dad,” Mateus said, “there’s Wi-Fi here.”

Yet he still seemed distressed.

Flor was sitting cross-legged on the other bed, reclining against the pillows, the phone to her ear. She hardly spoke—just laughed, as if someone on the other end were telling jokes. It was the first time I had heard her laugh since we left Lisbon. I was jealous of the person she was talking to. When she saw me, she slowly stopped laughing and said, “It’s Mom. She wants to talk to you.”

I picked up the phone. My jealousy dissolved. Marta’s voice sounded high and sharp.

“Are you all right?” she asked.

“I think so. We’re just tired. What about you?”

“I’ve been thinking about you guys all day, so far away.”

“Sorry.”

“Don’t be—it’s not you. I’ve been thinking about the trip, what you told me about the lady in Switzerland.”

"What about her?"

"I'm just sorry I'm not there with you. It's amazing what you're doing to help this woman. I'm so proud of you."

Almodôvar, it made me feel whole again to hear Marta say those words; it lent meaning to everything. Suddenly I just wanted to help Doroteia Marques as quickly as I could and get to my new home in Viana do Castelo with Marta and the kids.

We opened the pizza boxes on my bed and ate sitting on the floor. Xavier didn't show up. Alípio told a story about the first time he had been on a plane, a trip to Luanda that seemed endless, during which he sat next to a girl who was convinced that if she looked hard enough at the sky, she might see an angel fly past. Mateus rolled around on the floor laughing; he was the kid I knew again.

Around ten o'clock, Alípio and Vasco went to their rooms. We put on our pajamas and turned off the lights. For a few minutes, Flor and I made sinister noises with our mouths to scare Mateus. He begged us to stop, insisting through his own laughter that it wasn't funny, and then made a sound like a rattlesnake. We all fell silent at the same time, a silence that darkened the entire world. They fell asleep; I stayed up, quiet, lulled by their deep breathing.

On Wednesday morning, we left the hotel before seven.

"I can drive," I told Alípio.

He laughed and waved at me dismissively as he settled into the driver's seat.

I didn't press it. I was feeling good. I had slept more than four hours, and that on its own was enough. The kids were in a good mood, even though they couldn't play on the console. Mateus seemed resigned about it.

He said, "Better that way—no temptations."

I wondered if he was able to understand the full scope of the word *temptation*. Maybe it was forced optimism on his part, but it didn't seem that way.

Marta's words from the night before had entered my bloodstream and were now pulsing through my veins. The force they exerted on my body was a kind of magic. When we got back on the road, I thought: I could do this the rest of my life, drive around the world helping people. It would be impossible, but still.

The first hour of the trip was peaceful. We ate muffins and drank the chocolate milk we had taken from the hotel breakfast bar. Alípio, Vasco, and Mateus talked about soccer, the Spanish and French championships. Vasco asked for the road map of Europe and opened it in front of him. He and Mateus consulted for a few minutes and then suggested that we go see a game in Barcelona or Madrid on the way back. Alípio nodded.

"Not a bad idea," he whispered, as if he were thinking aloud.

Xavier ate in silence. There were sheet marks on his face; his hair was unkempt.

When I asked if he had heard any news about Doroteia Marques's brother, he only said, "He's not dead yet."

"Is he going to die?" asked Mateus.

"Maybe," Xavier replied.

"We don't know that!" I exclaimed.

"If she's so desperate to see him," said Vasco, "it's because he's going to die."

"She wants to see him because he's in the hospital. If someone I cared about was in the hospital, I'd want to see them too."

A few miles later, Alípio said, "It doesn't matter if he's going to die or not."

"It doesn't?" asked Mateus.

"Not to us. She asked for help and we're helping her. The end."

"That isn't true," Flor chimed in. "We wouldn't be doing this if her brother were in the hospital with a broken leg."

"Or hemorrhoids," said Vasco.

"What are hemorrhoids?" asked Mateus.

"Blisters in your ass," said Vasco.

Mateus laughed.

"If that were the case," Alípio replied, "she wouldn't have asked for help."

"But what if she had? Would we have traveled so far to help just because we can?"

"I don't know. Maybe. If someone asks for help, it's because they need it."

Xavier took his pills out of his bag.

"Don't do that," said Flor.

"I want to."

"Stay awake."

"No."

"We can talk."

"That won't do it."

"Why don't I read you a few pages of my book?"

"What book?"

Flor bent forward, pulled a book from her backpack, and showed it to Xavier.

"They're stories," she said. "If I read you a story, will you stay awake?"

I looked back at them: Xavier was holding the book, staring blankly at the cover, fighting a tremendous inner battle; he didn't turn the book over to read the back, nor did he flip through the pages. After a few seconds he passed the book back to Flor.

"Fine," he said, resigned.

She opened the book and flipped through the pages until she found the story she wanted to read. It was the story of a boy who had an inflatable friend. My daughter's voice flooded the air of the van, every word in perfect tune. None of us moved; we were all listening. I thought: If she wanted to, she could do extraordinary things with that voice. Then, in the story, the inflatable friend was chased by an angry mob wielding sticks and stones, and I fell asleep.

I woke up to my phone ringing. Flor was no longer reading her story. In fact, when I peeked back at her, I realized she had dropped the book. Everyone was silent. Xavier looked at me as if he wanted to smile, but he didn't.

"Answer it," he said.

I answered. It was a man whose name I didn't recognize. He spoke quickly about a job interview, and it took me some time to realize that this wasn't some new thing. It was one of the men who had interviewed me the week before. He said they were still interested in me as a candidate and told me what the company could offer.

I asked what company it was, and he replied, "We'll tell you everything at the next interview."

"There are more rounds?"

"Just one. You've been selected for the final stage."

"And it's just an interview?"

"Exactly."

"When?" I asked.

"Tomorrow. Preferably in the morning. But we could do sometime in the afternoon."

Life's a bitch, Almodôvar.

"I can't tomorrow," I said. "I had to leave the country for an emergency."

"Okay, Friday works, but we can't do any later than that."

"I'll be back on Sunday."

He laughed.

"There won't be anyone here on Sunday."

"Monday, then."

"That's impossible. We have to complete the process this week. What a pity."

I didn't respond.

"It's a pity," he repeated.

Almodôvar, there were three people in the final round of that recruitment process and I was one of them. My hesitation was great; my chances were real. That last interview would decide everything.

I considered the possibility of leaving the group in Switzerland with Doroteia Marques, borrowing money from Xavier, and catching a flight back to Lisbon. But that would have been out of the question: I couldn't leave the kids with Xavier and Alípio.

"Monday's my earliest," I repeated. "If they're willing to wait, I can be there at nine."

"I'll put it on the schedule," he replied. "No guarantees."

When we hung up, I thought: We turn back now, we're in Lisbon by tomorrow night, and I get an interview for Friday morning. It was such a rare opportunity, Almodôvar. I'd been in free fall for so long, and suddenly a net had appeared; I just had to let myself fall into it.

But that woman needed your help.

I needed help too.

Maybe you should have used our site.

You're a bastard, you know that?

I could feel them all in the backseat looking at me, waiting for me to speak.

"It was a call for an interview," I said, turning to face them.

"We can't turn back," said Xavier.

"Why?" asked Mateus.

"Doroteia Marques is expecting us."

"But it's a job interview, and my dad needs a job," he said.

"Imagine how you'd feel," said Flor, "if you needed help and someone told you they'd be there, and you waited, hope swelling in your heart like a tide, your whole body tingling with an energy that doesn't belong to you. You imagine the future becoming a certainty, but then the hours turn to days and no one shows up, and time extends before you into a hopeless void."

Mateus nodded silently.

Flor leaned forward and wrapped her arms around my neck.

Alípio and I exchanged glances. There was an openness in his expression that reminded me of you. He was one of those people who could see the world from every angle simultaneously and understand them all. For Alípio, any decision I made would be valid.

I looked through the windshield: the road, the trees, the houses passing by, people seeming too small under the enormous sky. And I was suddenly furious. When Flor spoke, I had felt my body heat up, my stomach and lungs igniting, the flames rising to my throat. We have so much to do, so many places to go, we're so eager to offer comfort, but instead we waste day after day not knowing how to take care of ourselves, not doing what's necessary to find our way when we're lost, so we can only hope that someone will appear to give us a hand, or their whole arm, or their life. I didn't want to help anyone. And I didn't want any help.

Daniel, human beings help each other.

Fuck human beings.

You turned back.

No, Almodôvar. We kept going.

A hundred and twenty miles later, Alípio asked if we could stop.

"Are we out of gas?" I asked.

"No."

"What, then?"

"Cramps. My accelerator foot."

We were on a national highway with just a few cars on it and vineyards on both sides that extended to the horizon. There was a burning smell in the air, but no smoke that we could see. Alípio pulled over on the shoulder next to a bus stop. We all got out except for Xavier. Alípio limped across the street. Flor sat on the bench at the bus stop. Mateus and Vasco jumped the guardrail and walked twenty or thirty yards along the vineyard. I circled the van. Xavier had opened the window and was smoking a cigarette.

"Are you okay?" I asked.

"No," he replied. "Are you?"

"That interview was important."

"So is this. If it wasn't, I never would have left the house."

"But at least you know that you'll get to shut yourself back up in your apartment for the next twenty years when we get back."

"No one knows what's going to happen in ten or twenty years."

"I know I have an interview."

"Daniel, it's going to be fine."

"You don't believe that."

"But you do."

Two cars raced by. Then Alípio approached. It was clearly hard for him to walk.

"I'll drive," I said.

"Nobody touches the steering wheel but me."

"You're in no condition to drive."

"I'm fine."

"You can hardly walk, let alone drive. We still have three hundred miles to go."

"I can do it."

"Nonsense. You're going to kill us all because of some childish idea in your head."

"You guys knew—"

"The van is yours—no one's going to take it from you."

"Daniel," said Xavier. "Stop."

"But do you hear this guy, Xavier?"

"Stop. Go away. Take a walk."

I crossed the road, jumped the guardrail, and pissed against a grapevine.

Xavier appeared two minutes later.

"The van isn't insured," he said.

"What?"

"You heard me. He's unemployed. He canceled the policy two years ago."

"And he's telling us now?"

"No. He already mentioned it. I just didn't tell you."

"Why not?"

"Because if I'd told you, you wouldn't have come."

"Are you fucking kidding me? Of course I wouldn't have come, Xavier. We can't travel twenty-five hundred miles in a van without insurance."

"Why not?"

"Xavier. If we get pulled over, that's it. Plus, we'll be in the middle of Europe. Those guys don't mess around with shit like this. Why didn't he buy some coverage before we left?"

"Don't you get it? Alípio has been unemployed for four years, and he doesn't get retirement yet. He lives on almost nothing."

"But you paid him."

"Not that much."

"What about your inheritance?"

"I told you: it's not very much money. And after this trip—with gas, hotels, and food for six people—there won't be anything left."

"Shit, Xavier. You should have talked to me."

"I know. But you wouldn't have come. And without you, I wouldn't have been able to come either."

"This is crazy."

"We've come this far. We might as well keep going."

"Alípio's not going to make it."

"Of course he will."

"He should at least let me drive."

"He's scared."

"Scared of what?"

"If something happens to the van, he has to pay for it out of pocket."

"Something will only happen to the van if he drives with his foot in that state."

"He says he prefers to take the risk. He says he doesn't know how you drive."

"He prefers to take the risk? Fuck you, Xavier—there are three kids in there."

The van's horn sounded like a steamship, dissipating in the air over the road.

"Come on," shouted Alípio, who was seated behind the wheel.

Mateus, Flor, and Vasco were already in their seats.

I stared at the red earth between my feet. Then I jumped back over the fence, crossed the road, and got into the van.

"Alípio," I said. "The first slip and I take the wheel."

He winked, as if it were a game and we were conspiring to cheat.

You let him drive like that?

It was that, or stay there in the vineyards in the middle of nowhere, waiting for him to recover. And we wanted to get to Geneva before dark.

You had the kids in the car.

I couldn't risk losing a day of travel.

You bastard.

What was that?

You bastard . . . You really believed you'd make that interview on Monday.

What?

That's why you didn't want to be delayed. You still had hope.

Of course I did, Almodôvar.

Fuck off, Daniel. The guy pretty much said they'd be done with recruitment by Friday, but you still thought you'd have another chance on Monday, and you wanted to get back to Lisbon on Sunday. So you let Alípio drive with his cramps.

You make it seem like I had thought it out. I hadn't.

Even so. You're a bastard, Daniel.

But Alípio did hold up. He turned down the AC so his leg wouldn't get too cold, and every so often he'd grumble. But he was never out of control of the van. Believe me.

We entered Switzerland at around five in the afternoon. At the border, the guards nodded at us but didn't make us stop. Geneva was coming up soon.

I took out a piece of paper with some facts about the city. I started reading them aloud when Xavier said, "The average life satisfaction for Switzerland is 8 out of 10."

I looked at him. Almodôvar, the bastard was fucking with me.

"What?" asked Alípio.

Xavier explained the average happiness index, the questionnaire consisting of one question, the list of countries. Mateus shouted that he knew the question and had already tried to answer it but was still trying to calculate his number.

"Maybe you'll never find the right answer," said Xavier.

"People are eighty percent satisfied with their lives here?" Alípio asked.

"On average, yes," said Xavier. And then he added, "Ask Daniel. He wanted to live here."

"Let's change the subject, Xavier," I said.

"Are the Swiss Buddhist?" asked Mateus.

Vasco and Flor laughed.

"No," said Alípio. "They're even better than that."

"What?"

"They're rich." He looked to the backseat.

"I could never be eighty percent satisfied with life in such a cold country," said Flor.

"Their average is so high because they don't know anything else. They're convinced this is paradise," said Vasco.

"They do know another reality," I said. "They travel, read books, watch TV."

"It was just a theory."

Alípio made sure to stop at a gas station to fill up the van; he wanted to be prepared for the next day. We all got out. Xavier handed me his credit card and asked me to get him some Swiss francs. In the coffee shop, Mateus opened his laptop.

"Just for a minute," he said, as if to appease me.

He took advantage of the Wi-Fi to sell thirty thousand virtual chickens. He explained that in another half hour he would have lost all those birds, which would have meant a considerable hit to his business. Alípio walked from one side of the room to the other, smiling at all the Swiss people around us as he tried to regain circulation in his leg. Flor asked me for money to buy a newspaper.

"I thought you stopped reading the newspaper," I said.

"I did. But I want to know how many times certain words appear in the press here."

"Because they're eighty percent satisfied with their lives?"

"Yeah."

"You don't know French."

"I don't, but Vasco does."

Vasco was standing next to her. He looked at me and shrugged, as if he were apologizing for knowing French.

I gave them a ten-franc note. Then I looked around: the people going in and out of the cafeteria seemed like regular people. They didn't look 80 percent satisfied with life. I tried to imagine the difference between them and us that might explain the discrepancy in our answers. There were bad things in our lives that didn't exist in theirs, and good things in their lives that were missing in ours. Alípio was right: they were richer. But it couldn't just be that—life consists of more than money. The Swiss were still people: they had fears, they suffered, and being Swiss didn't prevent them from getting sick or dying; the love they felt was the same love we felt. Why would they be happier than we were?

We took out a map of Geneva that Xavier had printed before we left Lisbon, the route to Doroteia Marques's apartment traced in red. We traversed the city in silence, peering into the side streets from our windows. There was an almost impossible order to it all, as if the buildings, parks, monuments, and even the mountains had been built for a movie set that was never dismantled. I tried to calculate how many people I helped travel there: tourists, students, businessmen, immigrants. Dozens. Possibly hundreds.

Alípio said, "I think I can feel their happiness."

I still didn't feel it, Almodôvar. But I believed Alípio when he said he did.

Doroteia Marques lived on a narrow street outside the city center, on the eastern shore of the lake, near the water. We parked the van right in front of her building. We got out. The air was cold, even though it was June and the sun still hadn't disappeared from the sky. We paused in front of the door.

"Are we going to ring the bell?" asked Flor.

I looked at Xavier. For some reason, I thought he should be the one to do it. But he was leaning on the hood of the van, his eyes closed, smoking a cigarette.

I approached the intercom and rang the bell to Doroteia Marques's apartment.

A minute passed.

Then we heard a voice, made metallic by the speakers, speaking French.

"It's Daniel from Portugal," I replied.

She let out a cry and immediately buzzed open the door. The six of us entered and took the elevator up. On the second floor, Doroteia Marques was waiting for us, sitting in an electric wheelchair. When she saw us appear she retreated a couple feet. It was clear she was startled to see so many people. I extended my hand. She hesitated, then shook it. I introduced everyone, myself first, then Xavier, Alípio, and the kids. I tried to explain everyone's reason for being there.

She replied in accented Portuguese, "So many people on my account. How senseless."

And look, Almodôvar. She was right: it was senseless. She sat there for a moment, looking at us. Suddenly the fear disappeared from her face. She asked us to follow her into her apartment. It was spacious, sparsely furnished, with books scattered everywhere, and enlarged photos of insects and frogs all over the walls. We left our bags in the entrance, and she led us to the kitchen, where she made us some tea. We sat on high stools that she surely hadn't used herself in a long while. Three white cats appeared, slender, almost hairless, and jumped up onto the bar and then back to their bed next to the toaster, where they lay tangled up with each other. Alípio asked her about her brother.

"He's waiting for us," she answered, then smiled a smile that spread over her entire face before slowly moving through the rest of her body.

She was a very beautiful woman, even with her wrinkles and gray hair, her limp legs and fragile voice; somehow, they were a part of her beauty. She wore a red skirt and a white turtleneck sweater; she had painted her lips with a pink color that looked natural. And she was barefoot—she later confessed that not worrying about shoes was one of the perks of not being able to walk.

Vasco hopped down from his stool and stood in front of a nearly five-foot-tall photograph of a praying mantis next to the fridge. The insect seemed ready to jump out of the frame and attack Vasco.

"My husband was a nature photographer," Doroteia Marques explained. "He even published in *National Geographic*. He gave me that one for our second wedding anniversary."

She stated it as if it were some historical fact we should all appreciate.

Vasco slowly walked along the walls of the kitchen, admiring each photograph. Then he went out into the hall. Flor and Mateus followed him. A minute later, Mateus returned and, without looking at me, asked Doroteia Marques if she had Wi-Fi. She said she did and that the password was written on a Post-it stuck to the phone in the living room. Then she asked Mateus if he knew what a Post-it was. Mateus laughed and left the room again.

Immediately after that, Xavier asked where the bathroom was and left us as well. For a few minutes, Alípio spoke to Doroteia Marques about the following day, our departure time, the trip to Marseille, and the hospital where her brother was. Then he complained about his leg and asked for a banana, praising the miraculous properties of potassium. I felt a pang of shame: the way we had taken up camp in her house made it seem as if we were the ones who needed help.

Doroteia Marques wanted to know which one of us owned the site.

"Xavier and I do," I said, pointing in the direction in which Xavier had gone.

"What a great idea!" she exclaimed.

I didn't want to contradict her, so I just said, "It wasn't mine."

"Still, it's a great idea," she insisted.

Alípio announced he needed to find a more comfortable seat for his leg. Doroteia Marques suggested the chair in her office, and he went to rest there.

I wanted to say that we also needed to leave on time so I could be in Lisbon for a job interview on Monday. Instead, I just pointed to Doroteia Marques's legs and asked, "What happened?"

She looked at me, a flash of sadness on her face. Then she suddenly smiled and raised her hands in the universal gesture of surrender.

"It's fine," she said. "I slipped by the pool after a water aerobics class six years ago and fell on my back. My spinal cord was injured. But I wasn't totally paralyzed—I can still move two toes on my right foot, and I have some sensation in that leg."

I looked at her bare feet. It was true: two of the toes on her right foot were wriggling, as if they wanted to break free from the flesh and bone that held them in place. Doroteia Marques followed my gaze down to her feet, looked back up at me, and then back down to her feet, expectantly smiling, as if she were performing a magic trick and wanted me to guess the secret behind it.

"Is your husband still alive?"

"God, no! Fortunately he died the year before my accident."

"Fortunately?"

"Jacques loved me very much, and I never had any reason to complain. But he hated to relax. He was always out strolling, writing in cafés, drawing, taking photographs. He'd go off to the mountains for three or four days every month, and sometimes he'd just pack up and fly off to the other side of the planet. That's how he was. And I liked him that way. If he were still here, this situation would make him crazy; he'd be constantly torn between his urge to see the world and his guilt over leaving me."

"So you never go out?"

"Only if absolutely necessary," she said, her eyes widening. "I have a lady who comes every morning to do my shopping, clean, iron, that sort of thing. But I buy almost everything I need online. I've been out three times in the past five years. I was like that even before the accident. I've never been one to have many friends. I never liked to explore; when

Jacques would ask me to go with him anywhere, I'd think about going back home as soon as we left. This silence, this stillness, even this solitude have always been a part of me. I have my books, and my cats, and the Internet. That's enough. The days pass, and I don't mourn them."

Almodôvar, I don't know if you realize, but she was happy with the life she had left. Even without her husband, even without her legs, even without the world around her. Old people usually complain that their hours feel too long. But she didn't feel that way. There was no revolt or anguish in her voice when she spoke of her life, no trembling in her eyes when she thought of the past. I had imagined she was a defeated woman, but it was a gross error of judgment. I didn't even need to calculate her happiness index. She was there in front of me, and her happiness was evident. How did she do it? I felt intensely jealous. And we were there to help her. There were billions of people in the world, and we had traveled twelve hundred miles to Switzerland—where the average citizen was 80 percent happy—to help a woman who, in spite of the odds, was happier than any of us.

She needed help.

Almodôvar, every last one of us needed more help than she did. What were we doing there?

She asked for help and you went to help her.

Imagine if she was the average Swiss citizen with a happiness index of 8.0. Imagine if no one responded to her call for help and she didn't get to see her brother in Marseille before he died. Imagine the damage this might cause to her average happiness index. A few decimal points? One whole point? Two? She had already lived through so much, I don't think it would have come to two points. Maybe one and a half. Her new number would be 6.5. Shit, Almodôvar, none of us in the van were that happy.

You don't know that.

Almodôvar, you're the one who doesn't know. But we'll get to that.

I thought you believed you were doing a good thing. That's why you brought the kids.

I did believe it. But then I got there and saw it. I saw her house and heard her stories. It changed everything.

I got up. I explained to Doroteia Marques that we had booked rooms in a nearby hotel, and that we'd be back the next morning around seven to pick her up.

"Don't even dream of it!" she exclaimed. "You'll be my guests tonight. It's the least I can do."

I told her it wasn't necessary; there were so many of us and we didn't want to be any trouble. She waved her hands in front of her face, as if she were trying to keep my words away.

"You're staying and that's that. I'll hear no more of it."

I didn't insist. I was exhausted. We were all exhausted. None of us wanted to leave her house.

We did nothing for two or three hours. Flor and Vasco sat in front of the TV flicking between music channels without stopping on one for more than ten minutes, while Mateus played on his laptop, laughing at videos of Chinese people dressed in outlandish costumes competing on a muddy obstacle course. Alípio and I determined the plan for the next day. Xavier appeared in the room to ask Alípio for the van's documents. He examined the expired insurance card and finally said he'd try to change the date—something about a 0 instead of a 1. I explained that it wouldn't do any good if we actually got into an accident. He said that even so, it was worth trying.

Night fell quickly.

Alípio reclined on the sofa and fell asleep. I leafed through the newspapers Flor had bought, some pages already full of numbers in the margins and underlined words: *guerre*, *conflit*, *paix*, *mort*, *développement*, *crime*, *découverte*, *recession*, *fortuné*, *festivités*, *chômage*, *assaut*, *inflation*, *futur*, *crisis*. Xavier worked on his counterfeiting mission. He didn't show anyone the final result. He stood up, paced around aimlessly, admired a group of eight photographs of lizards on the wall behind one of the sofas, and went back to the bathroom. When we mentioned dinner, Doroteia Marques opened a drawer, pulled out a dozen menus from restaurants that delivered, and asked us to choose what we wanted—her treat.

"That's not right," said Alípio.

"I do it every night," she explained. "You're my guests."

It wasn't possible to pick something that would please everyone: Mateus wanted pizza again, Flor and Vasco wanted Chinese food, and Alípio wanted to eat traditional Swiss food. So we ended up ordering dinner from three different restaurants. As we ate, Doroteia Marques gave us a kind of history lesson about Switzerland. When she finished, Mateus asked if it was true that the Swiss were 80 percent satisfied with their lives. She said she had no idea—she'd never heard of such a thing.

"But is it possible?" insisted Mateus.

She turned to look out the window, as if she could observe the whole country from there.

"It's possible," she answered.

Which says nothing about the country, Almodôvar, but a lot about her.

When we finished eating, we cleaned up and went to bed: the kids and me in one guest room with two large beds; Xavier and Alípio on the living room sofas. I fell asleep almost immediately but woke up just before three. The house was silent—that is, except for the sound of Xavier pacing between the kitchen and the living room.

The next day, Thursday, Xavier and I lifted up Doroteia Marques and carried her into the van. She sat in the front between Alípio and me. Then we loaded her wheelchair into the back, which was only possible by folding down the last row of seats. It was still before eight in the morning, and the sky was so blue it looked painted.

We traveled about thirty miles in silence. Mateus was sitting behind me, pissed off, a huge look of dismay on his face. He had spent the past six days waiting for three million chicks to grow up so he could sell them and use the money to buy an incubation system that would double the speed of egg production. The chickens were supposed to be ready by 9:47 that morning. Mateus would then have an hour to close the deal; after that, his losses would grow exponentially by the minute. Our plan was to get to Marseille after noon. Mateus had done the math, calculating his losses from the catastrophe in question, and was filled with a fury that none of us knew how to calm.

Flor and Vasco were reading the same book, some novel about the Great Depression in the United States, their heads very close together; he held the book while she turned the pages.

Shortly after we passed Grenoble, Doroteia Marques announced that she had reflected on her satisfaction with life. And then, without any explanation, she announced her number. No one asked how she had reached it, which parts of her world she had included, the weight she gave to each one.

A few minutes passed. Then Flor, without looking up from her book, announced her number.

Then Alípio announced his.

And then Xavier.

And Vasco.

And Mateus.

Then I did.

"6.0," said Xavier. "The average happiness index of this car is **6.0**."

The number seemed impossible. It's true that Doroteia Marques had a high level of satisfaction with her life, but even so, 6.0 seemed very far from representing us.

* * *

We arrived in Marseille around one. The sun was an explosion of light on the world, and the Mediterranean was very still; it looked as if it would be possible to walk on its surface. We went straight to the hospital. Alípio pulled over near the door to the emergency room so we could get out and unload the wheelchair, and then he went to park. The front desk told us the room number; visiting hours would begin at two.

Alípio met us at the café in the lobby. We were eating meat pies and soft drinks. I read out a few facts about Marseille on a piece of paper I had brought from Lisbon: it was the second-largest city in France, the oldest, with about 860,000 inhabitants, an amphitheater facing the Mediterranean and, contrary to popular belief, "La Marseillaise" wasn't born there, but had been made popular by federal Marseille soldiers in the late eighteenth century, during the French Revolution. They listened to me in silence, but no one seemed very interested. Doroteia Marques stared at her plate with a superhuman stillness, not touching her food. Mateus opened his laptop on the table, spent a few minutes looking at the screen without typing, and finally closed it.

"There's no wireless here," he said.

"Of course there's not," said Vasco. "It could interfere with all the life-support equipment. People could die."

Mateus looked at me.

"Is that true?" he asked.

I had no idea if it was true.

"It makes sense," I said.

Doroteia Marques suddenly wheeled herself back from the table.

"It's time," she said, smiling and nodding as if we were all children and she was a teacher prepared to begin the lesson. She looked nervous, a girlish anxiety in her every gesture.

We stayed in our seats, looking at her. And when she didn't move, Alípio asked, "Do you want us to come with you?"

She smiled again, and Alípio stood up. The two of them moved away in the direction of the elevators. After they left, it was just our original group from Lisbon remaining. And yet something seemed to be missing.

We finished eating and left the hospital. Mateus wanted to explore the city. But it was impossible; we were far from the city center, and the hospital was surrounded by apartments, warehouses, and woods. He insisted: he still wanted to see Marseille. So we walked for a while. We crossed a six-lane road and walked down small neighborhood blocks that looked identical, apartment buildings with two or three floors, no movement in the windows. A little farther ahead, in a leafy park, we found a lake. Xavier and I sat down on one of the wooden benches. The kids ran over to the lake, Mateus plunging his hand into the water and leaving it there.

"Fuck," said Xavier.

I looked at him. He was sitting up very straight, his hands under his butt, staring at a distant point ahead. His expression was one of absolute surrender, as if he were facing a firing squad.

"What's wrong?" I asked.

"I don't know if I can stand this."

"Stand what?"

"This. Being here."

"You wanted to be here."

"I didn't. But we had no choice."

"So now what?"

"Now I feel like I'm upside down and the whole planet is resting on my feet."

"Jesus, Xavier. Relax."

"It would be great if saying something aloud were enough to make it happen. But it's not like that."

"Why do you always do this?"

"Do what?"

"You always find a way to put yourself at the center of everything."

"That's not true."

"Of course it is. Your fear, your sorrow, your aversion to the world, to life—they're all greater than you are. They fill the air around you and affect anyone who gets close."

"That's not my intention."

"I know. But you're so focused on yourself, on keeping your fears at bay, that you don't even realize what you're doing."

"I'm sorry."

"An apology doesn't help me, Xavier. Just learn to live and cut it out."

"It's hard."

"It's hard for everyone. You're no different from anyone else."

His lips were pressed tight, the muscles around his mouth hardened. There was a deep pain in his eyes. He raised a hand and said slowly, "Daniel, let's talk about this later. I can't right now." He moved his hand in the air, marking the pauses between words.

And I thought: He's not going to make it to the end. He's going to kill himself one day, just as we always knew he would. It could happen soon. It might even happen today.

"Don't ruin this, Xavier," I said. "We came here, and now she's upstairs with her brother; it was what we wanted. And Almodôvar will be so happy when he finds out."

"I know. I know. He begged me so much to make this happen."

"Almodôvar? When did Almodôvar beg you to do this?"

Xavier bit his lower lip, his darting eyes nearly popping out of their sockets. He didn't want to talk. But we know how his body can't withstand the force of truth; it's impossible for him to lie.

"Xavier? When exactly did you speak to Almodôvar?"

He closed his eyes for a second, then opened them and said, "Last week."

"Last week? Shit, Xavier! You visited him in prison and he actually saw you?"

"I wrote him and explained what was happening."

"And the bastard wrote you back?"

"I didn't know if he'd answer. It was the first time that I had ever written to him; I thought he should know about Doroteia Marques."

"And he responded just like that? After all that silence?"

Xavier leaned back on the bench without moving his hands from under his butt.

"He had written to me before," he said.

"Fuck—when?"

"About once a month."

"Once a month? Since when?"

"Since his third or fourth month in prison."

I did the math: it was more than ten letters. Almodôvar, the first thing that crossed my mind was to beat Xavier senseless. But that wouldn't have solved anything. I was pissed at you, not him.

"Why didn't you tell me?"

"He asked me not to tell anyone."

"Xavier, we've all been so worried about him for over a year and no one has heard from him. Clara and Vasco need to know about this."

"He told me not to say anything."

"What else did he tell you?"

"Nothing much. He told me about life in prison, all the hard things that happen to him, conversations with other inmates, some memories, plans for the future. Almost like a diary."

"Does he talk about what happened?"

"No."

"And you never asked?"

"I never wrote back until now."

"Why not?"

"I never had anything to say."

"Shit, Xavier, you have nothing to say to him? No questions?"

"About what?"

"Robbing the gas station? His silence?"

"No."

"And he just kept writing to you all these months? Why didn't he write to me?"

"I don't know. Maybe he knew I wouldn't answer. Maybe he needed to talk to someone who wouldn't talk back."

And then it dawned on me. "It wasn't your idea to take this trip, was it, Xavier? Almodôvar was the one who told you to go to Switzerland to help Doroteia Marques. He told you to convince me. We're only here because of him."

Xavier was silent. He nodded almost imperceptibly.

Almodôvar, I wanted to understand. You refused to see me; you wouldn't talk to me for over a year. Yet you write to Xavier each month, confess yourself, share your life with him and the things that happen to you. Please explain to me why you did this.

You know I can't do that. I'm not even Almodôvar. I'm in your head.

I know.

So you're mad?

Fuck off. I'm not sitting here on the outside waiting to solve all your problems. You may think I am, but I'm not. I have other priorities.

You do?

Fuck you.

But maybe Xavier was right. Maybe I just wanted someone to talk to who wouldn't talk back.

Why?

Who knows? Fear. Exhaustion. Shame.

I would have known how to keep quiet.

I don't think so, Daniel. You have too many questions. And you need answers. You expect too much from people.

Where is this coming from?

You were always like that. You have your ideas about how everyone around you should be, down to the last detail, and no one is allowed to veer an inch from your imagination. You can't handle it if someone takes up more world, more time, more life than you've allotted them. But here's the thing, motherfucker: the problem isn't other people—the problem is you.

Remember that night, Daniel? That night at Xavier's, before I was arrested? I asked you to meet me at his house because I had something important to tell you. And you showed up around eight in your three-piece suit, impeccable as ever, and even before you walked through the door you asked me to spit it out, because you were in a hurry, you had to get home for dinner with your family, and then you needed to work on a proposal that was due in two days. But I just held up a vodka bottle in one hand and a shot glass in the other, filled the glass with vodka, passed it to you, and said, "Drink." And you acted like you were the coolest guy on earth; you dropped your grown-up act and looked at me as if you were about to propose we do something crazy, and then you took the glass and downed it in one gulp. As if that weren't enough, you held out the glass and said, "Fill 'er up." I poured you more, and you downed it again. Do you remember that?

"Nothing's wrong," I said. "We're here to celebrate."

"To celebrate what?" you said.

"Nothing special. Just celebrating for the sake of celebrating."

And you needed it so much, Daniel—to feel that lightness again. So you called Marta to say you were with me and you stayed.

Xavier didn't drink; he paced for hours holding his cup. His problem had nothing to do with trying to find that lightness, but the opposite: he had lost density and didn't know how to get it back. But he talked and laughed with us. Shit, it had been so long since I had heard him laugh like that. Then you got drunk so fast and chastised him for bleaching his hair white; you said his belief that he had been old since he was a teenager was a bunch of paranoid nonsense. So he finally explained that he didn't bleach his hair—it had naturally gone white six or seven years before, as if his body was finally reflecting the dark ideas that went through his mind.

And then we smoked a joint and definitively moved on to other things. It was around this time that Xavier began to speak of his fear of the world, and heaven. The guy said heaven seemed like the right place for someone like him, not heaven like paradise, but the heaven of clouds and wind, and we lay on the floor laughing about his theories. Remember that?

You managed to get up off the floor in spite of your laughter to go to the bathroom, and when you came back, you had a look of enlightenment on your face.

"What? What's wrong?" you asked.

And you looked down at Xavier.

"Let's go out," you said slowly.

"Now?" I asked.

"Now. Xavier, come with me down to the street."

You bastard. You're like this every time you drink: you lose respect for the world and the people in it.

"Don't be an idiot, Daniel," I said.

"He can do it. We'll cross the street and come right back. Just that."

We sat there fighting about it as Xavier just looked at you as if he were seeing you for the first time.

"I can't do it," he finally whispered. "I'm sorry."

And he began to cry.

I don't know if you ever noticed, but he tried so hard to please you, to get you to understand him. Your approval was so important to him. But you never looked at his face. You just grabbed the bottle from my hand and filled up your glass again.

To get him to stop crying, I asked him to give me a tattoo. Remember? For years he begged us to let him give us tattoos.

He looked at me and then wiped his tears away with the back of his hand.

"I can do whatever I want?" he asked.

"Whatever you want, with two conditions: it can't be more than an inch across, and it can't be in a visible place."

He gave me an ellipsis— . . . —behind the ear. It didn't take more than a minute.

Then he immediately tattooed the same three dots— . . . —inside his left wrist, right over the veins. Then he turned to you and said, "Now you, Daniel."

"Fuck off, Xavier!" You laughed.

"This only makes sense if you have the same tattoo."

"Not my problem," you said. "I never said I'd let you tattoo whatever you wanted."

"You're a fucking idiot, Daniel," said Xavier.

"We all are, Xavier."

Remember the silence? As if the building was going to implode at any second. Xavier cleaned up, leaving the needles out, packing up the machine in its case.

"Fine," you said.

He paused; he already knew things were never that easy with you.

"I'll let you give me a tattoo. But only after you go outside with me."

"Jesus. Give it up, Daniel," I said.

"Stay out of it, Almodôvar," you replied.

Xavier got up from the chair and walked around the room, his hands on his head, his fingers all tangled up in his white hair, fighting the epic battle inside of him. Then he stopped and put his robe on over his pajamas.

"Let's go," he said, heading for the door.

"No, Xavier," I said. "Don't."

But you got in my face, your eyes practically bursting from their sockets. "This will be good for him, Almodôvar. We'll help him."

I pushed you. You caught my wrists and resisted like a boulder stuck deep in the earth. It could have been the beginning of a fight. It could have ended badly. Remember the last time we fought? We were eleven; my dog had just died and you said it was just as well because the stupid animal only knew how to bite people.

Anyway. You pushed my arms down.

Remember, Daniel? Did you still believe you were helping him? We left the apartment, you and me screaming, Xavier as silent as if he were being marched to the gallows. You called the elevator.

"You don't have to do this, Xavier," I said.

He looked at me, panic flooding his eyes.

"I know. It's okay," he said without conviction.

You put an arm around his shoulders.

"We'll go downstairs, smoke a cigarette, and come right back," you said, reassuring him.

The elevator arrived, and we got in. Xavier leaned against the wall and slowly slid to the floor, drawing his knees to his chest and clinging to them. When the elevator began its descent, he started to cry. I looked at you in the mirror. You cocked your head and winked at me, as if the two of us had planned the whole thing together.

We reached the ground floor. You and I got out, while Xavier peeled himself off the floor and just stood there.

"Come on, Xavier," you said, holding the door open.

"I will. I will."

And he stood there a minute, two minutes, immobilized by fear, and gulped.

Until you let go of the door and it closed in his face. A second later the elevator began to rise. You shook my hand, said good night, and went on your way.

It was nearly three in the morning.

Two hours later, they caught me robbing a gas station.

Remember that?

Remember?

Of course I remember, Almodôvar. But you're wrong: I didn't do what I did because I didn't respect Xavier. On the contrary: he's a human being, and I believe that all human beings have a force within them that transcends our imaginations. We're capable of anything. I believe that the impossible is just an idea we've created to deal with our frustrations; believing that some things are unreachable makes life easier. Xavier believes he's lost that power, but I know it's not true; that force will exist within him as long as his heart is beating. I was just trying to show him that. And what you don't know is that I went back there. A few weeks later—I can't remember if your trial had started yet—I went back to Xavier's and let him give me a tattoo. He gave me the same ellipsis— . . . —right in the middle of my back.

I'm happy to know that.

Right. Now shut up and let me tell the rest.

I got up from the bench. I took three steps to get away from Xavier. The park was so quiet, as if it were a secret garden. The trees swayed lightly; they seemed to be hanging from the sky. There was a woman sitting on a bench opposite ours with a pram next to her. There were two old men strolling around the lake, taking tiny steps. There were pigeons perched on the statue of a mermaid, almost as if they were part of the statue. Mateus, Flor, and Vasco were no longer by the lake. They weren't anywhere. I turned to face Xavier.

"Do you see the kids?"

He had turned his face to the sun, his eyes closed. It took him a moment to open them. Then he pointed to the shore of the lake.

"They were over there," he muttered.

"I know they were there, Xavier. But where are they now?"

"I don't know."

"Wait here," I told him.

And I crossed the park. When I got to the other side, I realized it didn't end where I thought it did: there was a slight incline, and the woods gave way to fields full of yellow flowers. There were several people running on the dirt paths. I kept walking for more than a hundred yards. Then I saw them, in a playground. Flor was sitting on a swing, her toes grazing the ground, her hands gripping the chains. Vasco was standing between her legs, his hands over hers. They were in the middle of a kiss that seemed to have already lasted some time. There was no sign of Mateus anywhere.

Almodôvar, do you remember when they were little? They were inseparable, always chasing after one another. Even though they hardly spoke, we always joked about how they'd grow up and get married. And we'd congratulate one another, future fathers-in-law, future grandparents of the same grandson. I don't remember if we were ever serious. But that kiss could have been the beginning of it all. And look, I had never been an overly protective father; the idea of a fifteen-year-old boy kissing my daughter, who was as beautiful as any thirteen-year-old girl, never worried me. On the contrary: I knew it was inevitable. Only that kiss, Almodôvar, left me with no ground to stand on, flailing in a liquid panic. As if your son could contaminate Flor through that kiss. As if Vasco's life, those videos of the homeless people, his friends, that apartment, the drugs, the lies, his missing you, his low happiness index—as if all that could be transmitted to Flor and consume her until there was nothing left of the girl she was.

I approached them. They didn't immediately notice, and the kiss went on.

"Flor," I said.

Vasco dropped his hands, stepped away, and stood against a nearby wall. Flor remained in the same place and smiled at me while hardly moving her lips.

"Daniel, I'm so sorry," Vasco said.

It occurred to me then that I could leave him there, go back to Portugal without him, save my daughter. But instead I just said, "We'll discuss this later. Flor, where's your brother?"

"I don't know. I thought he was with you."

"He's not. I thought he was with you."

"He's not."

We walked back to Xavier. A woman sat next to him on the bench with a dove on her wrist eating cracker crumbs from the palm of her hand. Mateus wasn't there.

"Wait here," I said.

The park ended abruptly across the way. I ran across the street between two cars. Along the promenade, there were two or three shops, a café with three tables outside, and a newspaper kiosk down the block. I entered every shop, but I didn't see my son. I spoke to the man who was inside the kiosk, and he shook his head, though I'm not sure if he understood my French. I crossed another street and did the same thing on the next block, and then the next. I was becoming queasy, the beginnings of a quickly approaching sadness.

I returned to the park.

"We have to spread out," I said.

I asked Xavier to go back to the hospital; maybe Mateus was there. He dragged his feet as he walked away as if he actually did have the whole world on his shoulders. He wasn't well, Almodôvar, but there was nothing I could do for him then. I told Flor and Vasco to stay in the park in case Mateus came back. And I ran; I crossed the park and came to a parking garage that belonged to the hospital, three stacked concrete platforms the size of soccer fields. I walked through the ground floor, searching for him. There was no sign of movement, as if all the cars had been abandoned. I thought of Marta, of the words I'd use to explain that I had lost our son in France. Except the words didn't exist. Almodôvar, that trip was anything but the right thing to do.

I walked up to the second level and shouted his name. No one answered. Then I did the same on the third level. After that, I checked the roof. He wasn't there either.

I called Xavier. He had just arrived at the hospital. He hadn't seen Mateus.

I left the parking garage and continued on to a street full of shops. It was after three in the afternoon. I scoured dozens of nearby streets as if it were a game. On one of the busiest streets, I entered the stores, restaurants, bakeries, cafés, a public bathroom, an office building, a massage center where three women helped me to take off my coat before they realized my problem wasn't that easy to solve. I went running from one place to the next—always running.

I looked at the phone; no missed calls. I called Vasco; they were still in the park, and Mateus hadn't shown up. I called Xavier; the only thing he said was, "This hospital is endless."

I called Alípio and told him what was happening. He and Doroteia Marques were still with her brother. She was telling him stories about when they were kids, laughing as if she herself were hearing them for the first time. Her brother, in a deep coma, had moved his left pinkie three or four times. Alípio left her to go search the hospital for Mateus.

On a busier street, I saw a bus stopping for a minute at a bus stop; some passengers got on, others got off. I imagined Mateus getting on an identical bus with a destination written in a language he didn't understand. The idea was absurd, but it still seemed possible. So I got on the next bus. I paid for my ticket and stood there next to the front door so I could watch the road through the windshield. He asked me to move back to the rear of the bus. I stayed where I was. The street seemed never-ending. There were people on the sidewalks, including a few kids, but my son wasn't among them. The driver asked me to move again. I refused. He spoke loudly, and I spoke loudly back, about Mateus and the meaning of losing a child, all the obvious stuff, all of it far from the true meaning of losing a child. He stopped the bus and opened the door for me to get off. I did, because I no longer wanted to believe in the possibility that Mateus had gotten so far.

I called Xavier again, but he didn't answer. Then I tried Vasco and Alípio, but they didn't have any news.

I ran nearly a mile and a half back in the direction of the park. I got out of breath quickly, my lungs full of embers that stirred with my every inhalation. Near the park, I found a hypermarket. For half an hour, I checked aisle after aisle. I entered the bathroom, remembering Ávila, the things he did in shopping center bathrooms. Then I remembered the stories we read every day in newspapers, about kids who disappear into child trafficking networks, all the shit that happens online. What if Mateus had told someone online that he was going to Switzerland and France? What if he had shared our itinerary with someone? Almodôvar, the world had swallowed my son, and I was overcome with sadness.

And then I thought: He doesn't know my number. Even if he found a pay phone, he wouldn't be able to call me. But maybe he'd think to try Marta. So I called her.

"Everything all right?" she asked.

"Yeah," I lied. "Everything okay with you?"

"The same. Can I talk to the kids?"

"They're not here."

She didn't ask more questions, but she could sense something was wrong.

"Call me when you're with them again," she said.

Then I realized that there were four movie theaters in the hypermarket. I bought tickets for all of them. I walked into each theater, stood in front of the screen, and shouted Mateus's name into the darkness. The only answer I got was a few bad words in French.

I left the hypermarket. It was almost seven in the evening by then, and the sun was beginning to set behind the buildings, though the air was still warm. For the first time that day, I thought about going to the police. But it seemed too daunting.

I called Alípio. He said he was looking in a neighborhood behind the hospital.

I ran back to the park with the lake. Flor and Vasco were sitting on the same bench. They weren't kissing. Flor was crying, and when she saw me, she hugged me, apologizing. And I thought: No, she doesn't need to apologize. I do.

I told them to go back to the hospital and wait for me in the cafeteria; maybe Mateus would think to go back there—maybe he was already there.

And I sat down to wait. Almodôvar, I didn't know what to do next. My lack of options filled me with a tremendous fear, as if night were falling and I knew the sun would never rise again. Maybe Mateus would wander back. There were children running around everywhere. The two old men had returned, walking shoulder to shoulder like two hundred-year-old turtles. I hung around for about ten minutes, looking at anything that moved: kids, pigeons, old people, the trees, the water, the clouds, the whole world so alive and bustling and yet, even with all my grief, I felt like granite inside. I wanted so much to be a part of all that movement, except that I needed to find my son. When I did, I'd never let go of the world's hand again.

Once the sun disappeared, the sky turned red and lilac, like in a dream. That's when my phone rang. It was Alípio.

"I found him," he said.

"Mateus?"

"Yeah."

Alípio began to explain what happened. Almodôvar, that whole time we had been looking for him, Mateus had been at a cybercafé about half a mile from the hospital. When Alípio found him, he was on the verge of accumulating the credits he needed to get to the next level of his game, where he would be allowed to incubate up to ten million eggs at a time. Our reality had ceased to exist inside his head.

And as Alípio spoke, gravity weighed on my shoulders like cement. The fatigue in my muscles became real.

I called Vasco and told him. He cried out as if he were watching a soccer game and his team had just scored. So did Flor. I hung up. Then I started to cry with an indescribable, absolute joy.

Only it shouldn't have been like that, Almodôvar. We shouldn't need bad days to appreciate the good ones; there should always be a joy inside of us, and not just in moments of relief. But we're doomed by our insistence on relativizing everything. The here and now isn't enough, so we lock ourselves into a struggle that we'll never resolve, because we refuse to be happy with less, because we always want more.

I sat there for a long time as the sky darkened and the people left. The park finally stood empty. When I got up to walk back to the hospital, I felt terribly sorry to leave that place, as if I had lived there for many years.

Vasco and Flor were sitting at a table in the hospital cafeteria. They were laughing; one of them had said something that had made them both erupt. And I thought: Perhaps the two of them together isn't such a bad thing—maybe it's the opposite.

Flor stood up and hugged me. She squeezed me as if she wanted to press herself through my body. Vasco smiled, the same smile you had when you were his age. And that was a good thing.

Almodôvar, a few minutes later, Alípio arrived with Mateus. I wanted to hug him, feel him whole in my hands, but at the same time I didn't want him to sense my anguish from that afternoon. So I did nothing. He sat down beside me, his hands in his pockets, and stared down at the table.

"Don't do that again," I told him.

He nodded but said nothing.

I looked at Alípio. I raised my eyebrows as if to ask him what happened.

"The same old story of satisfying desire," he said.

I looked back at Mateus. The euphoria of his previous five hours had disappeared, and my son found himself stuck in a paradox: he wanted to satisfy the desire he felt because he wanted to be happier, but desire supposedly prevented happiness. And I just wanted to help him. I wanted so much to help him, Almodôvar. It's possible that if a person eliminates their desire, they become happier. It's a theory. But what kind of person is capable of eliminating their desire? I didn't want my son to be that person. Happiness shouldn't require such sacrifice. At least not for a ten-year-old kid. I knelt in front of him and grabbed his ankles. I wanted to beg him to forget the theory, which was wrong because its premise was wrong: happiness can never be an end in itself; if you think of happiness as an end, it will drive you crazy. But I said nothing. It would just be fighting one theory with another. Mateus was ten years old, and he didn't need theories. He just needed to be a kid.

Alípio's phone rang. It was Doroteia Marques asking someone to come get her; visiting hours were over. Alípio stood up.

"I'll be back," he said.

And he walked off toward the elevators.

I sat down and looked at my children, your son, the three of them sitting there in front of me with so much uncertainty on their faces, waiting for me to speak, to reprimand them for all their misdeeds. But I didn't feel any better than them; the difference in our ages seemed irrelevant, and it wasn't right for me to tell them how things were.

"Where's Xavier?" asked Flor.

"You haven't seen him? He was here before you guys."

Flor and Vasco shook their heads. I got up. But Flor grabbed my hand.

"Stay here," she said. "Vasco and I will go look for him."

I couldn't say no, so I stayed and watched them walk across the cafeteria toward the lobby. I sat back down, this time next to Mateus. I closed my eyes. My body was throbbing like a muscle at its limits. I stayed that way for a minute. Then I opened my eyes. Beside me, Mateus looked so small. I tried to imagine what it would be like if he were still missing. I couldn't. I put an arm around him and pulled him to me. He let himself fall against me, his hair brushing my cheek, and time expanded. There was nothing in the world like those moments with my kids, Almodôvar.

And then Flor appeared before us like a wave. She was crying and moving her hands as if she were trying to grasp handfuls of air.

"You have to come," she cried, tripping over every word. "Xavier won't wake up."

And without waiting for me to stand, she turned and ran out of the cafeteria. Mateus and I ran after her.

We followed Flor's resolute strides down a long corridor, then took the stairs up to another corridor on the second floor. A nurse passed by, escorting a woman with a bloody face; they walked as if they were lovers. At the end of the corridor, there was a waiting room. A sign above the entrance said "Rheumatology." Twenty or thirty people, most of them elderly, were waiting with bored looks on their faces. On the back wall there were two doors: bathrooms. Flor entered the women's room. We followed her inside; no one in the waiting room seemed concerned about what we were doing.

My daughter planted herself in front of a stall and stopped crying, as if my presence there would solve everything. I approached the stall and peered inside. Sitting on the toilet with his head against the wall and his eyes closed was Xavier.

"Xavier," I said.

He didn't move. It seemed impossible that someone could sleep that deeply, stuck in that kind of stillness. I leaned over him and placed a hand on his shoulder. I gave him a slow shake. His head dropped to the side, and the weight of it dragged the rest of his body downward, until he slid off the toilet and onto the floor. I held him for a few seconds, feeling his dead weight in my arms. Then I dropped him, Xavier's long body heavy as if it were filled with stones. He fell to the ground, one arm twisting up by the side of his head, one leg curling beneath the other. He didn't wake up; no part of his body reacted.

Behind me, Flor jumped and let out a sharp cry.

I knelt beside Xavier and waited. He didn't move. He was dead. The idea seemed absurd. We had traveled twelve hundred miles to be there, Doroteia Marques had seen her brother, Mateus was fine, Flor and Vasco had kissed, and the worst was over: he couldn't just die. It was obvious—though impossible to put into words—that his death would take away any meaning from that trip. What would I tell the kids? There would be no way to separate the two events—our trip and Xavier's death would be fixed in our memories as a single event. And I was suddenly so pissed at him, Almodôvar, so pissed I scared myself with the anger that spread so quickly through my body. Then I slapped him, hard, my hand falling flat against his cheek, and the sound, like a whip, was loud enough to make Flor grimace.

"Don't do this, you motherfucker," I whispered, barely moving my lips. I pulled away and slapped him again with the back of my hand.

Flor began to whimper.

Nothing happened.

I hit him again.

"Dad," said Mateus, behind me.

"Don't do this," I said. "We're all here. Now isn't the time to do this."

I gripped his coat and shook him hard, and his arms flailed in all directions. He was dead, Almodôvar.

"Dad," Mateus said, crying.

"Wake up, you son of a bitch!" I shouted.

I was about to hit him again, but then Xavier opened his eyes. His chest rose as air filled his lungs. As if my voice had the power to resuscitate him.

He saw me, the fear that remained in my eyes, and knew what I'd been thinking a moment before.

ELECTRICITY IN MY VEINS AND MY HEAD FULL OF WORDS, ALL THE WORDS

"So that means there's still hope," said Alípio.

"No," said Doroteia Marques. "Not exactly, according to the doctors."

"I don't understand. He wiggled his finger. He heard you and he wiggled his finger."

"The doctors say that's normal, it happens a lot. They're nerve impulses, involuntary reactions . . . I don't know the medical term."

They were talking quietly in the darkness of the van, Alípio at his place behind the wheel, Doroteia Marques sitting next to him. I was in the row behind them, between Mateus and Flor, and when I opened my eyes, I could distinguish their silhouettes in the glare of the headlights on the road, the small movements in their shoulders caused by their words. And outside the van, night enveloped everything. It was a good feeling, Almodôvar, traveling inside that van, as if the whole world were made of darkness. The light demands too much of us.

I had dozed during our first thirty minutes on the highway, but then I heard them talking, and I quietly listened. Mateus, Flor, Vasco, and Xavier were all sleeping. Or maybe not. Maybe they were just pretending to sleep and listening to everything, like me. Whatever the case, I wasn't one to decide what was better.

For a few seconds, Alípio lifted his foot off the accelerator, and the engine strained, and the van slowed. Alípio huffed, a restrained moan. His leg was hurting again. He returned his foot to the pedal, and after a moment of silence, he whispered, "That's just what the doctors tell you so you won't get your hopes up. There are still a lot of things that can go wrong. And doubts. Of course there are a lot of doubts. But Christ, a lot of people take weeks to come out of a coma."

"The doctors said they wanted to wait. They're going to run some more tests next week and then decide whether or not to continue life support."

"He wiggled his finger. He wiggled his finger. That has to mean something."

"No. It doesn't."

"Have some hope."

"I don't want hope."

"Why?"

"I wanted to see him one last time to say good-bye. It was very important for me. Now I'm at peace; I don't need hope."

"People always need hope."

"Not always. Too much hope makes for a life full of loose ends. It's not nice to wake up every morning with a life full of loose ends."

"So you don't think there's a chance your brother will recover?"

"No. If it happens, I'll be happy. But I'm not expecting it to happen."

They fell silent for a few minutes. The night's blackness entered through my eyes and invaded my head before spreading to the rest of my body.

Then Doroteia Marques spoke again. "I've thought a lot about what you've done for me—six people crossing half a continent just to help me see my brother. And I can't make sense of it. It has no explanation. It's almost a fantasy. I know I'll never be able to repay you for what you did. But my happiness is real, and I thank you for that with every last part of me."

I had been waiting to hear those words, Almodôvar, though I hadn't realized it until that moment. When I heard them, I was overcome with a desire to embrace her, to thank her back. Because her words lent meaning to the whole trip, and somehow, they lent a new meaning to the life that still lay ahead of us.

I checked to see if Xavier and the kids were awake. I wanted so much for them to have heard those words. Without them, it would be impossible to truly understand what we had come to Switzerland to do. But none of them moved, their breath serene and constant.

We arrived in Geneva around two in the morning. I wanted to sleep at the hotel where we had reserved three rooms. But Doroteia Marques insisted that we stay with her again. It was so late I couldn't find the strength to protest.

Alípio got out of the van limping. He looked at me and tried to force a smile, but he couldn't. Xavier looked like a ghost. I had forbidden him to take more pills before we left Marseille, and the signs of a raging hangover were beginning to appear on his face. Flor and Vasco propped up Mateus, who couldn't wake up, walking him to the elevator and then putting him in bed. I pushed Doroteia Marques in her chair, even though I was exhausted. Almodôvar, we were like soldiers after a battle, not knowing if we had lost or won.

* * *

I woke up to a profound silence—a good one—not in the world, but inside my head. It was early, just after seven. Flor, Mateus, and Vasco were still sleeping. I got out of bed, sat down, and opened the laptop. I went to the aviary game. Then I created a user account.

Half an hour later, Mateus woke up and came to sit beside me. He looked at the screen and then at me.

"What are you doing?" he asked.

"I want to raise some chickens," I said.

He let out something like a guffaw but didn't venture to comment.

We sat there for almost an hour, developing a virtual piece of land, first barns to hold thousands of birds, then an incubator and then a garage for the trucks that transported the chicks and chickens, Mateus showing me everything step by step, the enthusiasm growing in his voice. I looked at him a few times; he just looked like my son. I couldn't tell if he understood what I was trying to tell him.

Doroteia Marques hugged me. I said nothing. So we stayed that way for a few seconds—me bent over her wheelchair, her arms around my neck. When I stood up, she did the same with the others: Alípio, Xavier, then the kids.

We didn't tell her what had happened with Mateus, or with Xavier. She believed that we were extraordinary human beings, that the whole world could fit inside our hearts.

We all piled into the van. It was almost eleven. The sky was heavy with clouds, every natural shade of gray imaginable.

Back on the highway, Alípio turned the wheel and took an exit toward a gas station. We hadn't traveled more than thirty or forty miles.

"What's up?" I asked.

"I can't do this. It feels like there's a knife in my leg."

"Do you want to wait until it passes?"

"It's not going to pass."

"What do you want to do?"

"Let's switch. You drive."

He didn't offer any further explanation for his change of heart. But I can only assume that he was as eager to get home as the rest of us.

That's how I ended up behind the wheel, Almodôvar, with the feeling that the van was no more than an extension of my own body. My will and my movements would be enough to get us home.

I drove for nine hours, interrupted by two short stops to eat and fill up the tank. No one spoke much, not even Alípio. And the silence of that morning persisted in my mind, as if I didn't have a single remaining thought. Imagine, Almodôvar, the relief of moving forward on autopilot, making all decisions on instinct, executing them by mechanical impulse. There was just the road. We entered Spain around seven in the evening, the sun sinking over the horizon ahead of us. If we were faster, we could chase it around the world in an endless day.

We stopped at a motel near Vitoria-Gasteiz. We talked a bit over dinner in a tapas bar next to the motel. Then we went to sleep. The silence continued through my sleep, my mute dreams; I had no words left.

Our will to get home was absolute. We were back in the van by seven the next morning. Alípio asked me to drive. I agreed, though I felt exhausted.

We had covered sixty miles when a highway patrol signaled for us to pull over.

I stopped on the shoulder.

A policeman walked around the van and approached my window.

I looked over at Alípio. He was sleeping. I glanced behind me. Xavier and the kids were sleeping too.

I lowered the window.

The policeman greeted me with a little salute. He had a thick black beard. He peered into the van, then asked for my license and documentation.

Alípio's wallet was in a compartment under the radio. I opened it and looked for the documents. I passed them to the policeman. Then I passed him my license.

The policeman collected everything without looking at me.

He shuffled the papers from one hand to the other, stopping to study each one for a few seconds: my driver's license, the registration, the insurance card Xavier had doctored. I knew he was going to discover the 0 Xavier had tried to change to a 1. We would all have to get out of the van, and the policeman wouldn't let us leave until we paid a fine with the money that none of us had. I wasn't afraid. I think I had grown used to taking life's beatings without fighting back. It was a different approach, to go on like this, with my fists lowered. But then the policeman tidied the stack of documents, gave them back, and said we could go.

I can't explain it, Almodôvar. Later I looked at the insurance card: Xavier's forgery was so crude. How could the policeman not have noticed?

I thought: We're invincible. As long as we keep believing we're invincible, incredible things can happen. And suddenly, there was **electricity in my veins, and my head was full of words, all the words**. A torrent of thoughts swept away the day's silence. It was absurd, Almodôvar, that my body was so full of strength just because of one lucky break.

I checked the rearview. Everyone was still sleeping. None of them looked well: they were all too tired, too lost, as if they had no certainty about the reality around them. But they were trying, Almodôvar. They hadn't given up. I believed it with every cell in my body. Even Xavier. Suddenly the idea that Xavier could live to a ripe old age holed up in his apartment seemed wonderful. And Vasco. Look, Almodôvar. I was wrong: Vasco wasn't going to contaminate Flor with his troubled past, his low happiness index. It was the opposite. Flor would corrupt Vasco with her humanity. She'd make him more whole. They'd kiss again, many times, and we'd all be better for it. I believed it as I believe what I see with my own eyes.

My head flooded with thoughts of the future, Almodôvar. Maybe not the future as it would occur, but a possible future. And that's all we need. Me, in Viana, with Marta and the kids. Marta's body next to mine until the end, her voice a beacon—always guiding me back to us. I'd take any old job: a bellhop, a waiter, a tour guide—whatever. And in the future, my kids would be happy. My certainty about that was unwavering, because I knew I could teach them. Flor had the whole world inside of her; she'd be bigger and better than any of us. Mateus will never have to worry about happiness; wherever he goes, the power of his smile will be tremendous, and I can help him understand that. We'll raise chickens together for a long time, and if necessary, I'll even shave my own head. And I want you to know that while you are where you are, whenever Vasco needs anything at all, I'll go. He'll never be alone.

It's a plan.

It's a Plan.

And here we are, Almodôvar, inside this van, on the way back to Lisbon. It's from behind the wheel, with the highway stretching out before me, that I'm telling you everything. So you know that we're still here, and you can join us anytime you want. I'm not afraid, Almodôvar. I still believe, and life goes on like always. In spite of everything, the days on this planet are still made of light, and the darkness of night still fills us with fear. And we're still here, Almodôvar. We're still here.

ABOUT THE AUTHOR

Photo © 2014 Mar Babo

Author David Machado hails from Lisbon, Portugal, and writes fiction for both adults and children. His books are popular in Portugal and have been awarded literary prizes, including the European Union Prize for Literature for the Portuguese version of this novel, *Índice médio de felicidade* (*The Shelf Life of Happiness*), which he adapted into a screenplay in 2016. When he's not traveling, he lives in Lisbon with his wife and two children.

ABOUT THE TRANSLATOR

Photo © James C. Taylor

A resident of New York City, Hillary Locke studied Spanish and Italian literature and translates from the Romance languages into English. When she's not running along the East River or reading in Tompkins Square Park, she likes to travel around the world and listen to beautiful languages she doesn't understand.

Printed in Great Britain
by Amazon